**JUST PAST**
stopped dead. Virginia narrowly avoided running into him. Staggering in the loose sand, she lost her footing and fell heavily against the lintel. Starting up furiously, she froze on her knees. A terrible whimpering sound was coming from the man ahead of her, and she saw that he had thrown up his hands to shield his face from what he saw.

Peering past him, all she could see was the light. It was at the base of the statue of Osiris, a pulsing presence that was all colors and no color. It had no source, emitted no heat, yet danced off the retina with the overwhelming brightness of the sun. It was not just light, it involved the other senses as well. Its effect was indescribable.

"Hamid, what in God's name—"

But Hamid did not answer.

# OBELISK™

## A NOVEL

Judith Kaye Jones

Prima Publishing

ISBN: 0-7615-0419-2
Library of Congress Catalog Card Number: 95-72401
Printed in the United States of America

96 97 98 99 EE 10 9 8 7 6 5 4 3 2 1

# Prologue

## No Time like the Present

### 2479 C.E.: The Cataclysm

It was difficult not to believe in the malign power of darkness. One day Earth was the center of the human worlds,the cradle of humanity and its greatest monument. That last day became the most recent era-marker in human history. It was the day that b.c. came to mean Before Cataclysm. It was the last day for Earth as humanity had known it. Cities were crushed and shaken apart; the population was devastated. A chain of earthquakes and volcanic eruptions hurled a rain of death into the air and sent huge chunks of the earth's crust to crash down on a helpless humanity. The resulting dust clouds filled the atmosphere, shutting out the light from the sun.

The colonies mounted rescue expeditions to find and carry off those few humans who survived the initial destruction. In the darkness and ruin, virtually all of the rest of life perished. The nearly dead Earth continued around the sun, bereft. Cosmologists said it was almost as if creation had started over again, as if Earth had returned to the violence of its birth. But these birth pangs would not deliver the embryonic beginning of life. The Cataclysm seemed very final. It was the end-time.

## 2484 C.E.: The Reconstruction

The colonies helped, of course. Almost at once the human populations began the process of reconstruction. Huge climate-control satellites orbited around Earth. Rain pelted down on the spiraling dust clouds, until the debris settled on the surface. The atmosphere cleared. Dedicated crews introduced new life into the seas and rivers—microorganisms, the tiny building blocks of ecology. Terraforming, developed to make alien worlds habitable, found its greatest use on the Earth itself. It took twenty years to make the planet capable of sustaining life. Plants and animals, descendants of specimens that accompanied the human move into space, flowed back to Earth from every garden and greenhouse throughout the settled worlds. The remnant population returned from its diaspora and started over. People called this work the Reconstruction, and every human, from whatever colony, took it to heart as a sacred goal.

The heritage of the past, however, was unrecoverable. At first, it did not seem to matter so much to any but the curators and historians. Survival came first, and recovery. Once the boom of Reconstruction was under way, the holes made themselves felt. There was no connection, no continuity with the past. Art, architecture, most of the literature and historical records were gone, those indefinable things that provide the human soul with a sense of transcendence. All that remained resided in the memories of the survivors and in the record banks of the colonies.

## 2685 C.E.: The Collection

Perhaps of all the colonies, New Paris suffered the most from Earth's loss. Originally settled by scholars and scientists, New Paris was the intellectual center of the colonies. The vast university there was the magnet that drew thinkers and creators from every settled planet. Their records of human history and culture were the most complete. The scholars of New Paris had been fond of saying that if Earth disappeared, they would be able to recreate it from their data banks. They never imagined that one day they would be called upon to realize that boast.

During the Reconstruction, they learned that data and facsimiles were not enough, no matter how complete. Only then did they discover that a replica of a pyramid was only an aching reminder of the hole where once the real pyramids had stood. No copy of Michelangelo's Pieta, however perfect, had come from the master's own hand. They finally understood antiquity.

New Paris undertook a great work. They called it the Collection. New Paris would build a collection of art and antiquities, historical documents and records, everything possible to rebuild a fragment of the artistic and cultural heritage of humanity. But the residue was small, a pathetic remnant of the wealth that had once been a testament to the creativity and energy of the human family.

Ironically, New Paris also gained the most from Earth's

destruction. A stunned humanity stood poised on the brink of sociological and political destruction. On a dozen worlds the seeds of parochialism were dormant but not extinguished. The unifying center of Earth's colonies was dead. History taught that, inevitably, world would follow world in declaring independence. Then would follow the equally inevitable buildup of militarism to defend that independence. Plowshares would be beaten into swords. Above all, on every world, the scholars and the intellectuals would be suspect.

Dark times and great enterprises have a way of creating men and women of History. Or perhaps they just unveil them. One such man was George Lewellyn, the Director of the Institute on New Paris. A sociologist, Lewellyn determined that this time history was going to be wrong. He threw all the vast wealth and genius of the Institute into making it wrong. The great minds of the Institute saw their opportunity clearly. They lifted the standard of Reconstruction and made it the unifying goal of humanity. Generously they poured their knowledge and technological expertise into the colonial worlds. Grateful populations turned to New Paris as the source of not only past glory but future hope. Save us from chaos, they cried. New Paris gracefully accepted the burden. The age of academic oligarchy had begun.

History, perhaps slighted by Lewellyn, presented another candidate for greatness. John Howard was first and finally an archaeologist, and the study of ancient Earth was his life work. His abiding passion for the art of the past was far too comprehensive to admit lesser interests. Contemporaries he largely regarded as unavoidable irritants. With rare exceptions, Howard preferred the company and thought of persons whose flesh had long ago turned to dust. Yet he was a man of great personal charm. Brilliant and charismatic, his admirers were legion, and the media loved him. It was inevitable that he would rise to a position of power and influence on the world of New Paris. It was only with the perfect vision of hindsight that one biographer would later write: You looked into the eyes, dark and compelling, and your immediate response was pleasure at the unswerving focus of that gaze. It wasn't until later that you recognized it,—the look of the predator as he assesses your ability to run.

## 2690 C.E.: Agate

When humans first discovered the planet Agate, its only recognized resource was antiquity. It was a small world, fourth in a system of eight planets circling a cooling sun. Located at the extreme edge of that part of the galaxy occupied by the United Earth Colonies, Agate turned in its darkened space, devoid of life. It was not always so. The original dominant race had risen from primordial soup, built an empire, and disappeared into whatever oblivion it created for itself before humanity walked upright. The only movement was that of the constant wind, winding and mourning through the desolation of stone left behind.

Covered in many places with broken, empty cities that stretched from horizon to horizon, Agate was an archaeologist's paradise. Perhaps it was this very wealth of ancient remnants that explained the less-than-thorough survey Agate received after its discovery. Pronounced lifeless by the exobiologists and geologically stable by the exogeologists, Agate underwent only a brief review by the mineralogical division of Exploration and Colonization. The planet's mineral deposits received little attention, a rare oversight for the aggressive colonization program. The dark and barren peaks brooded over vast cities of ruin where once again, life pursued purpose.

Archaeologists and historians arrived and selected a site for the initial dig. The soil was sterile and gritty, filled with fine, glittering silicate particles in which no life could root and grow. The remnant of the atmosphere contained insufficient oxygen to breathe, so the scholars came equipped with environment bubbles to make Agate habitable. Many of the buildings were reduced to rubble, but there were areas of lesser devastation where columns and stairs and an occasional roof survived. These possessed an extraordinary beauty. Built out of a luminous, quartzy stone, the walls and three-sided columns flashed and dazzled like torches in the waning sunlight. It was in one such area the archeologists settled to pursue their patient and relentless quest for the past. They learned to ignore the gentle, almost subsonic ring that vibrated in bone and muscle and was never still. The work went forward slowly at first.

There is a pattern to digging up the past, a methodology that is itself ancient and time-honored. Measure, section, dig, sift, examine, record, ignore no fragment however small, these are the rubrics of the archeologist. So it was on Agate. Gradually the shelves inside the environmental bubbles filled with foam-packed fragments of sculpture, or perhaps tools, or again perhaps eating utensils. Historians pored over the bits and pieces, drawing, recording, measuring, speculating. It was a slow and dusty business.

Then a digger found a small artifact that was intact. Its smooth black finish was unscarred by millennia of lying in the ruins. It was slightly over human-hand size, and had a small slot near the bottom. It did nothing whatsoever that anyone could discover. Countless hours were spent examining and discreetly prodding the "black box." It remained totally unresponsive, and the archaeologists were unwilling to risk damaging it by trying to take it apart. Several days later a handful of small red crystals turned up in the same trench. All identical, they had clearly been shaped. Inevitably someone tried one in the slot on the black box. A luminous grid appeared on the black surface with a series of small lighted areas near the edge. Touching one of the lights produced something like a holographic image, roughly half again the size of a human, in the air near the box.

It was as simple as that. Perfectly realized out of nothing, the being in no way resembled a human person. The words it spoke bore no resemblance to any known language group. The being sat there, talking energetically to someone who had been dead for thousands of years, while a group of scientists of an entirely different species gazed at it without understanding. They could not possibly have guessed the nature of the warning.

The archaeologists dispatched the artifact and the crystals to the Colonization and Development Center on Elgin. Recognizing the potential of the crystals as even more important than the historical significance of the recording device of an ancient and vanished people, C&D sent them all on to New Paris, to the Institute and the attention of the scientists there.

The large deposits of crystal, from which Agate derived its name, were unlike any encountered on previously settled worlds. Their color and translucence varied, but they shared one important and absolutely unique attribute. They were perfect. Once the scientists discovered the power crystals that operated the black box, those mineral deposits were subjected to the most minute scrutiny. The empty mountains were suddenly populous. The silence was riven with the noise of machinery and vehicles and construction. The archeologists looked up from their work in the ruins as the skies filled with ships and flyers of all descriptions. Prospectors explored adjoining systems, finding a variety of crystals in many deposits, most showing signs of having been quarried in the ancient past. Exploration of the ruins now went forward under the direction of a contingent of scientists, headed by Arthur Daedalus of the Institute on New Paris. The solitude of Agate had ended. It was again at the center of an empire. Built on the foundations of the old, the new age of crystal technology had begun.

When the theoreticians on New Paris began exploring the new crystal technology from Agate, they saw at once that the potential was greater than any previous estimates had suggested. The red crystals had an affinity for recording and storage, and could store an immense amount of data. The azure crystals could be used singly as small power sources, or combined into a complex matrix. They drew energy into themselves and sent it out again, magnified exponentially.

Humankind could power a dozen worlds for all time using the crystals from Agate. They could travel faster, farther, and more cheaply through space than ever before. With a crystal matrix of sufficient size, a ship could travel almost forever, providing its inhabitants with food and water and air for all the generations to come. The future was bright for all humankind. The past was still an aching void, and about the past they could do nothing. Or so it seemed. The multicolored crystals, glowing with a fire beyond opals, remained mysterious in their potential. Then Arthur Daedalus decided to try applying his theories of time travel to the crystal matrix.

# PART I

## A Matter of Time

# Chapter 1

## 1995 C.E.
## San Francisco

*Thou dawnest beautifully in the horizon of the sky, the living Aten, the first to live! Thou dawnest in the eastern horizon and fillest every land with thy beauty. Thou art lovely, great, glittering high above every land, thy rays encompass the lands unto the extent of all that thou hast made! Thou art Ra, thou reachest unto their end, and subjectest them to thy beloved son Akhenaten. Thou art afar off, yet thy rays are upon earth.*

The poetic phrases filled her mind's eye with images of that desert land where the lifeline called the Nile flowed among the sand and stones, and the rays of the sun still encompassed the earth. Akhenaten, *beloved son of Aten,* had penned this hymn of praise over three thousand years ago. The royal city, Akhetaten, was no more than a few empty rock tombs where even the name of the heretic pharaoh and his god had been violently chiseled away in an attempt to deny him immortality. Ordered by the zealot restorers of Thebes, she mused, who themselves and the gods they defended were now dust. And still the words had the power to move the heart and imagination long after his memory and that of his god had been reduced to dusty fragments to be pored over by scholars and romantics like herself. Dr. Virginia Alexander knew herself to be both.

The light from her window fell across the crumbling papyrus now protected by glass. An excellent reproduction lay beside it, so she had no excuse for keeping this fragile, precious piece of history on her desk. She could learn everything there was to learn from the copy. More, in fact, as the original was brown and mottled with age, barely legible in places. Yet however excellent, the copy had not come from the pen of a scribe who had perhaps sat in Akhenaten's very presence as he wrote down the words of the pharaoh's ecstasy.

She smiled as the voice of H.L. Pierce, the Director of the museum, intruded on her daydream. Dry, pedantic, he argued even in her imagination. "Cribbed from an existing hymn to Ra. Nothing about Akhenaten suggests he was a poet. It is, however, a rather good example of his ruthless attempt to suborn the religious traditions of his day and attribute all to Aten."

"Aten *was* Ra," she had retorted, "and the hymn could easily have originated in Akhenaten's court if not by his own hand."

He had shaken his head but his eye twinkled at her insistence. "What about this one in particular so fascinates you, Virginia? He was not among the great pharaohs, his reign was short and nearly disastrous for Egypt, and he was odd looking to say the least." She could see the tall alabaster statue of Akhenaten from her office door. Carved during his lifetime, it made no attempt to portray the pharaoh with the conventional perfection displayed by statues of his predecessors. The slanted gaze and full lips with their Mona Lisa smile, the wide hips and protruding stomach, could only present an unforgiving, speaking likeness. But was it the likeness of a visionary or a madman? A religious mystic or a ruthless zealot? Strange how time seemed to interconnect when you stood in the presence of the unimaginably old, looking so very . . . present.

She went back to the papyrus. The poetry she found so moving followed an uncompromising statement of power. For this document was the *Ban of Akhenaten*, with which the pharaoh ordered the closing of all temples in Egypt except those dedicated to Aten and the abandonment of the worship of the other gods. *Amon shall be silent, so shall Horus and Osiris and Anubis. For they are false gods, and they shall be silent. Their names shall be removed from the monuments. . . .* The uncompromising arrogance of the words sent a shiver up her spine.

The pharaohs and their courts were dedicated to the cults of Amon, Ra, and Aten, all forms of the solar god from whom Pharaoh was descended. But the people of ancient Egypt made sense of their universe in the worship of the many gods of the land, the gods of river and of home, of grain and water and cattle, and most of all, of Osiris and Horus and Isis, the ancient holy family who presided over the soul and its passage from death to life. They comforted themselves in their daily sorrows and losses by their belief in an afterlife ruled over by Osiris, where pain and suffering ceased and life was blissful for the righteous. Uncaring, Akhenaten had tried to remove even the names of his people's gods from their monuments. Yet it was his own name that the people struck from his kingdom's testaments in stone. Akhenaten's Egypt was not ready to abandon the worship of many for one. Akhenaten had attempted to reorder time. His failure had been absolute. Yet he was, if not one of the great pharaohs, surely one of the most famous. The attempt of the priests at Thebes to destroy even his memory had failed even more absolutely.

Her door flew open and the Director stood on the threshold. One glance at his flaming face and she was on her feet. He stood there, shaken with rage.

"H.L., what is it?"

"The Nefertiti statuette. It's missing."

She stared at him dumbfounded. Shaking her head, she stood up.

"Nonsense. It can't be. You've checked with Min?"

Min Lee headed the conservation department at the museum. Only she could have ordered the statuette removed from its locked case. Except for the Director. *Or herself*, thought Virginia with a sudden sinking in the pit of her stomach.

"Yes. She has done nothing with it." Virginia opened her mouth to say something, but he waved it aside.

"Oh, don't bother telling me you had nothing to do with it. I already know that. It was in its case thirty minutes ago. I was in the room with Georges and Hassan, and we looked at it. Hassan was annoyed because I could not unlock the case. You know how he loves to handle things. Well, as a matter of fact, I deliberately left the sensor alarm on and my keys in my desk because I knew he would want to take her out. We turned away to look at the Bastet statue. Georges gestured with his hands, the way he does, and Hassan right back at him. I keep remembering that I could see their hands the whole time, and then we looked around and it was gone. The case was still locked, you understand, we were in the room, no one else, and the alarm did not go off. Yet it was gone. Impossible."

He sat down, and she could see how shaken he was.

"But H.L.," she began gently, "how could—"

He stood up again, his face now white with loss.

"I don't know. It happened just as I told you. It couldn't have happened. But it did. Call the police."

She watched helplessly as he went out of her office. H.L. Pierce had found the Nefertiti statuette himself at Amarna, long after all the major finds. It was a fluke, a piece of outrageous luck. He was climbing in the stony wadis near the Queen's tomb, and had put his hand over a stone that was loose. Rock cascaded down, uncovering a hole in which lay a small cache of artifacts. He had put in his scratched, callused hand, and drawn out a small, perfect alabaster statuette of Akhenaten's queen, Nefertiti. *The Beautiful One Has Come*. It was unquestionably the Beautiful One herself. The carving of the pleated linen robe was so perfect the fabric seemed almost transparent. The delicate features reproduced exactly those of the famous bust in the Berlin museum. H.L. had always said the statuette was of even better quality than the larger piece, that it was in fact one of the finest pieces of Amarna-period Egyptian art in the world. Of all the things in the museum's rich collection, that one exquisite thing was closest to H.L.'s heart. Yet he would no more have stolen it than he would have cut his heart out. Virginia put out her hand for the telephone.

# Chapter 2
## 2712 C.E.
## Agate

There is nothing so empowering as a blank canvas. Vincent fought his reluctance to begin and picked up his drawing stylus. Until you touched it, drew on it, the canvas was the ground of infinite potential. The world's next great masterpiece was only a few shades and shadows away. *The world.* How the mind clung to its roots and origins. Humanity was on a dozen worlds now, and moving outward with ever-increasing zeal. Yet we still think in terms of "the world" as if it were the boundary of our imaginations. And the world of our thoughts, the "ground of our being" (he smiled at the pun), *Earth,* was no longer the primary residence of the human species. It would take generations to make it even a faint shadow of what it had once been. Perhaps a museum planet, revered but no longer *the world.* Humanity would have to go forward without its past. *Delaying again*, he thought. Quickly he drew the pencil across the white surface, and an intricate pattern of light and dark grew under his hands. As lines and shadows took possession of the page, their counterparts in Vincent's young face smoothed out. He always experienced undiminished wonder at the magic of his art. Its creation was his only real happiness. He lost track of time.

It was the ringing in the crystal ruins that roused him from his abstraction. It insinuated itself into your bones, even in sleep, so that the constant shimmering sound filled your dreams. He looked out through the transparent plastic of the bubble at the darkening sky, fading through all the shades of purple into night. What must this world have been like before the end? They had all speculated on the cause of Agate's demise. Whatever it was, the destruction had been virtually absolute. With few exceptions the world was desolate. *A cataclysm of some kind* . . . the thought drifted across his mind like smoke.

"You know, Vincent, I feel a little like Alexander Graham Bell."

Vincent looked up as Daedalus walked into his cubicle, his voice echoing oddly through the breath mask. He smiled at his mentor's obvious self-satisfaction. He helped the older man out of the breathing apparatus necessary for work outside the bubbles. Daedalus swept a pile of data sheets and record disks off a chair and sat down.

"Think how he must have felt when he first made the telephone work. He went . . . no, he *called* his young assistant, just as I might have done with you, and shared with him his wonderful discovery."

"What wonderful discovery have you made today, Dr. Daedalus?"

"Oh," he said slowly, "just time travel."

Vincent smiled. It was his mentor's favorite subject.

"I see that smile, young man, and I know exactly what it means. See here—"

He was busy sketching his time net on the back of a drawing of Vincent's. The younger man swallowed any comment, and tried to follow. They had discussed the theory many times.

"You see, Vincent, I have always believed that Einstein would be vindicated! If only I could meet him, tell him. Every possibility that could happen, does happen. Some have posited that time is like a river, and that all events exist along that river at a fixed point. Others envision a set of parallel lines, each traveling along with its own set of happenings separate and discrete. As you know, I have conceived of it as a net, with an infinite number of lines connected to one another by another infinite number of lines. You can travel along one continuous line, or you can travel between on one of the connecting lines. In theory, that is. And I was close, very close in this idea."

Vincent drew in his breath but Daedalus continued in his excited voice.

"This has been my theory all along, you understand," Daedalus went on, "but until now there was no way to test it, to prove it. There was no power source great enough to disrupt time, even that little portion of it we inhabit from moment to moment. And there was no way to test the structure of time. We could envision, yes, theorize, but not *test*. Then, tonight," he held up one of the opalescent crystals, "I saw it. These crystals are the key.

"It came to me. Just as Einstein's theory of relativity came to him. I *saw* it, complete and perfect."

"Saw what?"

He held up his drawing.

"Time. Time, Vincent, in the crystal lattice. Not a net, a *lattice*."

Vincent allowed the import of the words to settle into his mind. "You are saying that the structure of time is similar to a crystal lattice?"

"No, no my boy! I am saying that the crystal lattices, the crystal systems of these Agate crystals are perfect replicas of the structures of time."

Vincent shook his head, but Daedalus rushed on.

"You see, Vincent, we have always known that there was something unique about the lattice structure of the Agate crystals. They are perfect. As you know, it should be impossible for any crystal formed as part of a land mass to be perfect. The pressures of other matter create flaws. Perfect crystals may only be grown in space, or sometimes under water. But Agate crystals defy these laws and are, each and every one, perfect and identical to all the others, save for size. They grow as if surrounded by space, or a buffering field. But what kind of field could exist, invisible and impalpable, that would permit each crystal to grow within but untouched by its surroundings? We know their perfect structure is the reason the crystals absorb energy and magnify it. But it is not the properties and attributes of the structure that is of ultimate importance. It is the structure itself. Because nature on Agate saw fit to create the crystalline structure in a way that is synchronous with time, there exists a sympathetic resonance that allows for the manipulation of matter through time. Because the field that surrounds the crystals, and establishes that perfect structure as an echo of itself, *is time*. Each crystal is essentially a hologram of time, existing in space but not fully part of it.

"Quartz and corundum and the other crystals we know have only a few internal planes, but the Agate crystal lattice runs in *all* directions. You see here where the planes intersect, you get a timeline. That line shares points with a multitude of others. The logic of those shared points forms a system of metalines, call them *event strings*, relating the timelines to each other. Each choice, each decision, creates a new version of the timeline. Of course, in reality it would be multidimensional, and I cannot draw that. Someday you will, perhaps," he twinkled at Vincent.

"Now, this infinite number of versions of one timeline is discrete and unique. Next to it is another timeline with its infinite variations connected by event strings. And next to that one, another. And on into infinity in all directions, all dimensions. Between each timeline set and the next are connections. These occur at points where the two timelines are synchronous. Synchronous, but distinct. They resonate together, like time membranes. It is possible to travel, not only through the event strings within one timeline to all its variables, but also through these synchronous event points to other timelines. No door is closed to us now."

Vincent looked at the drawing and then at Daedalus's face. He felt a cold touch on his spine, as if, as the ancients used to say, *a ghost had walked over his grave.*

"It was so simple a discovery, so undramatic to change the world . . . the universe for all time. Time, Vincent! We speak of 'all time' as if we could quantify and measure and possess such a thing. But always it was impossible, until now! Now we do have 'all time' at our command."

"You think we can go back in time."

It was banal, he knew, but he simply couldn't think of anything else to say. Daedalus beamed, so certain that he was holding out to his young assistant the keys to the future. And to the past.

"Yes! Yes! Haven't I been telling you that? Now, we must talk. Think of what this means to all of us. Time travel works. We can go back. We can go back in our own timeline, or in any other timeline we choose. At least, for now we can only go back to nearly adjacent tracks, but that we will work out later."

Vincent finally found his voice.

"I have always thought . . . believed, that if time travel were possible it would be terribly dangerous. Because you might—"

"Do something that disrupted the future?" Daedalus finished for him. "Yes, so you might. The old paradox about accidentally killing your own grandfather. Then you would no longer exist. But that we can talk about later. Here is the point. Suppose we *wanted* to change the past. Suppose we deliberately went back to change it. Not to do something terrible like kill someone, but to do something to the benefit of all humanity."

Vincent could see where the older scientist was going as if he had drawn it on his time net.

"The Cataclysm," he said, and Daedalus nodded.

"Yes. The Cataclysm."

There was a long pause, then suddenly Daedalus gave an explosive shout of laughter.

"Einstein! I *can* tell him!"

They went out on the next shuttle. Fortunately, there were many flights every day in and out of the skies around Agate. Vincent tried to listen as Daedalus expounded on corollaries to the original crystal matrix theory, but his thoughts kept drifting back to his question about the dangers of time travel. *Talk about that later*, Daedalus had said. But would they? What dangers could outweigh the glory of preventing the Cataclysm that had wiped out most of Earth and its treasures of the past, the heritage of every living human? He could think of nothing. But still he felt that cold thrill. He looked down at his lap where his long fingers were drawing the interior of the shuttle in the notebook he carried. As always, he drew comfort from his ability to translate his surroundings into interesting patterns of dark and light, line and color. The head of the man across the aisle from him took form, its silky dark cap of hair just brushing the ear, the curve and intricacy of the ear itself . . . gradually his anxiety receded and he was able to hear Daedalus again.

"And as usual, you are not listening, Vincent!" Daedalus was exclaiming in affectionate exasperation.

He cuffed Vincent on the cheek, but Vincent felt the very real frustration behind the jest. How Daedalus would love it if Vincent were as dedicated, as excited by science as he was himself. How often he had praised Vincent's brilliance and insight. He could follow Daedalus into the intricacies of that genius mind with little effort. But his heart was not in it. Had Vincent known it, Daedalus was keenly aware of the real mainspring of his ward's existence. But he had been designated to the sciences, and he was undoubtedly gifted. Daedalus had always taught him that the Institute knew best and they had sent Vincent to him when he was just a little boy. He could not have loved him more if Vincent had been his own son. Smiling, Vincent gave Daedalus his full attention.

# Chapter 3

## 2712 C.E.
## New Paris

New Paris! Most Earthlike of the colonial worlds, it had immediately felt like home to the first wave of colonists. It was home of the Institute, that vast complex of thinkers and doers, scientists and researchers and teachers and builders, the hope of humanity. Arthur Daedalus and his ward were as at home there as anywhere in the universe. Both truly lived inside their own imaginations, Daedalus in the intricacies of his theories, and Vincent in the equally complex world of color and form. They were nevertheless both aware of homecoming when they landed, and breathed the air of New Paris.

"Excellent," said Daedalus.

Vincent smiled. "Technology can't do everything, can it?" he asked mischievously. "It can clean and recycle air, but it can't put life into it."

Daedalus nodded. "True enough. It is good to be back among living things."

"The team on Agate would not thank you for suggesting they are not living," said Vincent.

Daedalus gave a short bark of laughter. "Fossils. Just like the bits and pieces they so assiduously dig up and mull over—dry and dusty."

"There are a few living fossils here as well," Vincent commented wryly.

Daedalus nodded again. "Also true. Let us hope George Lewellyn has not become one of them in our absence."

The Director had not become a fossil. He was very much alive, and alive to the overwhelming possibilities of Daedalus's theory. Without hesitation he put the enormous facilities of the New Paris Institute at Daedalus's disposal. The old scientist settled in, gathering around him those colleagues and students he most trusted, to undertake the unimaginable. They were going to build a crystal matrix of sufficient size and complexity to push matter through the invisible divisions between now and then, past and future, being and nonbeing. They were going to conquer time.

ꙮ ꙮ ꙮ

The silence in the darkened lecture hall was almost absolute. On the stage area a seemingly infinite number of beams of light converged on the shining crystal web floating at the center. A small transport pad sat directly beneath the matrix, and beside it was a control console. Two young men, one thin and dark and the other fair with startling blue eyes, stood beside the console. Vincent Ginevra, Daedalus's assistant, and Nikko Lantis, a crystallographic engineer, never took their eyes from Dr. Arthur Daedalus, who was speaking to the assembled scholars and politicians.

"Those of you who have known me for long, know that time travel has been the subject of much of my private research and work. A theory, we all agree. Filled with tantalizing possibility. But only a theory. It was, well, call it recreational. Even a scientist may occupy his mind sometimes with things beyond the range of probability. But today, you have come to witness a test of, not possibility, not even probability, but actuality. Time travel exists, now, today."

Some of the audience stirred. Even for those who knew Daedalus, it was an amazing, yes, even a preposterous claim. They had read the paper, they had heard his words, but the reality of the infinite did not come easily to the finite mind.

Daedalus continued, grave and courteous. "Let me digress for a moment. Yesterday, something untoward, something tragic occurred here at the Institute. We all sustained a great loss. Yesterday, a prized remnant from the past—the marble statue popularly known as the 'Winged Victory'—was destroyed, victim of an explosion set off in the midst of the Institute's sculpture garden."

An angry murmur broke out. The sculpture had been one of the most precious artifacts in the Institute's collection of ancient art treasures. Its destruction was a terrible blow, all the more so because it was inexplicable. No one could even imagine striking a blow at such a monument to human artistry. Such acts of destruction and terrorism belonged as much to the ancient past as the artifact itself.

"You are shocked, enraged. Perhaps you will be even more enraged and shocked when I tell you that I am the one who destroyed it."

Pandemonium broke out. Daedalus smiled, then, and lifted his hand for silence.

"Once, such destruction would have been absolute. But not today. In a few moments, you shall see proof that we have, in fact, conquered the destruction of the past."

Every eye in the room followed the direction of his gesture. Vincent Ginevra was standing on the transport pad. Daedalus gestured to the young man who stood at the control console.

"Lantis, if you would be so kind." The young man entered a series of coordinates into the console and the gate effect filled the space between the transport pad and the floating matrix. A flash of unnamable colors and Vincent disappeared.

"We will wait for a few moments. Vincent will signal when he is ready."

The darkness filled with whispering, and not a few people who sat there believed that they had just seen Arthur Daedalus, the most respected scientist of their time, murder his young assistant.

Then a small light flashed on the console, and Lantis nodded to Daedalus. He then became busy with the controls.

"Ladies and gentlemen," Daedalus said, "here is Vincent Ginevra, raised from the dead. Or, in fact, brought back from the past. And, as you see, he is not alone."

On the transport pad stood Vincent, and something else. An ancient block of marble carved in breathtaking swirls of drapery and lifted wings, looking as if it might fly off the platform.

"The Winged Victory," Daedalus said softly. "Time travel."

He explained it all, then. How Lantis and Vincent had destroyed the statue with a delayed explosive charge, carefully placed near the statue and set to go off in the predawn hours when no one would be in the locked sculpture garden. How Vincent had, just now, in front of their eyes, gone back through time to the hour between setting the explosive and its detonation, and affixed a receiver crystal tuned to the crystal matrix. And how the matrix had retrieved both Vincent and Victory and brought them back. Everyone in the room knew about the bomb and the statue. Many of them had actually seen the splintered marble shards, the blackened hole.

"The Director will tell you that he had the shards analyzed by the experts from the museum here," Daedalus was saying. "There can be no doubt that they came from the genuine statue. Analysis of the statue you see before you will establish it also as absolutely genuine. It was destroyed, but it is here. Because Vincent went back through time and brought it here, around the destruction. You will, when you leave here, still see the blackened hole. You will not see any splinters of marble. I am sorry for the outrage and grief felt by all of you over the apparent loss of so great a treasure. But it seemed somehow fitting that the road to the triumph of all time should be taken in the shadow of the Winged Victory."

He smiled as the tumultuous applause filled the hall.

ᘛ ᘛ ᘛ

A man stood at his window looking out, a shadowy form against the slowly dying light. The sprawl of buildings below him, glowing in the last rays of New Paris's sun, did not occupy his thoughts. He saw instead a vision of ancient glory, undimmed by the passage of time. A vision in which one man held the center, enthroned upon the accomplishments of a brilliant mind. He was that man.

He looked down at the data screen on the desk beside him. It was a copy of a paper by Arthur Daedalus, describing his discovery of the application of Agate power crystals to time travel. The matrix was complex. The prototype built by Daedalus on New Paris was only the beginning. It would carry a fairly small amount of mass a limited distance in space, and back an even more limited period of time. But it had worked. Arthur Daedalus had sent his assistant back in time, before the famous statue in the New Paris sculpture garden had been destroyed, and returned him safely, bringing the statue with him. Once the Institute accepted time travel as a fact, they would quickly overcome the limited scope of the prototype matrix. It was the application of the matrix that interested him. The test itself, designed to impress and convince skeptics, to elicit funds and support. It was astonishing that the old man should have thought of using the statue for his purposes. Perhaps there was a god, after all, one with a sense of humor.

John Howard sat down and looked with unseeing eyes at the data screen. He was already familiar with its contents. The pedantic language was no problem for him to understand. He would master this theory as he mastered everything he set his mind to conquer. Mastering the personalities involved would be no more difficult. He was already acquainted with the Director of the Institute. Not an easy man to manipulate, the Director would nevertheless be quick enough to realize what could be accomplished using this new theory—no, not theory, he corrected himself, this new *power.* He allowed himself to consider the concept of power. John Howard had not pursued power outside his own field. Yet he had acquired it, and knew he could acquire more should it serve his ends. As it was, he had been too profoundly disinterested in modern humanity and its current fate to consider becoming a politician himself. He could nevertheless appreciate the Director's position. The Director was the most powerful man, politically speaking, on New Paris. Now that Earth was dead, that made him the most powerful man in the settled worlds. Anything that consolidated and expanded that power would be most difficult for the Director to ignore. Or refuse.

Daedalus himself probably wouldn't recognize the potential of his discovery. The real significance of his own test would escape him. He would only be interested in something impossibly exalted, such as preventing the Cataclysm. That could take years, even decades to work out. But John Howard had a more immediate vision, one that could be accomplished in a few years. One that did not require a universe of patience. His eyes strayed to a small gold figurine on his desk. It was one of the oldest pieces ever found for the Collection, infinitely precious because there were so few such treasures. It was a likeness of the ancient Egyptian god Osiris, Lord of Forever. John Howard was not a patient man.

# PART II

## A Stitch in Time

# Chapter 4

## February 1, 1995 C.E.
## San Francisco

Hours later, Virginia and H.L. sat in silence, sharing their exhaustion and bewilderment. The museum had been searched, every case unlocked and locked again. Every closet, drawer, and cupboard had been opened and turned out. The search continued in the basement premises where objects not on display or waiting for conservation or repair were kept in storage.

"Perhaps they'll find it downstairs—" Virginia began.

H.L. didn't answer. His museum was phenomenally well ordered. Extremely valuable items were all under lock and key. Only Virginia, Min, and H.L. himself had access to those keys. When the theft was discovered, an immediate search for the keys located them where they were supposed to be. H.L.'s were locked in his desk. Virginia's were also locked up, in her credenza. Min had her keys with her in the big conservation rooms at the top of the museum. Access to the keys was only part of the mystery. The most precious items of the museum's collection were protected by sensor systems that went off if anyone touched the cases or moved too close to the larger items on pedestals. No one could lay hands on anything important without setting off the piercing wail of the alarm. The police and the chief security guard had tested the alarm. The system was working perfectly, it was set—and yet it hadn't made a sound when the Nefertiti statuette disappeared.

"It's enough to make you believe in black magic," H.L. muttered, "unless Georges, Hassan, and I are all in it together."

They continued sitting in the hallway outside the Amarna rooms, trying not to look in the direction of the empty display case. Finally Min Lee returned. She had a suspicion of tears in her dark eyes as she looked at H.L.

"Nothing. No sign of it. We looked in every possible place. They went through the plans for the building. They even took apart the ventilating system. It isn't here, H.L. And there's another thing. The front doors were locked and you need a key to get out. And the bolts were shut on the inside. The only person with a front door key who isn't here today is Paul, one of the security guards. He's home sick. The police sent someone to check. He has the flu. He also has his key. He couldn't possibly have gotten home in the time between the theft and the police checking on him. He lives all the way across town. And someone would have had to shut the bolts behind him."

"So," said Virginia slowly, "not only did someone remove the statuette from a locked case without a key and without setting off the alarm, they also got out a locked door without a key and shut the bolts from the other side. It's nonsense, H.L."

"It *is* nonsense," he nodded emphatically, the red color again burning in his cheeks.

"Here they come," said Min, gesturing toward the stairs.

The police had finished their search. Lieutenant Murphy was an old friend of the Director's, and he looked at H.L. with sympathy.

"Well, H.L., what kind of pharaoh's curse are you cooking up today?"

H.L. managed a small smile and merely nodded. He looked old, Virginia realized; the first time she had noticed it.

"We've finished for today. I have nothing to tell you, except that we are doing everything we can. Your two visitors have been allowed to go home. You should do the same."

Virginia stood up and took the Director's arm.

"Come, H.L. There is nothing else for you to do here tonight."

The police lieutenant gestured to her.

"Please wait a moment, Dr. Alexander. I have one or two more questions I would like to ask. If you wouldn't mind—"

He gestured in the direction of her office. She looked back at Min.

"Please see Dr. Pierce to his car, Min."

She led the way to her office and sank down into the old wooden desk chair. Its scream of protest echoed the one in her bones. She was tired to her very soul.

"Yes, Lieutenant?" she matched his distant tone exactly.

His smile was rueful. "Sorry, Virginia. I know this is hard for you. Let's get it over with as quickly as possible. You've known H.L. for a long time." It wasn't a question.

"Fourteen years. He chaired my doctoral committee. And then hired me out of grad school as his assistant here at the museum."

"Tell me about him. Your perspective."

"You know all this already."

"I have to ask. Indulge me."

She sighed, and leaned back. "We are friends and colleagues. On that basis, I know him as well as anybody. He wouldn't do it, you know."

When he didn't respond, she went on impatiently.

"Steal it. He wouldn't steal the statue. If you know him at all, you know that."

"And why not? What makes him exempt from the frailties of human flesh?"

She smiled a little bitterly at his professional demeanor. They had a few nonprofessional memories between them. He was talking as if they were strangers.

"He has family money. More than he'll ever need."

"Enough to buy the Nefertiti statuette?"

"No one has that much money. The point is, he wouldn't sell it for money. And he has no need to steal it to possess it. It's as much his as it could ever be, even if it never leaves the museum."

"Which he hardly does, anyway. And the two guests?

Drs. Georges and Hassan?

"Dr. Georges is with the Louvre. His field is Baroque painting. He would have no professional interest in the Nefertiti. He also has money. Dr. Hassan is an Egyptologist, works in Cairo, and would probably love to have her. He has an impeccable reputation. All this is meaningless. Either all three of them conspired to steal her, or none of them did. H.L. wouldn't do it for a fortune plus personal immortality. I see no way it could have happened at all."

He sighed and shook his head.

"Neither do I. Virginia, come out for a drink. Let's talk."

"No, but thanks," she shook her head.

"I thought we had something going between us. Something good. If I did or said anything—"

Her mouth tightened. "It isn't anything about you. I'm not ready to be involved with anyone."

"You just can't let the past die, can you?" he said bitterly.

She looked away. "The past isn't dead. It's part of the living, of who we are. I'm sorry. I thought you had decided to let the whole thing drop."

He smiled wryly. "I had. But I have this penchant for mean, red-headed women."

She smiled back, shaking her head. "It's the Irish in you. Charlie, I'm worried to death about all this, about H.L. This museum is his life. I'm just too tired. I'm sorry."

He looked at her for a long moment. "We'll find out

what happened, Virginia," he said gently. "It's only a matter of time."

# Chapter 5
## 2712 C.E.
## New Paris

"Two months! It has been over two months and still we are waiting for a decision whether to go forward!" Daedalus stormed. "I will be an old man before they finally decide anything. Too old to go!"

Vincent smiled. Nothing short of death would keep Daedalus from going on the mission, should there ever be one. And even that might be debatable. If nothing else, he would *haunt* the mission. He laughed softly, and Daedalus gave a reluctant answering smile, reading Vincent's thoughts. The Director's door opened and the young woman, wearing the look of all the young women who have guarded access to the powerful for centuries, beckoned to them.

"The Director will see you in the conference room. This way."

They followed her down the shining hall, each regarding her provocative walk in silence. *She is very pretty*, thought Vincent. His fingers itched for pen and paper. He felt Daedalus's eyes on him, full of amused understanding.

"Vincent," he whispered, "in your mind, you are

*drawing* that young woman! I'm ashamed of you."

Then they turned into a room that was surprisingly full of people.

The Director stood up at the head of the table and motioned them to the two empty chairs at the foot. About an acre of shining *ilannan*-wood table stood between them.

"We have reviewed your findings, Dr. Daedalus," began the Director, "most thoroughly."

"I should hope so," Daedalus mumbled. "You've had them long enough."

Vincent shot an alarmed glance at his old friend, but the Director was not offended.

"Arthur," he said in a totally different tone of voice, "you have not changed. You were the same at school. Impatient. Always wanting to go *now*. Do it *now*. How can you be so good a scientist and be so impatient?"

Daedalus smiled.

"I work twice as fast," he said simply.

The Director laughed then. He turned to the man on his right.

"Dr. Arbuthnot agrees with everything you have done here," he indicated the rack of data crystals on the table before him.

Daedalus nodded.

Arbuthnot leaned forward. "As usual, your work is impeccable, Dr. Daedalus. We have had to work hard to keep up with you in some places, but I am satisfied that your theory is completely sound. Certainly the prototype is very impressive. We have experimented on a small scale, as you know. You have done it again, done the impossible. You have given us time travel." The roomful of scientists nodded in agreement, all but applauding.

In spite of the words of praise, Vincent stirred uncomfortably. *Something is wrong*, he thought.

Arbuthnot echoed his thought. "But we are not in agreement on one thing."

"And what is that?" Daedalus shot back quickly.

Arbuthnot leaned forward.

"The nature of the test mission. Naturally, we all agree that your desire to go back and alter time to prevent the Cataclysm is the ultimate goal. It is a magnificent vision. Everyone here would give his or her life ten times over if that were possible. But more immediately, the test mission must be decided upon."

Daedalus opened his mouth to argue, but Arbuthnot forestalled him.

"You suggest that we send eight teams back in time to the year preceding the Cataclysm, place them to observe event strings, and relay data through the time lattice for us to analyze."

"I have read my proposal," Daedalus said dryly.

"Listen, Arthur," Arbuthnot continued, "while you have been working on perfecting the theory and experimenting with matrices, we have been analyzing history, and your own line of thinking, I might add. Going back and viewing the Cataclysm will be of no help . . . we have many visual records taken from satellites, the Moon observatories, the Centauri station. But the cause eludes everyone. We have established that it was not normal seismic activity, Earth was not attacked from outside, there were no meteor showers, it simply shook itself to pieces for no known cause. So, we have to look somewhere in the past for it. But how far back? Where do we start? A day before the Cataclysm? A week? A thousand years?

"You propose a year, but the evidence we have of the Cataclysm suggests nothing about time. I'm sure you know that the cost of such a program is going to be enormous. Are we justified in spending all those resources, taking that enormous risk with personnel, on the very slim chance that somewhere in that one year someone will stumble over a clue? How can we go back in time and change something we do not understand, have not even identified? We have had a team of researchers running the possible changes to history, the countless thousands of tiny decisions and actions that might avert the Cataclysm. Somewhere in the endless number of event possibilities, we must find one that would avert the Cataclysm in the past and not have detrimental effects on history since that time. And, Arthur, what if we discover that the event we must change in order to avert the Cataclysm will itself cause even more devastation to Earth? We have searched and hunted and theorized, and we simply cannot risk doing something that might destroy more than the Cataclysm itself."

Daedalus looked at Arbuthnot in exasperation.

"Good God, why do you waste all this time preaching to the converted! If you've read my proposal as carefully as you say, you also know that I propose that the first step be a series of close observation satellites, shielded and placed in time at five-year intervals, starting with a block of one hundred years. Only when we have gathered enough data would we know approximately when to go. The year of observation is the second step, to test the theory and gain some preliminary experience." He stared at Arbuthnot in bewilderment. "How could you think otherwise?"

The Director intervened. "It is the mission that is the issue."

"The mission? What are you talking about?" demanded Daedalus, with rising anger. "It must be clear that we cannot proceed with plans against the Cataclysm without a preliminary mission! It's inconceivable!"

"Of course," the Director's tone was placating. "However, we have another proposal here, suggesting another mission, one that will provide us with all the observation, useful data, experience that you propose, and benefit humanity in extraordinary ways."

Daedalus narrowed his eyes, his normally pleasant expression quite altered. "You can't have been paying attention to me. I state clearly in the paper that meddling with time is a desperate, a phenomenally dangerous undertaking with only one possible goal worthy of the risk. We can observe, nothing more, until we find a way to avert the Cataclysm. If we can do that. And surely that is worth the expense?" His voice was scornful.

"Naturally it will be worth any expense when we know we are on the right track. We hope that we can use it for the purpose you intend, Arthur," the Director went on. "And, by undertaking another mission first, a lesser one to be sure, but very important nevertheless, we can increase our chances of success against the Cataclysm. We need more time to discover its cause. But time is our enemy. Or it has been, until now. We are only considering this as an alternative, Arthur. Just listen for a few moments. I think you might be interested."

Another man leaned forward. As he looked at the dark, aquiline face, Vincent's fingers itched for his drawing notebook. The Director waved in the man's direction.

"Have you met Dr. John Howard?"

Daedalus mumbled something indistinct. Vincent, attuned to his reactions, instantly read reserve bordering on dislike. He looked more closely at the famous John Howard. Deep dark eyes set under arched brows gazed back at him for a moment before transferring themselves to Daedalus.

"I have read your papers with great interest, Dr. Daedalus," Howard began.

He had an unusually beautiful voice. Daedalus nodded.

"You have heard, perhaps, of the Collection?" Howard asked.

"Certainly," Daedalus replied.

Howard glanced at the Director, as if asking for aid in reaching the gruff old man.

"Arthur," the Director began.

"Oh, all right, of course I have heard of the Collection. Who alive in the colonies has not? A very worthy enterprise, as far as it goes. How am I concerned in this?" Daedalus asked impatiently.

"Well," Howard began, "although as I understand it we cannot go back in time and alter so major an event as the Cataclysm itself as yet, it did occur to me that we might go back and avert some of its worst depredations."

Daedalus looked up. "And how would we do that?" he asked.

"Your own very effective public demonstration suggested it to me. As you know, the Collection is a project dedicated to finding and preserving all that may be found of Earth's art and historical records. The Remnants of the Past, I believe the media has dubbed them. And as I am sure you also know, that remnant is tiny, the merest scrap of what was lost in the Cataclysm."

Daedalus nodded.

"Suppose," Howard continued, "we were to save something from that catastrophic loss? Suppose we were to go back in time and bring some of our heritage forward, *around* the Cataclysm?"

Vincent, who had been following the discussion with growing disappointment, sat up. *He is proposing we become grave robbers*, he thought with rising anger and disbelief.

He glanced at Daedalus, and saw his feelings mirrored in the old man's eyes.

"Dr. Howard, I chose my test carefully because it demonstrated beyond any doubt that it was possible to go back and forth through time. I chose to use the statue because it is so famous, because such a loss would gain instant and widespread attention, and I knew absolutely that I could undo the destruction. What you suggest is quite different. You suggest removing art treasures belonging to another time, stealing them, in fact.

"Ethical concerns aside for the moment, why do we suppose that doing this would not also affect the present in unforeseen ways?" demanded Daedalus suddenly.

"There are three reasons," began Howard. "First, because we would be removing the artifacts from the ancient past, long enough back for time to repair itself. There is the theory, isn't there, that time will try, like a river, to flow down the most compatible terrain? If disrupted in a minor way, the river will still tend, over time, to regain its most advantageous path. So removing artifacts—inanimate objects and records—from the ancient past would be unlikely to affect the distant present in any very important ways except—and this is a very important way—that we would have preserved the heritage of humanity. We would have it safe, here. Think of it. The paintings and sculptures made by human hands thousands of years ago. Not replicas. Not facsimiles. The real things, preserved forever. With us.

"The second reason time would be relatively undisturbed is that we would take only objects that for one reason, or another, did not survive in their own timeline long enough to seriously affect history. Many important objects, just as wonderful as those that survived up until the Cataclysm, failed to do so, due to war, natural disasters, thefts, and mysterious disappearances. Since they could have had no effect on history, we shall be doing no one a disservice by removing them to safety."

"And you will be able to identify which objects may be taken, and which left behind?"

Howard smiled. "I believe I am considered to be quite knowledgeable in my field, Dr. Daedalus. I have devoted my life to the study of humanity and its accomplishments. You may safely leave that judgment to me."

"And the third reason?"

"Well," Howard began, glancing out of the corner of his eye at the Director, "we have determined that it would be ultimately safer if we go back, not in our own track, but in one adjacent. The nextmost line, if you will."

Daedalus's head snapped up.

"Safer?"

"Yes. We cannot afford to undertake this enterprise if there is the slightest possibility that by so doing we might alter our own present so much that we do not exist."

Seeing Daedalus's expression, he hastened on earnestly.

"Not that we wouldn't all take the risk personally if it would avert the Cataclysm. But in order to do that, *we* must exist. We must try the theory and go back in time. If we are successful, and if the technology works as you say it must, then we can also continue to search for that moment in time, in our timeline, when we can safely avert the Cataclysm."

"So you suggest going back and removing these antiquities from some other timeline as the *test*?"

"Yes. A test of whether we may be able to do what you want, what we all want above all things. A test of the time lattice, the crystal matrix technology, and whether we will be able to use it to change the past."

"The risks are too great for a cartload of trinkets!"

Howard flushed then, and looked down at his hands. When he raised his eyes, Daedalus was shaken by the depth of emotion they showed.

"Not trinkets, Dr. Daedalus. The creativity of humankind."

"And what of the loss of these treasures to the other timeline? Do we rob them even as the Cataclysm has robbed us?"

Howard bowed his head again.

"There is the probability, as you know from your own theories about those timelines closest to us, that the Cataclysm exists in them as well. The immediately adjacent timelines, if I may speak of them like that, would be different from us in only small ways, in all major event strings virtually identical to our own. We would travel to an adjacent timeline through one of the synchronous points, the membrane of time possibilities, I believe you call it in your paper? You might say we would be robbing their past, I suppose, though I prefer to say we are removing the artifacts and preserving them from the Cataclysm. Theirs and ours. Isn't it better that they be preserved in at least *one* timeline than lost in all? And, of course, if we concentrate on those works that existed only for a short period, not long enough to really influence history, then we run even less risk of disrupting the future. We must try the theory. I can think of no nobler goal than to test it in the preservation of our past."

It had ended with Daedalus agreeing to consider the proposal. Vincent was surprised, but prudently held his questions until they were alone.

Daedalus and Vincent sat in their living room and considered the proposed expedition into the past. It was far from what Daedalus had originally imagined when he had considered using the crystal matrix for this purpose. He had dreamed of preventing the destruction of Earth. Now he was being asked to rob it instead. Vincent spoke up, suddenly.

"I have been reading the newest publications about the Collection. They have made significant advances, but the total is still small. It is hard not to be stirred by the desire to add to it in a truly significant way. It really is a noble undertaking, Dr. Daedalus."

"Yes. I know. I contributed something to it, didn't you know?"

"You did? No, I didn't know. What was it?"

"Something that had been in my family since before we colonized New Paris. Before the Cataclysm. A piece of sculpture, a girl, dancing. It was made by an artist named Degas. From the Nineteenth Century."

"Degas!" Vincent said in amazement.

"Yes. I should have known that you would recognize the name," he twinkled.

"But . . . you sat there acting as if . . . and letting Howard talk to you as if you knew nothing about the Collection. And you are a Contributor! Why?"

Daedalus nodded. "Because *he* knew."

"I think they are going to go, Dr. Daedalus. It . . . would be an admirable opportunity to test the theory. And—"

"And?"

"And I would feel safer if you were along."

Daedalus looked thoughtfully at Vincent for a moment.

"Have you been imagining there was an atom's worth of possibility that I would *not* go along?"

The door chime sounded, and Vincent was astonished to see the Director standing in the hall.

"Good evening, Vincent, Arthur," he nodded, taking the chair Vincent pulled forward. "I got your message. I'm on my way to meet with Dr. Howard now. Have you decided in favor of his proposal?"

Daedalus smiled at his old classmate. "George, you know as well as I do that this suggestion of traveling into the past for a bunch of old fa-lals is ridiculous, to put it no lower." Seeing the Director about to interrupt, he raised his hand and continued.

"However, I can see one important way in which it

can be turned to account."

The Director looked surprised. "I'm interested, Arthur. Go on."

"I am assuming that your real interest in all this is to test the validity of time travel."

The Director nodded. "That is my main interest, Arthur. Although I admit that the good publicity this mission of recovery will bring won't do me any harm, politically. After all, the Reconstruction is the most cherished goal of our times. It welds humanity together, unifies us, just at a time when disaffection and strife would bring us to chaos. It is absolutely critical that humanity, on all its myriad worlds, continues to work together with a common goal. That it continues to see itself as a single people on many worlds, not as many worlds with different and perhaps mutually exclusive goals."

"I agree. That has been the thrust of our sociological development for centuries. Now, George, we will go on this little shopping trip your Dr. Howard proposes. But we will have another purpose. My original proposal included the planting of close-surveillance recording satellites throughout time. That will no longer be necessary. It would take much longer to do that than if we go ourselves and record what we need."

"Arthur, what have you got in your mind this time?" the Director said slowly.

"My young protégé Nikko Lantis is a most talented crystallographic engineer. Now, he has been working primarily in the area of building crystal matrices that provide immense storage for data, communication relays, the like. I would like to work with him on building a little idea I have had during these interminable months of waiting for the Institute to make up its collective, erudite mind. Something that I believe will advance our plan by several decades. As we now understand the true nature of these time crystals, I have been turning over in my mind the idea of aligning certain lattices, creating a system that utilizes the systems of both monoclinic and triclinic. . . . " His voice trailed off, seeing the slightly glazed look in the Director's eyes. "George," he said firmly, "I think we can build a time recorder."

"Time recorder," the Director repeated.

Vincent's eyes kindled. "You mean," he asked slowly, "it will record the *time lattice* itself?"

"Exactly, my young friend. We can record the lattice at any given moment in history. We can then compare the recordings of time and see at which point certain event strings change or are acted upon by some catalyst, and that will tell us—"

"What caused the Cataclysm?" the Director finished.

"Yes. Eventually. Theoretically, you understand, we have always known that this was possible. But the amount of storage space necessary, even using the Agate memory crystals, would have been enormous, planet sized, if you can imagine a matrix that big. But with the unique properties of the crystallographic axes of the new lattices . . . the time crystals, well, I believe we will be able to solve that problem. The recorders will be small, almost indistinguishable from simple memory crystals. They can be sown in time like so much grain, and the matrix will harvest the crop. But, and it is a big but, each crystal recorder will have to be tuned to its own time. We can't just send them back through the gate. Someone will have to take them and tune them, and leave them to do their work. And, of course, they will only function so long as the crystal matrix functions. When we leave, they will cease to record."

"Well, Arthur, that is almost too much to take in."

"Just take in this much, George. If you think you will gain good publicity for additions to the Collection, consider what it will be like to be the man who gets credit for undoing the Cataclysm."

The Director nodded, his eyes very bright. "I'd probably never have to run for reelection again."

Daedalus snorted. "Can't think why you want the job in the first place."

"Power is not only a savory dish, Arthur, it is also addictive."

"Power! You talk of a paltry span of years in which to meddle in the affairs of humanity. Think big, George. We are talking about having mastery over time!"

"We would then be altering the past. You are certain about this, Arthur? I can't keep from thinking we might do something that is even worse than the Cataclysm."

"That's what the time recorders are for. They will tell us what will happen if we do this because, don't you see, in some event string far from our own line, we have. Everything that can happen, does happen. The true cause of the Cataclysm may well lie in a small, insignificant event string. It may be that the worst outcome of preventing it is that John Howard and his Holy Cause of the Collection will have to look for another job. Not a bad trade, in my opinion."

Silence spun out in the room as they all considered the implications.

"There is just one more thing, George. I am willing for Howard to lead the expedition. Let him think this is all about collecting antique doorstops. The teams who go will believe. They are all so obsessed with digging up things to enshrine in museums, they'll believe anything."

"But why? Why on earth go to all that expense needlessly? We can—"

"Listen, George. We are proposing to record not only the events of the past, but the probable past, the possible past, and the wildly improbable past. I'm sure you understand the implications of this. There are very few people in the universe I would trust with this information, with this possibility! You, Vincent, Lantis, and one other will know the true purpose of the mission."

"And who is really in charge," said the Director, nodding thoughtfully. "Will you be able to keep up the pretense, Arthur?"

Daedalus smiled. "Probably."

ᘐ ᘐ ᘐ

"Drink, John?" The Director offered the decanter.

"No, thank you. About the meeting this afternoon—"

The Director smiled at Howard's single-mindedness. "Well,. I think that went as well as could have been expected."

Howard nodded. "You know we will have to have Daedalus's full cooperation. I didn't notice any overwhelming enthusiasm for the mission on his part. Do you think he will consent?"

The Director laughed. "I know of no way on New Paris to stop him from going along. Even if I wanted to."

Howard smiled at that. "He's necessary to the mission's success. No one could possibly understand the theory as well as he does. And certain key people won't go along unless he does. I hope you are right."

"I am. I have known him for a long time. He will come with you."

"Then we must begin assembling the personnel. I will need a total of eight teams for the subsidiary gates, plus my own team to oversee the mission."

"Of course. I've had lists prepared of the top people in the field. Perhaps you would care to make your selections from here?"

He handed a data crystal to Howard, who turned it over in his hand, a curious expression on his face.

"Interesting, don't you think? Twenty years ago no one had heard of crystal technology. Now it governs our lives. Humankind has ever sought to be master over its destiny.

Is it possible that we will at last achieve that mastery, so that even the past may be reordered?"

"Be cautious, John," said the Director. "Some things may always be denied to the merely mortal."

Howard looked up from his rapt contemplation of the small glowing crystal in his hand, and smiled.

# Chapter 6

## 2712 C.E.
## New Paris

Howard stood on the floor of a vast, hangar and gazed up at the towering building that almost filled it. He squinted to see the young man only partially visible among the jutting spars of the framework and the hundreds of projecting crystals. The air rang with a strange vibration, just below the sense of hearing. *Dogs would be barking all over this planet*, thought Howard wryly, *assuming there were dogs on this planet.*

"I am John Howard, Mr. Lantis. I understand that Arthur Daedalus told you I would be coming to see you." He resisted the temptation to shout.

The young man finally put down his tools and started down the ladder. "Sorry," he said, "but when you are working with crystal, it calls the tune, so to speak. I couldn't stop in the middle of an adjustment to the matrix. Come into my office where we can talk."

He led the way to a small, cluttered cubicle. There was a welcoming absence of vibration inside.

"It's shielded," Lantis explained.

"What did Daedalus tell you about the purpose of my visit?"

Lantis replied slowly, with emphasis, "*Dr*. Daedalus explained that you are putting together a team for a top-secret project of some sort, and you need an engineer."

"Not just an engineer, Mr. Lantis. I need the best. One whom Dr. Daedalus recommends. The only one, I might add, that he will accept for this mission. You."

Lantis was young enough to blush at flattery.

"Dr. Daedalus is very kind. We worked together at the University on New Paris."

"So I understand. Now. Let me ask you a question, Mr. Lantis. What, in your estimation, is the most serious problem facing humankind at the moment?"

Lantis looked up, surprised. He had very vivid, clear blue eyes, luminous as the crystal at the heart of his work.

"I would have to say the Reconstruction."

"Yes?" encouraged Howard.

"I know you are the head of the Collection Project on New Paris," Lantis continued. "Does this secret mission have something to do with it?"

Howard smiled.

"Very quick, Mr. Lantis. It has everything to do with it. There has been an interesting serendipity in time. A stitch in time, in fact. Two things have come together in all this vastness we call the universe. One, Arthur Daedalus has spent a good part of his life developing theories about time, theories with no practicable application whatsoever because without the right kind of energy source there was no way to test them. And, two, an archaeologist on a little backwater world discovered an unusual type of crystal that can apparently channel not only energy, but time itself. What was merely theory now becomes practicable reality. Time travel."

Lantis brushed the long hair back from his eyes, and gazed at the ceiling. He knew all this. His longing to get back to his work was palpable. The dark gaze, which missed nothing, noticed the young man's eyes straying to his chronometer, to the window that showed the matrix he had been forced to abandon. *Give this boy something to build and he would be happy if Armageddon lay an hour ahead*, he thought.

"You have built matrices that can send messages to the heart of the galaxy, store the knowledge and experience of entire planets, move a starship across light years. You have now built a small matrix capable of moving through time. Dr. Daedalus feels confident that you will be able to construct a network of crystal matrices large and complex enough to enable us to take a team back into time and, if not prevent the Cataclysm, at least to prevent its worst depredations. I need an engineer to build the time gate complex, to take Daedalus's theories and, as you are used to doing, make them real. Come with us, Mr. Lantis. Build us a gateway into the past."

The blue eyes were alight with excitement.

*He will come*, thought Howard.

## 2712 C.E.: New Paris

Three days later on New Paris, Howard called out to a young woman walking ahead of him on the tree-lined walks that surrounded the University Inner Complex.

"Miss Alda." She stopped and, recognizing him, was speechless.

"I've been trying to reach you. Could we chat for a moment?"

"Dr. Howard," she stammered. "Of course.—"

"Let's sit here," he motioned to a bench.

He was not unacquainted with the symptoms of hero worship, and was quite ready to indulge her. She was an attractive thing; her black curling hair framed her face in a way that was very appealing. He surveyed her critically, noting the blush in her face, the feverish brightness in her dark eyes.

"I've been reading some of your papers," he went on. "I am very impressed. Your knowledge of ancient Earth cultures is most comprehensive."

She laughed then, nervous and delighted.

"I don't know what to say," she began.

He waved her embarrassment aside.

"I would like to speak to you as a colleague, Miss Alda. I have a project I would like to discuss with you. Something I think you may find of interest. And I need an assistant, preferably an archaeologist with a broad understanding of ancient cultures, and an interest in the Collection."

The look on her face told him clearly everything he needed to know.

"Perhaps we could meet and talk later. My office at four?"

She nodded, still speechless. Later would come the bubbling enthusiasm, the attempt at dignity, the shy presentation of her work. At this moment, sitting on a bench with one of the most famous men on New Paris, her idol, she was stricken dumb.

ꙮ ꙮ ꙮ

"Dr. Howard, allow me to present Gianni Roma. I think you have read his file?" The Director rose from his chair behind the great shining desk.

Howard nodded, looking up slightly at the tall man from Menelaus. His eyes lingered on the small bronze emblem on the breast of his black jumpsuit. It depicted the head of Medusa, the insignia of the Persean Order.

"Indeed yes. Very impressive. I hope you are considering joining us, Mr. Roma?"

The Persean's eyes weighed him, his gaze critical. Howard found himself growing restive. He was accustomed to being the one who weighed, judged, decided. He found it mildly irritating to be so obviously measured by the bright hazel eyes.

Finally Roma spoke, his voice surprisingly soft. "I found the outline . . . interesting. I understand there will be nine sites in all?"

"Initially, yes. We hope to establish additional subsidiary gates once we are settled in and assured that the crystal matrix is working properly. We will be a small number, working under pressure in very unusual circumstances. I'm sure you can appreciate that we need the best possible security personnel. Your authority with regard to the safety of the personnel will be absolute. With regard to the mission, second to my own."

Roma nodded, as if he had expected no less.

"And," Howard continued smoothly, "we will be depending on your expertise in both finding and securing good sites for the gates themselves. Somewhere relatively isolated, as few people around as possible for obvious reasons. And ideally, somewhere near the locations of the artifacts themselves. That part of it will be fairly complicated. We are leaning toward recently abandoned sites where we know there will be important archaeological discoveries in the future. Only now, we will get there first."

A line appeared between Roma's eyes at the shifting references to past and future. Howard struggled to keep the impatience he always felt in dealing with slower minds than his own, out of his voice.

"What I mean is—" he began.

"I understood what you said, Dr. Howard," said Roma quietly. "I was considering how this removal of objects from the past of this timeline will affect its future. It is an ethical issue."

A suspicion of dull red showed above Howard's beard, but his voice remained pleasant.

"One we have considered also, believe me. However, as we are by no means removing *every single* artifact of worth or historical interest, we feel we are not damaging the future in any significant degree. We have selected the most desirable pieces from our standpoint, but there will be many similar objects left behind. And whenever possible, we will retrieve art objects and documents that were lost or destroyed in their own time. It has been most carefully planned, I assure you."

Roma nodded, and turned to the Director.

"I do have one more question, sir."

"Of course. Anything I can tell you."

"Who will be the other security person at the main site? I have reviewed the list of security personnel at the other gates, and have made a few suggestions that I hope you will consider."

"Certainly. I never ignore the advice of my own experts. At least, not very often," he amended. "As to your first question, a young man I believe you will find an able second will accompany you. Per your approval, of course. His name is Temogen."

"He is not a Persean." It was not a question. The Perseans knew the name of every one of their kindred.

"No. Temogen was trained on Janis Prime. I think you will find his training and experience to be excellent."

Deducing correctly that Roma would despise any suggestion of personal interest or favor, the Director prudently refrained from mentioning his close ties with Temogen's family. He needed to return a favor, and Temogen's family was powerful and ambitious. Including Temogen on this high-profile mission would settle a pressing political debt.

"His qualifications are detailed here." He handed over the memory crystal.

Lewellyn did not allow himself to feel concern over this appointment. The record of Temogen's qualifications was indeed impressive. Previous employers had awarded him a fair number of bonuses and citations for excellence and described him as intelligent and courageous. He was also, Lewellyn knew, utterly ruthless. There had been a few incidents that had not found their way into his record. Money and power could still buy silence. Lewellyn was counting on Gianni Roma's experience and skill to keep Temogen in line.

Roma pocketed the crystal.

"I will review it immediately. If you will excuse me."

After he had gone, Howard looked thoughtfully at the Director. "An . . . abrupt young man to say the least. Is he as good as you say?"

The Director smiled.

"He's very, very good. If my life were at stake, I would want Gianni Roma on my side. Or better yet, in front of me."

Howard nodded. "Then my team is complete. We are ready."

"It has happened so quickly. You have no doubts at all?" The Director looked momentarily troubled.

"None. Timing is everything."

# PART III

## Perfect Timing

# Chapter 7

## February 13, 1995 C.E.
## San Francisco

"I need you to go to Abydos."

*Abydos*. The single word hung in the air between them, filled with the unspoken. Instantly, a vision of the massive ruins beside the river rose in her unwilling imagination. She could hear the calls of the boatmen as they sailed past in their small craft made of papyrus, even as they had been doing for thousands of years. She could smell the odors of dust and river water, reeds and birds and camel dung. She could see the workers, the lines of dirt carriers clamoring about the trenches of the dig. Abydos. It was as present to her as the museum director's face as he watched. She could not possibly go there again. Ever.

Virginia cleared her throat.

"The Seti I statuette." It was not a question.

H.L. nodded. "Hassan says Cairo is in a complete flap."

She remembered it well. Small, beautiful, gold, the Seti I statuette dominated an entire room in the Cairo Museum. Even among the wealth of golden objects there, it was special. In an eerie parallel to their own loss, the Seti I statuette had vanished from its locked case in the Cairo Museum. One distraught woman insisted it disappeared in front of her eyes. No alarm, not even a puff of smoke had marked its passing. One moment the burnished gold features of the king had looked out from the case, somehow both serene and sensuous. Then it was gone as if it had never been there. Less than an hour later, it was found by a workman at the Abydos dig, half buried in the sand. You couldn't fly from Cairo to Abydos in that amount of time. There was no possible way it could have been there. Yet the golden image of the great pharaoh, just eighteen inches long and unbearably bright in the sun, *was* there.

"They're sure it isn't a copy?"

H.L. shrugged. "Hassan says it's unmistakably the original, down to the last small scratch. He says he'd know."

"He would, too. So would you."

"Probably."

"It's not as well known as the Tutankhamen treasures. Others might not be so discerning. It would be a red-hot item on the black market." She knew that, however unlikely, it had to be considered. There existed a powerful fascination among those who collected stolen art for Egyptian artifacts. Preferably, those made of gold.

"This gets us nowhere, Virginia. The point is, it couldn't have been stolen. Neither could the Mona Lisa, nor Michelangelo's *Pietà*. The *Pietà*, for God's sake! Disappeared out of the Vatican and out of its bulletproof case, leaving it locked. No one has that combination. Even the Pope couldn't get it! It's happening everywhere. Every major museum in the world has been hit, most of them more than once. Out of the Tutankhamen treasure there's hardly a gold pinkie-ring left! The greatest art treasures of every culture are being plundered, and there hasn't been a single clue as to how it is being done. Until now. A statuette that was in Cairo at nine in the morning turns up in Abydos just before ten. And there's more. Workmen at the Abydos dig have been reporting strange noises, flashing lights, that sort of thing, for several weeks. We've largely ignored the reports; you get a lot of that sort of thing on a dig. But now, two of our best diggers have disappeared. At first we thought they had taken unofficial leave and gone home. But the foreman says they are two of his most responsible workers, and their families have not heard from them. We can't ignore their disappearance. And it must be connected with the thefts. At least it is a place to begin. So I need you to go to Abydos."

"I'm not sure I can. Surely someone else could—"

"No one else knows Abydos as well as you. No one I can trust." He looked at her for a long moment, sympathy and determination equally balanced in his eyes. Finally he shook his head. "Virginia. It is over. You must go on with your life."

"H.L.," she ground out his name from between clenched teeth. In the past using his name like an expletive had been a joke.

"I know. But it is time you buried the past."

"I thought our job was to dig it up."

There was a long, tense pause. Then, seeing the need as well as the determination on his face, Virginia relinquished her suddenly insupportable resistance.

"Oh, well. I guess it is time to face down the demons of memory."

He smiled then, and patted her shoulder with gentle affection. "Good. Tomorrow. It is arranged."

# Chapter 8
## 2715 C.E.
## Traveler One

Vincent looked out the viewport and considered the ship framed there. Hanging against the veil of stars, *Traveler One* embraced a shining asteroid-sized chunk of crystal. Huge spars of crystal jutted out from the main body, connecting the ship to the matrix. It was opalescent with almost blinding color. *A crystal matrix the size of an asteroid*, he thought. *Powerful enough to travel through time as well as space. Powerful enough to travel through someone else's time*. He glanced at Dr. Daedalus, and found the old man's eyes upon him.

"Worried, Vincent?" the scientist asked.

Vincent smiled in apology.

"I know the theory is sound," he assured his mentor. "It's the fundamental thing we're about to do that concerns me."

"I thought you believed in the Collection as a great and noble enterprise?"

Vincent nodded.

"I do. Of course I do. But, somehow, it doesn't seem right to be taking art treasures from some other world. And it is another world. Not our world at all."

Daedalus nodded.

"I know. But they would all be lost in the Cataclysm anyway. This way at least they will survive. It will be interesting to see how the works themselves compare with our facsimiles. I wonder if they will be subtly different in some way. Marked by their own timeline, as it were."

Vincent looked at Daedalus, his eyes asking.

"No, I don't think they will be different," Daedalus answered. "And who knows, perhaps you and I in that next line are this very minute on a shuttle, about to embark into the past of their nextmost line. Perhaps even ours. What will happen to us then? Will their depredations in our past somehow affect our history?"

Vincent looked up at the cabin ceiling, ruefully smiling at Daedalus's tortuous thinking process. Daedalus laughed.

"You see, Vincent, this is the ultimate frustration and the ultimate challenge for a scientist. You simply cannot estimate the validity of a theory if there is no way to disprove it. We will never know how our traveling into the past will affect the future until we do it. Theory is not enough. We must have experience if we are to prevent the Cataclysm. That is the true goal, after all. And surely it is in every other time as well."

"I have one more question. You said you and I in that other line, or in many other lines, might be doing the same thing. One of those pairs, Daedalus and Vincent, might go back in time to our past, and so affect *our* present, or our future."

"I did say something like that. So?"

"So," said Vincent, "if they did, how would we ever know? Would we remember the past the way it used to be? Or would our memories adapt to the new past?"

Daedalus considered for a moment.

"Remember that the crystal matrix is more than a doorway. Within its structure we will be unaffected by any changes we, or anyone else for that matter, might make in the past. So, Vincent, if that other Vincent and Daedalus accidentally change history, even though such a change might cause us to cease to exist in the natural course of time, because we are not in the natural course of time but here, in the crystal matrix, we will be unaffected. When we return to our own line we would, of course, experience the consequences of the change, but not the process."

"But for everyone else, still in our timeline?"

"That would depend. Time would be changed, but not necessarily the memory of it. Remember the test, Vincent. We blew up the statue. Everyone in that lecture hall remembered it being blown up because, at the time of the demonstration, we had not gone back and retrieved it. History had not yet been changed. After the statue's demise, we went back and got it, dipping into the event string and out again. That is the key. We changed the event string after it had already happened for everyone in the lecture hall. Memory remained intact, but the effects of the change were there to see on the gate pad. Because they were in the room with the crystal matrix, and were shielded from the change in time. Now others who were not in the demonstration, as you know, remembered that the *sculpture garden* was blown up and the statue gone. They did not remember shards of the statue being found, because of course there were no shards in the altered timeline. They only know that it was gone after the explosion, and now it is again safe in the garden where it belongs. They did experience the change in history." Seeing Vincent's expression, he smiled. "Paradox is hard to defend, no? You and I, and the Vincents and Daedaluses of the other lines, will take good care that we do not disrupt history."

In the silence that followed, the shuttle began its docking sequence with *Traveler One.* Vincent looked and smothered a small gasp as the great crystal asteroid ship now filled the viewport. He nervously began shoving his notebook into his carry sack, but Daedalus stopped him with a gesture.

"There is no hurry, Vincent. It will be several minutes before they cycle the airlocks. Soon, we will be very busy. But for now, we can take our time."

ꙮ ꙮ ꙮ

Daedalus's prophecy was correct; they were very busy. The journey to Earth was only a few weeks. Plenty of time to develop their space legs, and to get acquainted with each other and the mission. Commander Durand gave a reception the night *Traveler One* began its historic journey—historic in the truest sense of the word, as no other journey had ever been. The whole team gathered in a large room, with great viewports looking out at the stars. Once, thought Vincent, this traveling faster than the speed of light was believed impossible. Now, nothing was believed impossible.

The Commander, a middle-aged woman from Carillon Four, had been gracious. "You are the greatest explorers of our time," she had said to the assembled travelers. "Your commitment to rescue some of our heritage and preserve it is a noble undertaking. To contribute to the Reconstruction is the most cherished ideal of every human in the settled worlds. You are embarking on an opportunity that is breathtaking in its scope. It will be a privilege to carry you and your great accomplishments back in triumph. I congratulate you all."

Many of the travelers had been slightly chilled by their realization of the enormous gulf they proposed to put between themselves and everything that was familiar. The Commander's words had warmed them to excitement. They were clustered in groups around the viewport lounge, the archaeologists who would supervise the removal and packing of artifacts, the engineers and technicians who would maintain the gate system, the security personnel who would watch over the safety of the teams.

The ship was surprisingly spacious, built for journeys taking months and years. There was one thing no amount of artistry or comfort could completely palliate, however—the constant, nearly subsonic whine of the crystal matrix at the heart of the ship. Waking or sleeping, the travelers' bones and nerves hummed along with it, until they all felt like extensions of the matrix with no true existence apart from it. It became difficult both to imagine how to endure it for one day longer, and how life once had been without it.

They were a small group, each person a specialist. The engineers, technicians, and security personnel would have the primary responsibility for initializing the gate system transfers, but Roma and Daedalus were united in their insistence that no one go on the mission without the skill necessary to operate the gate controls. Lantis, under Daedalus's direction, drilled them all endlessly. Absolute accuracy was essential because, as he pointed out, the tiniest error could send something or someone a thousand miles or a thousand years in the wrong direction. Eventually, Vincent believed he could use the gate safely in his sleep.

"The transfer suits," Lantis explained one morning, holding up a black garment with a small control panel on the chest, "are used to augment the time signal of the matrix when transferring to locations without gates. A small power crystal fits here," he pointed to the panel, "and this is tuned to the time of its gate. So, if you are located in the Yucatan, for example, your transfer suit crystals are tuned to that time, that matrix. If you hit this return button," he pointed to the control, "the crystal will lock in on the console and initiate a return to that location. It's a one-way transfer only, back to the gate of origin. The final piece of equipment relative to traveling in the gate system is the transfer crystal in the transcomp." He held up one of the hand-sized multitask transport computer relay systems. "These are also tuned to your particular gate. You can use a transcomp to transfer, but only between your gate and the main gate. They are not strong enough to transfer between subsidiary gates in different time periods. These should not be used to transfer between times, except in emergencies. As you will always have your transcomps to use for recording and computing, we have also equipped them with transfer capability as an additional safeguard, but the safest way will be to use the matrix-to-matrix transfer."

Howard used every available hour to expound upon what he called their "crusade against time." It was clear that no one was exempt from what he called their "Mission of Rescue." When Howard used the word "mission" it had a capital "M" and, indeed, his handsome face glowed with inner fire when discussing it. Vincent always felt tempted to genuflect.

"We are few in number, and we do have time constraints, as strange as that may seem," he permitted himself a small smile. "Some retrievals will require only a few of us; others will involve everyone. Whatever your specialty, you may well be called upon to help retrieve artifacts. We have good equipment, but we will all be getting our hands dirty. We are all orphans cut off from our ancestors, and the works of their hands. We go back in time to save, to preserve, not to plunder. We will share in the labor and the glory equally."

He had looked sharply at Roma as he said that, as if it were part of a continuing argument between them. Vincent glanced at the tall, black-clad man who leaned against the edge of the viewport, apparently absorbed in the view of stars. Did he imagine a slight flicker in those bright eyes, a tiny flutter at the corner of his mouth? Roma shifted, aware of the scrutiny, and glanced over his shoulder at Vincent.

Vincent blushed and lowered his eyes, but not before Roma surprised him with a sudden smile. It had an amazing softening effect on the stern, lean features. *Perhaps Roma is not totally lacking in humor, after all.* The thought flicked across his mind, then Howard called for the voice-activated lights to dim. The holographic projectors reproduced images of the art treasures they sought in the center of the room. Today's "most wanted" list included Egyptian artifacts and papyri.

"Seti I," he began, indicating the shimmering gold statuette floating before their eyes. "Eighteen inches high, solid gold with lapis lazuli and carnelian inlay. . . ."

ꙮ ꙮ ꙮ

As the great ship neared Earth space, Vincent and Daedalus stood together in the cargo bay that housed the crystal matrix destined for the main gate. Lantis was almost totally concealed within the matrix, the intermittent flash of his tools giving the only indication of his location. He had spent most of the journey inside the matrix, patiently and meticulously following Daedalus's instructions. The crystal whined as Lantis played upon it, and Vincent grimaced at the pain in his ears. Daedalus nodded, and pointed to Howard, standing unmoved a few feet away. No shade of discomfort distorted the handsome features. He watched the flashing crystal with a look of dreamy content on his face. He did not look like a man standing on the brink of eternity. *But then*, thought Vincent, *nothing seemed to ruffle*

*Howard. Except,* he revised the thought, *except possibly Gianni Roma.*

In the beginning, it had been small things. There had been the meeting at which they discussed the locations for the gates. Several of the archaeologists had wanted the main base to remain on the ship. They were uncomfortable with the idea of being completely separated from what they regarded as their own present. Daedalus had dismissed this as impractical, explaining patiently the nature of the crystal matrices and the way they functioned in time.

"The crystals, in order to operate at their highest potential, must be *tuned* to the time in which they are located, much as the ancients tuned crystals for primitive radio devices," Daedalus had explained to the assembled teams. "Also, the further you move matter, the larger and more complex the matrix must be. The power cost to push matter across timelines is enormous, even for a matrix the size of *Traveler One's.* To send material directly to *Traveler One* from all the subsidiary gates, each site would need a matrix the size of the one that powers *Traveler One.* Impractical, I'm sure you agree. We will require a primary base located in the same timeline as all subsidiary gates, to act as the central clearinghouse, as it were. The objects will be sent to *Traveler One* from the main gate. The command team will be located at that gate."

He had glanced at Vincent and Lantis as he concluded, his eyes twinkling. It would be necessary, they knew, to have the main base within the timeline itself for another reason. The time recording crystals they planned on scattering through time would be linked with the main matrix. They needed its vast size and capacity to store the precious time recordings that lay at the heart of their hopes.

Howard, particularly fascinated with Old Egypt, determined to set up the matrix and the main time gate in the Eighteenth Dynasty, during the reign of Amenhotep IV. During the brief, aberrant reign of this particular pharaoh, many important temple sites were closed before being rededicated to his One God, Aten. There was an ideal spot for the main gate in an abandoned cluster of buildings on the banks of the Nile, near the ancient Temple of Osiris at Abydos.

"No." Gianni Roma dropped the quiet word into the flow of Howard's eloquence.

"I . . . beg your pardon?" Howard said, his voice expressing only mild surprise.

"I said no," repeated Roma simply.

Vincent felt Lantis's bright, sardonic gaze from across the table. The engineer made a small gesture with his hands, which Vincent had no trouble identifying as an explosion.

Howard leaned back in his chair, his long fingers steepled in front of his face.

"I . . . don't quite understand, Roma. This site is perfect. It's over a mile from the main temple, and a good portion of the rooms are usable. The temple itself has been reduced to a handful of preoccupied priests. I explained about the *Ban of Akhenaten*, and we are certain to find—"

Roma was shaking his head. "I've read the report. It's too close to the main temple and to the town. You say it's abandoned, but the main temple is not. It would be almost impossible to secure."

Howard was persuasive. "I spent quite some time selecting this site. It is exceptionally convenient, with good anchorage at the river's edge. We can pass up and down the river quite easily, and, with care, undetected."

"The risks are unacceptable."

Howard smiled, without amusement. "Well, then, what would you suggest?"

Roma allowed himself to reflect, until Howard's eyes darkened.

"Your reports note an older temple site with a labyrinth beneath it three miles inland in the heights above Abydos. It is forbidden to the local people, so it will be easy to secure. It's been closed and sealed by the date we propose to occupy it. We would be undetectable there. If the plans we have are accurate, there is room for everything we need. Not generous, but enough."

"This will delay everything! We'd need days to clear enough room even to begin! We'll need twice the equipment for environmental control because it'll be hotter than the hinges of hell in there. We need the space for the artifacts. This could slow up the entire mission for days, perhaps weeks. You can't be serious." Howard's expression had darkened, and the dull red that only Roma seemed able to summon had blossomed in his cheeks.

"Security must come before convenience, Dr. Howard. And, as I'm sure you agree, we have plenty of time."

There was a suspicion of a gleam in Roma's hazel eyes as if he were suppressing amusement.

Howard was not amused. "Very well," he replied stiffly. "I am guided by your opinion."

He pushed his chair back and dismissed the rest of the meeting with a wave of his hand.

"Thank you for coming. You are all making excellent progress. Our success will be assured if we all continue as we have begun."

Vincent noticed the look of sparkling anger on Cassandra Alda's face as she gathered her notes and prepared to leave. He moved to join her in the doorway.

"What is it about those two?" he asked, smiling. "They always seem to strike sparks off each other. I think it's the only time I ever see Howard get mad."

"He has every right to get angry!" she flared back. "Roma, picking, always questioning, he would enrage a saint. Dr. Howard certainly knows what he is doing, or he wouldn't be leading the mission. But Roma questions him at every level."

Vincent tried to be fair. "Sometimes Dr. Howard gets . . . well, caught up in his enthusiasm for the mission and overlooks other issues. It's Roma's job to be concerned about the security of the mission, so—"

She tossed her head impatiently, and brushed past him. "Roma's job is to protect the mission, not interfere with it. I don't think he appreciates its importance at all. Certainly he doesn't appreciate its leader's importance. I am amazed at Dr. Howard's patience with him."

Vincent watched her hurry down the hall to catch up with Howard, his face registering what was becoming a familiar sense of loss. Lantis was at his elbow, following his gaze.

"Trying to compete with the great God of History, Vince?"

Vincent turned to him in frustration.

"It isn't like that." Under Lantis's patently disbelieving eyes he flushed, and smiled in spite of himself. "Well, maybe it is like that. Not that she'll ever notice."

"You never know. She may wake up one day and realize there is a present. And even more radical, a future. Come on. Time for a little relaxation. Listening to Howard prose on about the glories of the past makes me long to do something spectacularly disrespectful."

Vincent laughed. "Like what?"

"Oh, I don't know. Maybe while we're delivering our little time recorders, I'll find a way to carve my initials in the fabric of time. *Lantis was here.*"

ꙮ ꙮ ꙮ

It was late. Howard stood, looking across the dimly lighted lounge at Gianni Roma, who had taken up his favorite spot at the viewport. Coming to a decision, he picked up a bottle and two glasses and moved to the table nearest the viewport.

"Forever gazing out at the stars, Roma," he said softly.

Roma did not turn to look at him. "They keep things in perspective. I find it useful."

Howard sat down and pulled out the other chair.

"We have really not spent much time talking, and I think now would be a good time to . . . well, reach a complete understanding, don't you agree?"

Roma gave a last look at the shimmering expanse, and turned to the table. His face registered nothing but polite attention.

"Understanding?"

Howard nodded, his eyes narrowing. "I want to impress upon you how important your contribution is to this mission. I'm certain that you know I have the highest regard for your ability, or else you wouldn't be here."

Roma nodded. Howard felt his temper rising, and made a conscious effort to suppress it. *What was it about the man that got under his skin?*

"This mission may be the greatest opportunity we will ever have to repair the losses to human history caused by the Cataclysm. It might even pave the way for us to prevent that catastrophe from happening. It will be absolutely essential for the success of the mission that we are in accord."

The dark eyes glowed, the beautiful voice resonated with passion and urgency. At such times Howard's face was illuminated from the fires that burned within.

Roma looked at Howard in silence for a long moment. Perhaps it was the quality of the silence that Howard found so annoying.

Then Howard leaned back and smiled with what appeared to be genuine amusement. He indicated the bottle on the table, and the empty glass.

Roma shook his head. "No . . . thank you."

Howard laughed. "As you are such a high-order *Persean*, I assume what I've heard is correct. No vices, no lighter moments, no . . . shall we say, distractions? Do you ever relax, Mr. Roma?"

Roma's lips curved, lightening the stern features. "Do you know what we call a relaxed Persean on Menelaus, Dr. Howard?"

It was Howard's turn to shake his head, his eyebrows arched in question.

"Dead," said Roma, as he stood up.

He walked to the door, then turned back. "Perhaps you are correct, and we do need to come to an understanding. I have serious questions about this mission, and what lies behind it. But the part of it that rests with me is the safety of the personnel. That is *my* mission. I will allow nothing to come between that mission and me. I hope that is . . . completely understood." It was not a question. The door shut softly behind him.

After a heartbeat Howard turned back and regarded the viewport in silence. The long fingers drummed a silent tune on the table. Calm, serene, his face revealed nothing of his thoughts.

The ship was as quiet as it ever was, deep in the time period arbitrarily designated as night. Howard walked through the hallways, silent and thoughtful. *Traveler One* orbited the Earth. He could see it out the viewports, the sphere that was once again blue and green and white. Not so lush as it had been, not so fully enveloped with the moisture-rich veil of cloud, but alive. Clusters of lights would show, upon closer view, where humanity had once again gathered together to rebuild life and hope. They were unaware of the presence above their skies of their greatest hope, the travelers who were determined to defeat time itself. Howard smiled at the view.

All was in place. The sites for the gates had been agreed upon, not without difficulty. It seemed that Roma had produced disagreement where he had least expected it. Accustomed to having his lightest pronouncement in his chosen field taken as supreme truth, it was unsettling to be constantly questioned by a young hired gun from a backwater world like Menelaus. He frowned slightly. No, Menelaus was not a backwater world, exactly. His own unyielding intellect would not tolerate inexactitude, even from himself. Menelaus was a small world, by reports bleak and lacking in amenities, but it was a very famous world nevertheless. It had one resource that made it absolutely unique. The Persean Order was the source of the best soldiers and security officers in the settled worlds. Followers of its unyielding code lived their lives devoted to one ideal, the protection of human life. They were warriors who abhorred war, skilled practitioners of the martial arts for whom a resort to violence was itself defeat. They were also realists. So long as the penchant for violence existed among humans, protection from it would be a necessity. Perseans chose carefully whom they would serve. It was a unique world in another way. No one from off-planet went to study at the Persean School. Human traffic, with regard to Menelaus, was strictly one way. It made perfect sense that the mission would be protected by one of the best Perseans to be obtained.

Gianni Roma was not, however, adding to his peace of mind. Howard continued on his solitary walk, feeling the endless crystal noise crawling on his skin. Soon, in a day or two, he would be in Old Egypt. He imagined the deep quiet of the desert, disturbed only by the most elemental sounds—wind, water, the cries of animals, the footsteps of men.

Roma and Temogen had gone first, transported across Daedalus's time lattice to an adjacent timeline and back into its ancient past. He shivered slightly, remembering the great surge of energy as the ship's crystal matrix had realigned the fabric of the universe, sending Roma and Temogen to discover eternity. Even now, as he stood here looking out at a different time, a different Earth, they were examining the proposed site, observing its potential for security and convenience. *Security first, convenience a not-too-close second*, Howard mused with a somewhat sour smile. It was exhausting, dealing with what he frankly regarded as little men, particularly one with a hero complex. *Perseans*! Still, he had every confidence that Roma, though officious, was efficient. His own sense of self-importance would not tolerate less than minute attention to detail. When he and Temogen returned, all would truly be ready.

The members of the team were prepared, drilled, to perform their duties without error. The main crystal matrix and the subsidiary matrices that would make up the time gate system lay suspended in cushioning layers of gel. The network waited only for Lantis's final touches to bring it to life on Earth thirteen hundred years before the common era, thirty-eight hundred years before the Cataclysm, four thousand years ago tonight. The thought that anything could have gone wrong with Roma and Temogen or their journey never crossed his mind. He smiled at the beautiful world spinning before him, all blue and green and white against the darkness. He was a man whose time had come.

# PART IV

## Time Is of the Essence

# Chapter 9

## February 16, 1995 C.E.
## Cairo

Virginia stood staring out the window of her hotel room, shivering slightly. Like all modern hotels in Cairo, this one overcompensated for the desert climate by frigid blasts of air-conditioning. The looming shadows of the pyramids at Giza swam at the edge of the scene, dimmed but not defeated by the air pollution and the permanent haze from the great dam at Aswan in the south. Once, she reminded herself, they would have stood glittering in the pure air like gigantic crystals—before the uncaring builders of the city of Cairo had stripped them of their polished white limestone coats for the bridges and mosques and public buildings.

Her own reflection in the glass caught her eye. She looked insubstantial, superimposed over the awesome giants of Egypt. What on earth was she doing here? Egypt was alien to her now. Once she had loved this land with a passion that hurt. *Or perhaps*, she thought, *that was untrue*. She had loved the *past* of this land. Had the Egypt of the present ever been anything more to her than a gateway? Now, even that gate was shut.

It was nonsense, sending her to investigate, to straighten out anything. She was utterly inadequate to the task. This was the scene of failure. Oh, she was moderately successful by most standards. Virginia knew herself to be well liked, well thought of, especially by H.L.'s circle. Some of his cachet was bound to extend to his long-time assistant and probable heir-apparent. He had made no secret of his own affection and respect for her. He had made her accept a position in his museum, and she liked to think she had contributed to its success. But the desert winds no longer alternately baked and froze her; she did not hear the sighs of ancient queens sifting through the ruins on moonlit nights.

She was an associate director of a museum, an administrator. Others would have to camp on the edge of history, digging for potsherds and fragments of bone, bruised, dehydrated, gritty with sand. And, before the first glorious, exalted moments of discovery had even faded, they would bring their treasures to her.

Sick with longing for a moment, she let her face rest against the cold glass of the window, fists jammed against her mouth. H.L. had told her he was depending on her to find an answer to the inexplicable thefts. To somehow make sense out of nonsense. To help protect the museum. So she had come to Egypt, and tomorrow she would go to Abydos. But in her heart, after all, she didn't believe any of it.

A phone call early that morning had reminded her of how hopeless a task he had set her.

"Virginia," the voice at the other end was not professional and distant at all.

"Hello, Charlie," she replied warily. If the terms they had parted on last had not been bad, exactly, neither had they been particularly good.

"H.L. told me you were going back to Abydos."

*Back* to Abydos. "Yes," she had said, swallowing a little helpless flutter of annoyance. H.L. could no more avoid busying himself in her life than he could help being an Egyptologist. "Did I need police permission to leave town?"

He laughed a little. "No. But I wish you had told me, all the same. I like to know where you are, even when you aren't in the middle of a criminal investigation."

"I'll try to remember that," she said lightly.

"I don't suppose there is any point in telling you that I'm sorry for whatever it is I have done, or failed to do, or be."

"I keep telling you. It isn't you. It's me."

"Well, perhaps this trip to Abydos will serve to lay a few of the ghosts."

There was a long pause. "There is only one," she said quietly.

The really sad thing, she reflected, the impossible thing to explain to Charlie Murphy was the nature of the ghost. He thought, everyone thought, that the specter who haunted her was that of a boyish, laughing young archaeologist named Hickson. No one would ever understand that it was herself.

Except perhaps H.L. He couldn't possibly think anything she found in the ruins at Abydos would help solve the thefts. It was madness. He was sending her there because he believed it was the only thing that would allow her to finally lay the past to rest. She faced the featureless hotel room, turning her back on the lure of the titans of the ancient world.

# Chapter 10

## 1357 B.C.E.
## Abydos

"Temogen. I want to talk to you," Roma's voice sounded behind Vincent's chair. He and Temogen had been the last to finish dinner, delayed by a not-very-successful attempt to get to know the moody security second. He turned, startled at the note in the normally soft, pleasant voice. Roma was looking over his head at Temogen.

Temogen waved his hand, as if inviting Roma to talk all he wanted to.

"I think you would prefer to hear what I have to say to you in private."

Temogen made no move to get up, and merely shrugged. Vincent, scandalized at his insolence, rose hastily to his feet. As he reached the door he heard Roma say, "I want to hear an explanation. You'd better hope it's a good one."

Vincent stopped outside the door and glanced back, unable to stop himself from listening.

Temogen smiled and spread his hands wide.

"He saw me. What was I supposed to do?"

"You were supposed to use appropriate caution. You were not supposed to be seen. Failing that, you were supposed to use the tranquilizing darts. You killed him, didn't you?"

Temogen sat up a little straighter.

"No. I told you, I fired at him and he ran. He's probably still running. But he wasn't hurt."

Roma regarded him for a long moment in silence.

"I found the bundle he carried. I saw the scorch marks from the disrupter."

"The fire bounced off the rocks. I tell you, he wasn't hurt. No one could run that fast if they were. He may babble about it, but his friends will just decide he's off his head. The perimeter is secure now." He met Roma's stare with his own, apparently sincere.

"Very well." Roma turned and walked toward the door. Then he looked back, and his voice took on a tone of cold menace.

"If I find you have lied to me. If anything like this happens again. Anything at all. It would be unfortunate for you. Unfortunate, and permanent."

He brushed past Vincent without a word. Vincent drew a silent breath, profoundly thankful that he had never heard that cold voice addressed to him, and equally determined that he would never give Roma cause to use it on him.

The next day began with good news. Vincent looked up from the viewscreen in the Gate Control Room. Cassandra and Howard were fidgeting impatiently for confirmation that the work could actually begin. Roma was waiting for his report.

"Everyone has reported in, safe and ready for work," said Vincent, turning from the viewscreen, his thin face lighted up with excitement and triumph.

Howard nodded, smiling tolerantly at the young man's enthusiasm.

"I'll go through to the other gates with Lantis, starting in the morning," said Roma, "before they actually begin work."

Howard felt the all-too-familiar sense of frustration building, and sighed audibly.

"Surely that is unnecessary, Mr. Roma," he said patiently. "They all report the gate system is working perfectly. They are competent people or they wouldn't be here. It will take days to check each system personally."

"Yes, and it *is* necessary," said Roma softly but with emphasis. "You should come as well, Vincent," he added.

Vincent was delighted and showed it. He laughed, and Roma raised an eyebrow.

"I was just thinking," Vincent said, "that I want to be everywhere at once, and with the gate that is almost possible."

"Too much haste," said Roma grimly, "and you might be nowhere at once. We will test each and every gate before we begin work. Starting tomorrow morning."

Howard watched them leave the gate room in silence. He stared at the shimmering spars of crystal that rose on all sides to disappear above the gate pad in the swimming currents that surrounded the matrix, the currents of time. Why was he afflicted in this way? Why couldn't he inspire these people with a little of his fire, his longing to go out and find those precious links with the past that was denied to them in their own time? For a moment, he was touched by unaccustomed self-doubt. A soft voice drew him from his abstraction. It was Cassandra, looking at him with a worried expression that was becoming habitual.

"Is something wrong, Dr. Howard?"

He forced a smile as he looked down at her. "No. Just a little tired of waiting. You understand."

It was not a question. Her cheeks flooded with geranium color.

"Yes, it's terrible for you. Why do you stand for it?" Howard smiled again, weary but patient.

"Roma is doing his job. I know that. It's just . . . so difficult to be this close, and have to deal with these interminable delays. But I'm certain he really believes them to be necessary. He's right, of course; we can't take any risks with the safety of our people."

She smiled then, her heart in her eyes. His manner became brisk.

"Well, I have some work to do so I suppose I should be at it. Perhaps after dinner you would like to look over the plans for the Seti I dig. I think you'll approve. Oh, and have you got that outline for the Asia Minor station?"

Their conversation became businesslike as they tacitly agreed to drop the subject of Gianni Roma.

Three days later, Lantis reported all the gate systems were ready and safe to use. They were ready. Cassandra and Howard left early for the Minoan gate in the heights above Lasithi on Crete. Wrapped in a cloak of darkness, they led the Minoan team to the Psychro Cave.

"Handy, having its location in advance," said Howard gaily. "It will not be discovered until 1883 C.E.—to be precise, by peasants out looking for a goat. Another fourteen years before Hogarth gets here and opens the lower chamber. We shall be at home admiring the prizes long before that goat points the way."

He whistled softly as they moved into the upper cave. He felt excitement such as he had rarely felt before go singing along his spine. A rockfall blocked the entrance to the lower grotto.

It took two days to shift the boulders that had fallen from the roof, and Howard and Cassandra worked as hard as any laborer shifting the tons of stone and dirt, all of which would have to be replaced for Hogarth and his diggers. Carefully they worked their way down the sloping entrance to the lower chasm. Cassandra caught her breath, and Howard stopped so suddenly he almost dropped the lantern he carried. A wave of awe swept over him, blurring his vision. His heart constricted. It was like walking into the cathedral of giants. It was like walking into the presence of God. It was like being God. A lake, dark and cold, reflected back the hundreds of stalagmites and stalactites that grew and reached for each other, welcoming him. In the cold air the dripping of water echoed and played back from the walls and floor of the ancient sanctuary, singing to him. He was both humbled and exalted as he stepped onto holy ground.

Howard lifted his hand and gestured at the lake. "The Greeks believed this was the Dictean Caves, the birthplace of Zeus. Here he would converse with his son, Minos, back in the mists of time."

Everywhere reverent Minoan hands had placed votive

offerings—bronze daggers and double axes, statuettes, painted clay vessels and ornaments beyond counting. The artificial light from the lanterns reflected off a thousand shimmering objects. Cassandra looked at Howard, and her eyes filled with tears. He smiled.

"Yes," he said, with a suspicion of a tremor in his voice, "it is unbelievable. I can hardly bear it."

When they felt they could move again in the presence of such antiquity, they began a careful survey of the space, recording the location of each object, and opening the foam-filled crates they had brought to receive the treasure. Howard moved reverently from one object to the next, trying to decide which of so many to take. There were far more than even his painstaking research had led him to expect. Gradually the crates took on their burdens of ancient gold and bronze and clay, and the workers wondered if they would ever become accustomed to the touch of ancient things. Cassandra, still fighting back tears, came toward him, her hands spilling over with a glittering gold necklace. He took it from her and laughed.

"This is no time for tears," he cried, and his voice caromed off the forest of stone around them. He laid the necklace across her breast, and laughed again, gently.

"Rejoice. This is just the beginning. Do you understand? It's the find of an ordinary man's lifetime, and for us, it will be just the smallest fraction of our accomplishments. This is the predecessor of the Minoan pillar crypt, such as we shall find at Knossos and Phaestos. Shall I tell you what we shall find there, my dear Cassandra? Besides the mysterious

Phaestos disk, there will be statues of the goddess Kore in ivory and gold, golden bulls and vases painted with dolphins and leaping bull dancers, jewels and lamps and all the precious little incidentals needed to fill a museum. And more, so very much more."

Late in the day they had made their selection and were ready to go back to the small cave in which they had established the gate. A few hours' sleep, and Howard would send them ahead to the time selected to explore Knossos. Knossos, where another, ancient Daedalus had made a dancing-place for Ariadne the 'utterly pure,' daughter of the sea king Minos and Lady of the Labyrinth.

There was an atmosphere of celebration and excitement the night they returned with the first shipment. Howard produced some bottles of champagne from who knew where, and even Lantis allowed them to pry him out of the crystal matrix chamber to join in the party. Everyone had looked with awe at the treasures, the gold seals and bronze daggers, the statues and the cascades of garnet beads like drops of blood strung on a gold chain. Cassandra held up a narrow gold circlet set with emeralds and sapphires, and called it 'Ariadne's diadem.' Vincent, amazed later at his impudence, took it from her and placed it on her dark curls. "Ariadne of the lovely tresses," he said softly. She had blushed then, and he had the satisfaction of seeing a look of tenderness momentarily light up her eyes, before she turned back to Howard. Howard lifted his glass to her, laughing.

From the side of the room, Roma watched. Vincent turned to him and offered him a glass. As usual, he waved it away, but smiled. Vincent took up his stand next to the tall Persean.

"She's beautiful, isn't she?" he asked wistfully. Roma nodded, silently.

"It was intended to be worn, after all," Vincent continued. "It will be kind of a shame to lock it up in a case, don't you think?"

Roma looked down at him, amusement and something like compassion gathering in the bright hazel eyes. "After the untold cost, the incalculable risk of this expedition, all in the holy name of the Collection, you actually dare to suggest such an idea?"

Thoughtfully, Vincent went on. "Well, it's holy to Howard, of course, but to the rest of us, merely very important. And the ancients will just do the same. Put it in a case, I mean. Still. . . . " He faltered to a stop.

"Still," Roma continued for him, "you have doubts?"

"Well, not doubts, precisely. It's just that I can't help wondering how this will affect the future in this time. The Phaestos disk was found in this timeline. Perhaps someone was going to decipher it after all, and now he . . . or she . . . won't have the chance."

There was a brief, strained silence. Roma looked at Howard. "I thought we were not taking objects that had been found."

Howard waved his hand in an airy gesture. "No one ever succeeded in translating it. And it was destroyed in the

Cataclysm. Now, someone will succeed and the cultural base will benefit. Your concern is praiseworthy but unnecessary." He held Roma's gaze for a long moment, then turned back to the revels.

Roma walked slowly over to Daedalus, motioning for Vincent to join him. They talked softly, watching the celebration.

"You heard?" asked Roma.

Daedalus nodded. "Unfortunate. I wondered whether he would be able to keep his hands off all the famous pieces. Apparently not. But is it worth disrupting the mission—the real mission?"

"I suppose not," said Roma slowly. "But he will bear watching. How is the seeding operation going?"

Vincent smiled. "We're just beginning. While Dr. Howard and Cassandra have been gone, Lantis and I have placed about a dozen of the recorders at Dr. Daedalus's specified locations in time. Fortunately, we are going through the gate so often anyway, no one notices any little detours."

Roma was silent for a moment, eyeing Howard.

"You're really worried about that disk?" asked Vincent.

"No. But I am worried about Howard. I would never have agreed to come on this mission if it weren't for the recorders, the chance to undo the Cataclysm. I just hope we haven't brought an equal threat to humanity with us."

His voice was light, but his expression made Vincent profoundly uncomfortable. They separated, Roma returning to his silent observation. Daedalus and Vincent moved to join Lantis, trying to bury their uneasiness.

Temogen reached into one of the crates and drew out a bronze sword with a pommel of rock crystal. The light caressed the silky metal, made rainbows in the crystal. It looked new, like the day that ancient artisan had delivered it into the king's hand. Temogen swung the beautiful, deadly thing expertly through the air, making it sing. It was not difficult to imagine him as an ancient warrior prince embracing the glorious thrill of battle. For a moment, something dark and primitive lay across his face like a mask. Then it passed, and he replaced the sword in the crate. Lantis and Daedalus were singing a risqué song that no one had even suspected they knew. The hilarity grew, and it was an evening they would remember with wonder, later, when the times changed.

# Chapter 11

## 1357 B.C.E.
## Abydos

Howard took hold of the back of a chair, and strove for control. He could feel rage shaking at his knees, and his face felt like a torch.

"I want to know what happened," he ground out between clenched teeth. "This is unconscionable. A devastating loss to the Collection."

Cassandra looked down at the crushed and scattered gold leaves on the table. Once they had made up a necklace, found in a barrow near the Eastern European gate. She touched the small remnant of a cabochon emerald that had been the size of his thumbnail. She looked back up at Howard, and was relieved to see the furious red flush fading from his face. But his lips were tight with anger.

"I can't understand it," she began. "The packing container was almost completely destroyed, just . . . disconnected pieces as if part of it never got here at all. Lantis is looking at the gate now. It's terrible—"

He turned and strode from the room, never glancing at her. She followed him at a run as he headed for the gate.

Lantis was deep in conversation with Daedalus when Howard threw open the door.

"Well? What happened?"

Lantis turned back to the matrix, leaving Daedalus to explain their process.

"There doesn't seem to be any malfunction with the gate. We are examining the power flow modules—"

"I don't give a damn about that!" Howard said with suppressed violence. "The European station is obviously the place to be looking, not here. Some fool packed the thing incorrectly, or entered the wrong coordinates . . . I want someone to go there immediately and investigate."

Temogen's voice came from the doorway behind him. "I was just planning to leave."

"No!" Howard said, without looking around. "It is too important that you continue with Roma, securing the China gate. We cannot fall behind because of some idiot's lack of precaution. I shall send Vincent. He's careful and thorough. And people have a tendency to confide in him. You would scare them, and I don't want them scared. Yet."

Temogen smiled. "But I would be so very . . . gentle," he protested. "Roma will do very well without me."

Howard frowned at him then, his eyes flashing.

"You will do better to stick to your duty, Temogen. I am not feeling very patient just now. I want the China gate opened up immediately. I will send Vincent."

Vincent was delighted to be sent on an expedition, but it was to prove unfruitful. The team at the European gate was anxious to clear themselves of any failure on their part, and they gave him complete access to their logs and procedures. The computer's visual records showed the packing of the necklace had been absolutely correct, as had the coordinates used to send it to the Abydos gate. They had a small crate of other pieces, which they entrusted to Vincent to take back with him. He smiled wryly, as he accepted the crate.

"Well, if it happens again, at least I won't have to listen to Howard yell," he said, picturing the crushed and fragmented necklace. "All the same, don't make a mistake."

The technician, preparing to initialize the gate, smiled a little wanly.

"No chance," he said, and entered the coordinates. In an instant Vincent and the crate disappeared.

"I think you will find this shipment intact," Vincent said to Howard as he stepped off the gate pad and handed him the crate.

ꝏ ꝏ ꝏ

Roma had just returned from the China gate and Vincent's arrival had interrupted what was apparently a somewhat tense discussion. He looked at Vincent as Howard burrowed in the crate.

"It's as well that you are also intact," he said, "as I want a complete report. And I do mean complete, Vincent," he said somewhat sternly. "I notice that you do not make journal entries regularly. I can't impress upon you enough the importance of doing that. There are good reasons for keeping complete records of the mission, from the perspectives of everyone concerned. Absolutely complete. See to it."

"Yes, sir," said Vincent, resisting the urge to salute.

Daedalus's voice sounded over the intercom.

"Is that Vincent? What on earth has been keeping you for so long? I am waiting for your work on my latest corollary. Am I to be kept waiting forever?"

"I'm on my way. So is my work. So is my report," he added to Roma, heading for the door. "And my journal entries."

Roma smiled as he left. He was an engaging boy. Howard was making satisfied noises at the contents of the crate.

"Another necklace?" Roma inquired, deceptively mild.

Howard lifted his hands, and held up a gold ewer, chased and set with amethysts.

"Beautiful," he breathed.

Roma's voice took on a kind of wonder. "You did not worry for one moment about that boy's safety. You just sent him through the gate to find out what happened to your gold trinket. Temogen, too. I'm not surprised that you didn't warn me, but I should have thought you would not want to risk Temogen. No one should have used the gate until the cause of the problem was established. You know that. And yet you risked both their lives. You amaze me, Howard."

Howard's brows drew together, perplexed. "Roma, there was no reason to think the gate had malfunctioned. There is still no reason to think so. Daedalus and Lantis looked it over thoroughly. Clearly it was an error on the part of someone at the European station. And you are wrong to suggest that I find anyone expendable. Least of all you."

Roma did not bother to suppress a snort as he left.

ℌ ℌ ℌ

Vincent's report seemed to absolve the people at the European station, however. And still no malfunction could be found within the gate system. Howard finally shrugged and suggested that perhaps the necklace had been too fragile, on the point of collapse from some other cause, and the strain of packing and transport had simply been too much for it. It wasn't a very good suggestion, but he was immersed in the finds of the other gates, and had no more time or emotional energy to waste on their one failure. Artifacts flowed through the gates from all the stations, with more being planned and established every day.

ℌ ℌ ℌ

Daedalus was at work on something that kept him immured in his room for days, and he would only respond to questions with a twinkle and a shake of his head. Vincent and Lantis both recognized the signs, and knew that he would tell them nothing until he was ready. He sprang his announcement during a brief meal break on the evening of their twenty-ninth day at Abydos.

"I have found Atlantis," he said calmly.

Silence reigned at the table. Howard's head snapped up, and his eyes narrowed.

"If this is a joke—"

Daedalus waved his hand good-naturedly. "No, no, of course it isn't, my good Doctor Howard. Who would joke about such a matter. I merely turned some of my spare time to the problem. Something you said—" he turned and waved a fork in Cassandra's direction—"struck a spark of curiosity in me. Atlantis, such a long tale of the unlikely and the fantastical. So I just compiled all the records about it, starting with Plato, of course. I examined them. I looked at the evidence. A matter of scientific method, as always. However, there is also the issue of the leap of imagination, of intuition. Once I reconsidered the Santorini theory. . . ."

His kindly face was glowing with pleasure as he took them over his voyage of discovery. Lantis caught Vincent's eye and mouthed a rude word. Vincent smiled sympathetically. They both knew who would have to build the gate in Daedalus's watery new wonderland.

The next day they sent their first shipment through the gate to *Traveler One*, hovering above Earth in its adjacent timeline. Inside the matrix, the great crystal spars pulsed with light, and the whine insinuated itself through the shielding that separated the matrix from the rest of the labyrinth. They all felt it in their teeth and bones, that subsonic vibration that acted on the nerves like fingernails raking down a blackboard. *An odd simile*, thought Vincent. *What exactly was a blackboard?* They had all gathered in the gate to watch the precious crates being loaded onto the gate pad, shimmer in the light, and dissolve into time. Vincent's heart took two long, dragging beats. The viewscreen lit up with the image of the Commander, speaking to them across the gulf of reality. Her deep voice was soft with emotion.

"Congratulations to you all. Your cargo has arrived safely. You have made an excellent beginning. Think of it. You have not only made an extremely important contribution to the Collection, to all humanity. You have defeated time. The Cataclysm won't win, after all."

Her image faded, leaving behind a little silence. Howard stood for a long moment, staring at the empty gate pad.

"Missing your trinkets already?" Daedalus asked cheerily.

Howard looked at him in silence, not even troubling to disguise the anger in his eyes. Then he turned and left the room.

Vincent looked over at Roma, who had been watching Howard with a curious expression on his face. Was he asking himself the source of Howard's anger on the eve of his first triumph?

"Really, Dr. Daedalus," Cassandra cried, "did you have to spoil it for him like that?"

"My dear child, it was only a joke," said Daedalus, puzzled.

"A poor one, if I might say so." Her voice trembled. "It has been a strain, wondering if all would go well. He only thinks of the Collection, of the success of this mission."

"Does he?" asked Roma gently.

Cassandra rounded on him, her eyes very bright. Roma's look, patient and steady, defeated her anger.

"Why can't you see that he never thinks about himself? He only wants what we all want."

"Perhaps," said Roma equably, turning to go.

Cassandra watched him for a moment, her fists clenched. She turned to Vincent, who had watched the exchange helplessly.

"I'll never understand him. Why can't he see what everyone else sees?"

"Perhaps because he is looking for something else," Vincent offered.

"What is that supposed to mean?"

Vincent shrugged. "It's just that Roma only cares about the safety of the people. The mission, the artifacts, even the Collection, none of that really matters to him at all. He's a Persean, Cassandra. You know what that means."

She was diverted. "Do you think it's true, that they can't have any personal relationships?"

"It's part of the code, I think. He said to me once that they have to care about no one and everyone equally if they are to be effective. Personal interest cannot interfere with their judgment."

"It sounds lonely," she said.

Vincent looked sadly at her. "Are you any different, really?"

She jerked her head up at that, surprised and somewhat alarmed. "I don't know what you mean."

"Archaeology is your code, isn't it? You don't really care much about living people. Like Dr. Howard, you prefer their histories to their present."

She stared at him, unbelieving.

"Cassandra," he began again, "it's because I care that I—"

Her eyes softened, and she looked away. "I know. I know you do. But you don't understand. Perhaps if you felt about your work as I feel about mine, you would."

Vincent thought about his drawings, white sheets littering his small room like fallen ghosts. He thought about how he felt when he had stylus or pen in hand.

"But I do," he said, and his sadness deepened.

# Chapter 12

## 1357 B.C.E.
## Abydos

A full month passed before Howard mentioned the Library at Alexandria. He put on his most affable face, making sure to include everyone in the discussion.

"The repository of all the knowledge, all the scholarship of the ancient world. All irretrievably lost in 39 B.C.E. when Julius Caesar's overzealous troops accidentally burned it to the ground. It was restored, and destroyed again, finally, in 640 C.E. by a religious bigot named Amr, who decreed that anything not already in the Koran was not worth knowing and had it torched."

He looked up, and saw he had everyone's attention. "There were over six hundred thousand documents in that library before the Romans burned it, possibly almost a million. He paused to see the effect of those numbers on the team.

"How many do you propose to remove?" asked Roma—somewhat predictably, Howard thought.

"It's a problem," he said. "There are no lists of what was in that library. Quite a lot of surmise, of course, but that's all. So a preselection will be impossible."

"It is an inhabited area," said Daedalus slowly. But the

old scientist was not immune to the romance of the lost knowledge. "Scientific papers," he mused, "from the hands of the ancients, describing how they understood their world, their universe. Intoxicating!"

Howard felt Roma's eyes on him as he responded. "Yes, it's a dilemma. The city was never really uninhabited from the time Alexander ordered it built until the Cataclysm smashed it into debris, and of course, nothing of the library survived the burnings. We would have to go before the library was destroyed the first time. It was at its greatest then."

"What do you propose? How would we choose from among so many?" Cassandra was all eagerness.

"We would have to go only hours before the initial destruction, or else what we take would be missed," Howard said smoothly, looking at Roma. "The question is, is it worth the risk?"

They all looked at Roma then, expecting a flat prohibition.

"Tell me about the library," he said instead.

Cassandra hurried to spin the tale, about the great columned halls lined with floor-to-ceiling bookshelves, each filled with papyrus scrolls, parchment documents from the East, who knew what was there.

"The earliest copies of the Hebrew scriptures, certainly," she asserted, "as well as myths and histories of all the Ancient Near East. Documents from as far away as China and India, poetry, biography, mathematical theories. Texts and manuscripts from everywhere writing had been invented. Everything that was known about the earliest times."

"The librarian was a woman, did you know that?" Howard asked with a smile.

"No! A woman!" Cassandra cried, her eyes ablaze. "What happened to her?"

"Her name was Arsinoe, and she was a scholar and a teacher. Unusual, of course. This was the second library, you understand."

"What happened to her when the library burned?" asked Cassandra.

Howard took a long drink, and leaned back. "Well, it seems that the troops of the faithful took exception to a woman in a position of authority. When they burned the library, they killed Arsinoe. Scraped all the flesh from her bones with clamshells, I believe."

Cassandra turned white and looked away.

"Yes. Times were very different then. And yet, the contents of that library represent such an untold contribution to the Collection. . . . " He let his voice trail off into silence.

Roma's tone was still mild. "You wouldn't have long. How would you propose to get in, make a selection, and get out? If the times were so unsettled, it would be extremely dangerous."

Encouraged by the fact that Roma had not dismissed the idea, Howard continued, serious and persuasive.

"We would have to try to arrive inside the library on the night of the destruction. It would be a tremendous test of the gate's accuracy," he looked at Lantis, "and we would have to time it for the middle of the night when the smallest possible number of people might be around, possibly no one. We could do it in six hours, if everyone here helped. Except someone would have to remain to operate the gate. It would be imperative that we time it so the library burns just moments after we leave."

Roma started to object, and Howard hurriedly went on. "The sheer number of scrolls makes it necessary to have as many hands as possible. No one would need any special knowledge, because we wouldn't have time to select. It would be a case of grab as much as you can and get out. We would certainly need Temogen in case of any trouble. There is a possibility, of course, that someone would be in the library," he added candidly, "but tranquilizer darts would take care of any wakeful scholars, I assume. And the next day, the library burns. Everything would be lost, and in the confusion and general terror of the battle going on all around them, I feel certain no one is going to have time to worry about any missing scrolls. Even if we got them all."

Roma held up a hand. "Tranquilizer darts are effective against one or two, but you don't know how many people might be there. If there were several, one might give the alarm before we could get them all. And of course, there would then be several people with a very similar, terrifying story to tell the next day."

Lantis looked up. "Couldn't we use an anesthetic gas?"

Daedalus nodded slowly. "Yes. The Egyptian architecture will present problems, of course, unglazed windows open to the sky . . . still, we should be able to overcome that. A series of gas canisters, set off as soon as we arrive. The effect would be instantaneous. We would need protective masks, of course."

"No problem," Lantis was confident. "I can set up the canisters and the masks in a few days."

Cassandra looked longingly at Roma, her face eloquent. "You must see, Roma, it is the only way to save all that knowledge for the Collection. Think—"

"Now tell me how you propose to set coordinates for the six hours prior to the burning. How can you possibly know even the precise date, let alone the hour—"

Howard smiled then. He had saved the best for last.

"I propose to use this, my dear Roma."

He held up a scroll. "This was recovered by the team in Constantinople. It is a record made by a visiting scholar on the night the library burned. He was actually on his way to the library when it caught. This record tells us the very hour of the fire. Interesting. The Constantinople team was completely unaware of the importance of this little remnant. Of such insignificant scraps are empires of knowledge built!"

Howard's face was transcendent for a moment, then he settled back and waited for Roma's reaction.

Daedalus intervened. "I would operate the gate. You will need Lantis with you, I assume, because of the canisters and whatnot."

Howard appeared to consider. "Well, we could do it that way, of course. I was thinking that Roma would operate the gate, Dr. Daedalus. Surely you want to see the library?"

"Roma will be much more useful to you on such a time-critical venture. As I designed the gate, I'm certain you have no qualms about leaving the transfer in my hands? Or we could get a technician from one of the other gates, of course."

Howard threw up a hand in protest. "Not at all, Dr. Daedalus. If you really prefer that Roma go instead—"

"More important, if you'll forgive me," said Roma dryly, "*I* prefer it." He caught the look in Daedalus' eyes, correctly interpreting the silent message. He wanted a recorder crystal left there in that doomed library.

"Make your plans. God forbid we miss out on a million more bits of paper for the Collection. But understand this. You will all be under my command on this little foray. I will expect absolute adherence to procedure. Anyone who puts a foot wrong—"

The rest of the threat was swallowed in the uproar of cheers and applause from excited travelers. Even Temogen's habitually sour face brightened at the prospect of action. Jubilantly, they laid their plans for the assault on Alexandria.

The mission went like a dream. Daedalus worked for a week, poring over Howard's notes on the library, calculating dates and times, setting the coordinates for the gate. When they arrived, Lantis's canisters sent the invisible sedative gas billowing through the shadowy library. There was only one loyal guard standing at the outside entrance watching the burning docks, and he would remember nothing. He had not even seen the gate's flash of light. The sky was red with the fires of battle, but not so near that the library scholars feared the trouble might reach them. That wouldn't happen until tomorrow, mused Howard, when the blaze would break out from the wharves, spreading through the old city in a wall of fire, catching and burning the library and its priceless collection of thoughts and ideas.

The gate had deposited them and the huge stack of crates in the center of the largest chamber. Howard's notes had been accurate. They all looked for a moment in sheer awe at the towering shelves, filled with manuscripts of all descriptions. Then they started filling the crates they had brought. Haste rather than care was the order of the day. No one could afford the meticulous handling the scrolls merited. Looking like ancient undersea divers in their black clothing and masks, they gathered the precious documents into great armloads and thrust them into the crates.

Howard winced as he saw flakes of papyrus crumble from scrolls that were old even in this time, but he forced himself to keep working. Roma motioned Temogen to assist the gatherers, and he explored the library for any undiscovered inhabitants. The gas would be effective for several hours, so he contented himself with making a quick survey of the library. There were four symmetrically arranged rooms, one behind the next forming a long rectangle. Beautifully decorated columns marched through the shadows. Tables and chairs were scattered through the rooms, and everywhere were the tall shelves filled with scrolls and manuscripts. One ancient scribe lay across a table, his face pillowed on an incomplete copy of a manuscript. Roma checked his pulse—still strong—and gently removed the text he had been copying. He grabbed a crate and started filling it with scrolls. It took them just under six hours to rescue the majority of the library's vast contents.

When their time was up, they took a last look around. The shelves, full a few hours previously, were nearly empty. Lantis took up a large canister, and proceeded to blow what looked like ash into the library. The shelves soon held a burden of black fragments.

"A surprise," he grinned at the others. "According to Dr. Howard's notes, the fire will sweep into the library in eighteen minutes. Just before dawn. The battle—and the panic in the streets—prevented the library people from getting to the library in time to save its contents. But there should be some ash. If anyone does get here, it will look as if the scrolls burst into flame before the actual structure was destroyed."

Roma, who had gone back to the inner chamber, returned carrying the old scribe. Hugging the walls, moving like a shadow, he took him out the main door and laid him down on the steps of the great structure. He and the guard would wake soon, but not until the library was ablaze. They had timed everything down to the second. As the gate effect began to shimmer around them, Howard suddenly looked over his shoulder and cried out.

"Look! The fire—"

They were gathered together around the mound of crates. Roma's head jerked around just as the gate took them.

ꝏ ꝏ ꝏ

"We timed that very closely," Howard was saying as they materialized in the gate. "Too closely. The fire was almost to the library doors."

Roma paused in the act of removing his mask. Howard met his gaze steadily, a slight questioning look in his eyes.

"Better unpack the loot," Roma remarked dryly, looking at the crates.

"It will take weeks to repack all this properly," replied Howard. "We'll need some help from some of the other gates. Cassandra, perhaps you would—"

"Of course," she agreed, still exalted from their success, "I'll send messages immediately. Dr. Howard?"

"Yes?" he was busy with one of the crates.

"Did we really come close to the fire breaking out?"

Howard straightened and smiled at her.

"Indeed we did. I'd say we got out just in the nick of time."

# PART V

## Just Killing Time

# Chapter 13

## February 17, 1995 C.E.
## Abydos

The next day, Virginia looked out the passenger window at the passing countryside. Dry, this land was so very dry, even a few miles from the river. On either side of the river valley, the mountains stood up like bones spared no shred of flesh by the hot desert wind. She closed her eyes against the brilliant scene, trying to shut out memories past and present. She was here, unwillingly or not, and she would have to go through with it. She would have to look once more upon this land that had once been her heart's blood, her life. She would get out of this sheltering car and walk through the sand, feel the desert wind on her face, the harsh, bright kiss of the sun. She would have to endure the sibilance of the river singing its way through the Two Lands, the calls of the boatmen and the workers, the voices of ghosts.

It was becoming impossible to push the thought out of her mind. Abydos was the site of a series of temples and funerary monuments to Osiris, the heart of his cult. She knew the ruins well. The Seti I temple dominated the site. Following the debacle of Akhenaten's religious reforms, Egypt had been ruled for brief periods by several kings, including Tutankhamen—who died young, probably murdered. Seti I, named for the god Set, betrayer of Osiris, had attempted to smooth out the religious strife by building a magnificent temple dedicated to Osiris. Predating the Seti I temple by unknown centuries were the remnants of an earlier temple to Osiris, three miles north where the Nile curved closer to the spine of mountains on the west bank. It was this earlier and—in H.L. Pierce's mind—finer temple that was the site of his dig. Invariably he referred to it as the Temple, always to be distinguished from the New Seti I temple. When you were talking about three thousand years, 'new' was a relative term. At Abydos, however, far older monuments lay buried beneath the sand. Scattered across the plain between the Nile and the ever-present cliffs were other mounds and buried ruins, evidence of the prehistoric link between the God of Forever and this part of Egypt.

To a young archaeology student, Abydos had seemed like the highest pinnacle of heaven. Towering pylons framed the open gateway of the old temple. Once bright paintings of lotuses and reeds had adorned them, along with the portraits of the Eternal Ones who resided there. Now the tumble of huge columns and broken walls was soft, wind-scoured apricot gold, and only the sun was eternal. Osiris the Lord of Forever, and Isis the Mother of Heaven, and Horus the Beautiful God—all were gone from Egypt. Nothing remained but their memories, carved on stone and painted on walls throughout the Singing Land. And the singing had stopped centuries ago. *Or rather*, she followed the thought, *the singing goes on but now it names a new holy and eternal One.*

Her driver turned and smiled, momentarily dazzling her with the flash of gold in his mouth. "Soon we be there. A few more minutes." She smiled back with no illusions. "Soon" could mean anything from fifteen minutes to five hours. She estimated she had another hour before she saw Abydos again. She settled back and closed her eyes against the glare of outer sun and inner memory. Quite suddenly, she abandoned the attempt to hold the gates of memory shut.

*Abydos*. She had gone there as a student, working on her dissertation and eager as all get-out. Just dying to sit in the sun and brush sand off potsherds with a number-twelve camel-hair paintbrush. Virginia had been in love with Egypt then, and with the enigmatic figure of its strangest and most fascinating pharaoh, Akhenaten. She had longed to prove something definitive about him and his attempt at religious reform. The Old Temple at Abydos was one of those closed by the infamous *Ban of Akhenaten,* of which there were no discovered copies. She believed that some of the inscriptions there might lead her to the lost *Ban* itself. Virginia had rushed at her work, eagerly accepting the rough accommodations, the physical demands of the work and climate, the nearly all-male camaraderie of the team that allowed her only a marginal place.

And, of course, there was Hickson. If she had ordered him custom-made, he couldn't have been more perfect for her. Tall, blond, and fiercely intelligent, Hicks had laughed at her out of die-for-love blue eyes and she had been utterly lost. If she had imagined that her dream lover would be someone she could work with, side by side, in a sort of harmonious intellectual Elysian Fields, he had taught her otherwise.

"Jinn," his voice rang in her ears, "you have to give up this inane infatuation with Akhenaten. He was a mean son of a bitch and all the romantic drivel in the world is not going to change that."

"It's not romantic drivel, you arrogant pig!" she had fired back. "Your theories about Akhenaten are just that, theories. You don't *know*."

"And you do?" he had asked, in a curiously gentle voice. "You are a bad-tempered red-headed wench with a tongue like an adder, but you have the mind of a scholar. You don't know, either."

"No. But I'm keeping an open mind. Try it some time."

He had laughed then, but not unkindly. "I can't afford to keep an open mind about someone as nasty as that." Hicks had taken Akhenaten's religious reforms very personally. "Pogroms, more likely," he had said, "and I hate all forms of *cultural revolutions*, *racial purity*, *religious orthodoxy*. Whatever name you apply it is still the same old thing. Believe what I believe, think how I think, be as I am, or I will bloody kill you."

"Can't you even allow for the possibility that he might have been a genuine mystic? For every great new insight there has to be a person with an original mind."

"People such as Hitler or the Great Inquisitors? God, of all things, preserve me from a man with a mission." He had grinned, and her heart had turned over. Hicks had the power to enrage her to the point of blindness, then totally disarm her with a smile. His insistence that she defend, question, examine everything pushed her into doing the best work she had done in her life.

They had worked together all that winter, worked and quarreled and loved and dreamed. It was frightening to love someone as she had loved him. "Be on your guard against this one," her inner voice had warned. "He could break your heart." She had refused to listen. She could not believe that Hickson would ever hurt her. Yet he had. Not by being unfaithful or abusive or dishonest. He had broken her heart simply by dying.

# Chapter 14

## 1357 B.C.E.
## Abydos

Vincent was sharing breakfast with Roma and Daedalus when Cassandra appeared. Pleasure lit up his face as he pulled forward a chair for her.

"So, how's the digging-up business?" asked Daedalus.

"Dusty," she replied. "But the Seti I tomb will be more than worth it. I was up almost all night working on the plans. Preselecting, that sort of thing." She yawned. "And then one of the team at the Greek station woke me up just as I was getting to sleep, to tell me that a piece of her luggage has somehow accidentally been lost in the gate. It just disappeared, before she had finished entering the coordinates—"

Roma raised his head like a hound scenting its quarry. "When did this happen?" he asked.

"Oh, early this morning. I wasn't paying attention to the time. Howard said it sounded like nonsense to him."

Roma threw down his napkin and was on his way to the gate before the others could react.

"Another accident?" said Daedalus, his voice tinged with worry. "Surely not another accident?"

"But it's nothing!" said Cassandra, her voice rising. "It's just nonsense, some tools or something. She got careless, that's all."

"We'd better go," said Vincent.

Daedalus and Vincent rose, Cassandra following in alarm at the effect of her casual words.

When they reached the gate, the others were there.

"—serious," Howard was saying.

"Not serious?" demanded Roma incredulously. "Of course it's serious. It's the second 'accident' in the gate system. Two too many."

"What are the particulars, please?" asked Daedalus.

It was Lantis who answered. "Someone was getting ready to initialize the gate at the Greek station, going to China. Her luggage was next to the gate pad. Not on it, *next* to it. She says she hadn't finished entering the coordinates to transfer, but there was a flash and the luggage was gone. It didn't turn up at the China gate, or at any of the others. It's gone."

Daedalus frowned for a moment. Roma broke in on his thoughts.

"Dr. Daedalus. We have to close down the gate until we know what has happened."

Daedalus nodded. "Of course. But not entirely, you understand, because we will have to go to the Greek station to investigate. Lantis," he said urgently, "I think we should go now—"

"You must not use the gate until—" Roma began, interrupted by Howard's strident "Close down the gate! You can't be serious!"

Daedalus lifted his hand, and his kindly eyes surveyed

the room with the calm assumption of power that never failed to astonish his friends and enemies alike.

"Yes, Dr. Howard, close it down. Yes, Roma, we have to use the gate to find the source of the problem."

"Dr. Daedalus is right, Roma," said Lantis. "The problem most likely is in the Greek gate system itself. We have to go there."

"I agree that someone will need to go, but not you," said Roma grimly.

"I appreciate your concern, Roma," said Daedalus patiently, "And I assumed you would want to go, but really, Lantis and I will have to go as well. But certainly the others must not use the system until we have identified the problem."

Howard looked mutely at the pile of crates ready to go back to *Traveler One*, thinking of the dozens, hundreds of crates in other gates waiting for him to examine and catalog them. But he remained silent as Roma, Lantis, and Daedalus prepared to enter the gate. Not until they had shimmered out of existence did he remove his eyes from the gate pad. Then he turned to Vincent.

"Begin examining the information sent to us by the Greek station. All their transfer logs. Look for something anomalous, anything to explain this accident."

"Yes, Dr. Howard," agreed Vincent, turning to the work. He shook inside as he thought about the implications. It was only a suitcase. Some tools. This time.

Lantis and Daedalus found nothing wrong with the gate. They returned, having examined the gate at the Greek station with exhaustive care. Lantis had to be physically pulled out of the matrix.

"Enough. It is enough for now," Daedalus had insisted.

"Perhaps if we—"

"No. There is nothing more to look for."

ஐ ஐ ஐ

Howard was waiting impatiently to hear their findings. Lantis shook his head, the bright blue eyes undimmed by exhaustion or frustration.

"I've entered every combination we have programmed into the matrix a dozen times. Everything is working perfectly. There *is* no malfunction within the system."

"And I have examined the written theory phoneme by phoneme, the equations down to the last symbolic reference, and there is nothing incorrect, nothing we have not tested a hundred times."

"It's been three days. What *did* you find?"

"Nothing," said Daedalus. "Nothing at all."

"Nothing," exploded Howard. He stared bleakly at the two travelers. "Do you know how far behind we are? I can't go to the Seti I dig until this is solved. And you have promised me an Atlantis gate. Nothing can go forward on that project until we know what went wrong. And you say you found nothing?"

Daedalus nodded, patiently. "As we have told you, the gate is not malfunctioning. Lantis says it. I say it. We can find nothing wrong with it. Yet the technician has a complete visual computer log of what happened. It shows the luggage sitting beside the pad, and then disappearing.

Howard paced in frustration. "Obviously, someone entered the wrong coordinates. If not the woman in question, then someone else . . . using a transcomp, for example."

"Roma and Temogen are looking into that possibility. It would have to be someone at the Greek station, of course. The transcomp initiators would not work between gates. Perhaps when they return. . . . " Daedalus's voice trailed out in exhaustion, leaving the hope unfinished.

ꙮ ꙮ ꙮ

It turned out to be an unfounded hope. Roma and Temogen returned without finding any clues to the mystery. They had examined every transcomp, but none of the automatic logs showed any activity during the time in question. No one had initialized the gate with a transcomp. After days of examining the data brought back by Daedalus and Lantis, Roma finally acceded to Howard's demand that they open up the gate system again. He did insist that no one use the gate alone. And he stationed a security person in every gate, twenty-four hours a day. No one could use the gate without both computer and human surveillance. Roma personally took up almost permanent residence in the gate control room. The long vigil had begun.

"It's the randomness of the thing that is so frustrating!" said Vincent tiredly, late one evening.

His head ached, and his fingers longed for chalk or pen to give his mind ease.

Daedalus nodded, silent for a long while.

"Well. The measures we have taken, and what Lantis calls his 'bandage' fix seem to have stabilized the gate for the time being. It is tedious, having to recalibrate the matrix before each use. But worth it, of course, if it makes it safe."

"But for how long?" Vincent voiced both their fears.

"It has been twenty days without an incident of any kind. That is all I know. Still, we keep looking."

Vincent stretched his aching muscles. Daedalus smiled and patted his shoulder.

"Go to bed now. I should not have asked you to work with me this evening, after spending all day in the tomb."

Vincent grinned. "You're just lucky you're too busy to go, or Howard would have you out there digging too."

"Too old, you mean. Well, let me tell you something, Vincent. This old man goes tomorrow to the tomb and then you shall see some work!"

Vincent smothered an exclamation. Surely Howard had enough help in the Seti I tomb without involving Dr. Daedalus!

ᘝ ᘝ ᘝ

As the days without incident passed, the teams relaxed. The Seti I tomb had proved even richer than their wildest estimates. Crate after crate filled with treasures, until Roma demanded to see the lists. There was an unpleasant little confrontation in the gate control room as Howard was counting the shipment.

"How many items have been removed from the tomb?" Roma asked.

"Oh, a thousand or so," said Howard vaguely.

Roma stared at him, his eyes narrowed. "I don't believe for an instant that you don't know the exact number, Dr. Howard. How many?"

"One thousand, nine hundred eighty-seven," replied Howard, eyeing Roma. There was a long pause. Then Howard smiled, and added, "but most of them are small."

Roma was not amused. "Dr. Howard—" As always, he strove to keep his voice even. The difference was that now Howard could hear him striving, "Our purpose is to take a sampling of artifacts, sufficient to enhance our knowledge of the past without disrupting it. Nearly two thousand items from one tomb seems . . . excessive."

Howard shook his head. "Roma, Roma, please leave these matters in my hands! I really am qualified to judge what is excessive and what is necessary."

"I suspect your judgment has been a trifle . . . impaired."

Howard started to answer angrily, but Cassandra and Lantis walked in at that moment, and he bit back his angry denial. Roma was not similarly inhibited.

"I want to see the lists. I suggest a meeting between you, Cassandra, and me to decide which items shall be returned to the tomb."

"Returned!" Cassandra and Howard exclaimed together.

Roma turned to Cassandra. "How many tombs are we planning to enter?"

"Why, over a hundred during this first expedition," she

replied unhesitatingly. "We need a thorough sample from each of the major dynasties, so the final number will be much higher—"

He waved her to silence. "Over a hundred, just during this first expedition. And you took two thousand objects from the Seti I tomb. And that is only Egypt. There are thousands of other sites currently being opened, thousands more proposed sites. Anyone want to do the math?"

Cassandra stopped, shock registering on her face. "Two thousand? Was it really that high?" She thought about the excitement of opening the tomb, the hours that stretched into days as they examined the seemingly countless chests of jewelry, the statuettes, the clothing and furniture, all the fabulous glitter and craft the ancient Egyptians had believed necessary to accompany the dead on their journey to Osiris's kingdom of Amenti.

"Slightly less, actually," Howard suggested mildly. "Are you suggesting we have been greedy, Mr. Roma?"

"I am trying to avoid suggesting that, Dr. Howard."

"You realize that the choice of objects is outside your province? I am entrusted with that responsibility."

"I am aware of that. I merely raise the question. The gate system seems to be stable, but I am far from confident that it will remain that way. It seems prudent that we take a smaller sampling from the current proposed areas. Or else we will be here for a lifetime. Several lifetimes."

Cassandra, doubt warring with loyalty on her face, turned to Howard.

"I would be happy to assist if you decide to return some

of the objects. I was probably too enthusiastic myself. It's hard to choose among such lovely things."

Howard was silent for a moment. He was aware of their eyes upon him, Lantis with his impossibly blue gaze, Cassandra, worried and yet trusting, and above all, Roma's steady stare, watchful, assessing. He sighed audibly, but smiled in resignation.

"Perhaps we have all been . . . a little overcome. Certainly, we will make a smaller selection. Immediately," he added sardonically for Roma's benefit.

Roma nodded, the simple gesture somehow contemptuous. Howard gritted his teeth. Even Roma's silence was enraging. *Especially* his silence.

# Chapter 15

## 1357 B.C.E.
## Abydos

The Seti I dig was a turning point. The mission was already a success by any standards. The artifacts continued to pour in, documents, paintings, sculpture from sites all over the globe. They had ruled out the prehistoric periods for this visit, but that left thousands of years to assess. Howard's eyes took on a transcendent look as he contemplated the objects that came through the gate and were duly sent on to *Traveler One* at regular intervals. Yet even the success of the mission was not enough to remove the look of critical reserve from the security specialist's face.

Howard watched Roma watching him, one evening when they were trying to relax. It seemed that every time he looked around he saw that same watchful stare, weighing every decision, every action. He never knew when Roma would force himself between Howard and the mission. There was that ridiculous argument over the Dead Sea Scrolls. Howard felt the fire of frustration rise in his chest as he remembered Roma's outrageous interference in what was strictly Howard's business. But Roma had pried and spied and asked infinitely annoying questions about the *propriety* of taking the scrolls, their critical importance in the historical development of Earth culture, on and on until Howard's patience had snapped.

"This is not your business!" he had exclaimed angrily. "You will cease meddling and tend to the security of this mission or—"

Roma had cut in, his voice cold. "I'm sorry to disabuse your mind of the illusion that you are autonomous here, Howard, but in fact the nature of the mission is very much my business. I agreed to take on this responsibility because I was assured of the mission's ethical probity. I have grave doubts about it now. Your obsession with these artifacts you gloat over leaves very little room for concern over the people entrusted to you . . . and to me. And you have none at all for the people of this timeline you so blithely rob of their heritage. This is no longer selecting a sample of artifacts from each culture. You are pillaging the past. That is unacceptable."

"I have the power to decide what to take."

"And I have the power to decide when to end the mission. Don't force me to do it earlier than we planned."

There was a long, ugly pause.

Howard drew a deep breath and forced his voice to sound calm. "The scrolls we have removed were never found in this timeline. Taking them will not affect history. I will be happy to show you the list."

"I want to see the scrolls."

Howard jerked the lid off the crate, revealing three rolls of leather removed from jars in the caves at *Khirbet Qumran* just weeks after the Essene scribes had deposited them there. The new, supple leather gleamed through their protective layers of gel.

"How many?" inquired Roma.

"Three."

"And none of these were found?"

"To be strictly accurate, only one of them was never found. The other two were damaged beyond repair by the peasants that found them. When the first scrolls were discovered, the archaeologists of the time paid for every piece brought in by the local shepherds and scavengers. So of course the stupid peasants tore the manuscripts they found into thousands of tiny pieces to increase their payment. Many were never successfully reassembled. It's a wonder any of the scrolls were recovered. We are robbing them of nothing whatsoever except perhaps frustration."

"And there are no other crates?"

"There are no other crates," said Howard evenly.

The door opened and Cassandra, hearing these last words, looked momentarily surprised. Howard sent her a warning look and she said nothing. Roma, apparently satisfied, was preparing to leave. Howard drew a relieved breath.

"I really do appreciate your concern for the mission's integrity, Roma. I wish you could believe that."

"So do I," said Roma pleasantly, and left.

Cassandra stood silent, looking at the crate. Howard saw her expression. She had not leapt to his defense, had not expressed outrage at Roma's parting remark. Howard felt alarm stir for the first time.

"I wouldn't want you to misunderstand that," he began.

She looked up, eager to believe in him.

"I had to tell him this was the only crate. He has a mania about the number of artifacts we take, and no appreciation of how difficult . . . impossible it is to choose when each and every one is important in its own right."

"I do understand that, of course. But these scrolls form such a critical part of the history and theology of Earth, are you certain we are not damaging the future by taking so many?"

Howard allowed his expression to soften and grow warm. He took her hands in his and let her see the admiration in his gaze.

"You know you can trust me. I told Roma the truth about the scrolls. I explained that the ones we have taken were not found, or were never deciphered. I just, well, let him think there were only three. I simply can't endure these constant quarrels, this suspicion under which I must labor!" The beautiful voice was tragic.

Her heart went out to him, then, and tears appeared in her dark eyes.

"I do trust you, John," she said softly.

The door opened, and Howard saw Vincent standing in the doorway. Howard stiffened involuntarily and released Cassandra's hands. Vincent, his face masking any feeling, avoided looking at either of them as he handed Howard a memory crystal.

"The information you requested, Dr. Howard," he said in an expressionless voice.

Howard had taken the disc, silently cursing the lovesick young fool and himself for his lack of caution. As if he wasn't having enough trouble keeping the team's loyalty and efficiency without being involved in an embarrassing emotional entanglement.

It had been an ugly scene, one Howard regretted. Afterward he made a serious attempt to be more open with Roma, giving him information before he requested it. It was essential that the Persean not be goaded by his own suspicions into wrecking the mission. With Cassandra he was pleasant but distant, praising her work but avoiding any more emotional situations. Vincent, he ignored. *Let him recover in his own time*, thought Howard. *I simply can't afford to let all this interpersonal nonsense distract me. Only the mission matters. Everything else is a waste of time.*

# PART VI

## The Best of Times, the Worst of Times

# Chapter 16

## February 17, 1995 C.E.
## Abydos

Virginia's driver looked at her curiously. The car had been stopped for several moments, and still she made no move. She took off her dark glasses and polished them with deep concentration. Finally he broke the silence.

"It is very quiet."

She looked up, turning unwilling eyes to the ruins. True, there was no singing, no shouting, no sound at all except for the wind. She replaced her glasses, afraid of what he would see in her eyes.

"They must have shut down for the day."

It was early, barely noon. The sun was at its hottest, which even in winter was considerable. She forced herself to take hold of the door handle. Her hand was shaking.

The driver was instantly out of the car and moving to open her door. With a huge effort she gathered up her shoulder bag and climbed out of the car. The wind hit her with stinging intensity, hot blown sand scouring cheeks and nose. The car had drawn up at the edge of the temple precinct, in the shadow of one of the great obelisks that marked the entrance to the temple itself. A grubby Jeep shared the patch of shade, apparently abandoned. Telling herself the worst was over, Virginia reached into her bag. The driver's gold-dazzling smile flashed.

"Thank you . . . Hamid." She handed him the expected tip. "What time will the other driver be here?"

His smile faded. "Other driver?"

"To drive me back to Abydos, to the hotel. There may not be anyone here who can—"

He was smiling again. "No other driver, no. There is a car. For you." He gestured toward the Jeep.

She tried to swallow with throat muscles suddenly constricted.

"There is a mistake. I don't drive."

His smile faded again, and he looked concerned.

"Who can have made such an error?" He shrugged, clearly absolving himself of any such responsibility.

Virginia concentrated on not feeling helpless and foolish, and failed. A dull anger gave her a sense of resolution.

"Then, Hamid, will you wait while I see the foreman? You can drive me back after that, and we can straighten out the mistake about a driver at the hotel."

Relieved to have such an easy solution presented, Hamid nodded and his smile increased in intensity. The effect was blinding.

"But certainly. It would be a pleasure, Dr. Alexander." He picked up her shoulder bag and turned to look around the ruins.

The Old Temple of Osiris at Abydos was laid out in a

manner similar to many of the great temples in Egypt. The path up from the river passed into the outer courtyard through a gap in the brick walls surrounding the precincts. On the north side of the court was the temple to Isis, now nothing but a broken flight of steps and a row of columns half buried in the sand. On the south, the two obelisks on either side of the main gate pointed to the heavens. Facing the river from the west side of the courtyard was the Lord of Forever, Osiris himself. The great statue sat staring over their heads with empty eyes, brooding perhaps on a very different scene. The ruined visage still conveyed a sense of serenity and grandeur.

Silence fills a place in different ways. The expected hush of empty, deserted places can possess a restful, even a spiritual quality. Though the Temple of Osiris had been empty of life for thousands of years, the silence that filled it now had no touch of peace. Virginia found it ominous. No voices, no birds, nothing. Even the sound of the wind had muted, as if heard from a great distance. This ought to be a hive of activity—not dead. There were signs, however, that activity had ceased very recently. A shovel leaned against the throne of Osiris. A brush, the soft camel-hair variety used by archaeologists to clean the dust from artifacts, lay near a broken clay vessel, as if both had suddenly dropped from nerveless hands. Only a very fine sifting of sand had accumulated on the pot, so it had fallen, abandoned within the past few hours. Most disturbing, several bundles and backpacks lay about, still holding their owners' notebooks and tools. Casual about many things, no archaeologist is casual about tools. Virginia remembered her own attachment to a certain set of brushes. Hickson had sulked for days when his favorite small pick had disappeared, and no one, ever, left precious notebooks like these unattended. The sudden memory left her momentarily breathless—and unaccountably cold.

"Well, I guess I'd better just check the inner precincts, in case someone. . . . " She left the sentence unfinished, and Hamid nodded, his eyes shifting uneasily from the car to the temple and back.

She turned and walked with some difficulty through the sand that had gathered in the gap where once the main gates had stood. The inner court was littered with equipment; boxes and tools lay everywhere. Papers fluttered where they had caught, trapped along the edges of fallen stones. She stooped and picked up one of the loose sheets. It was part of a drawing, a pencil sketch of a woman's head. Certainly not Egyptian, she mused, looking at the rounded cheek and soft curling hair. There was a familiar quality to the work, but the reference eluded her. She looked up at Hamid.

"I suppose we had better go back to the hotel. Perhaps someone there knows—" she was never to finish the sentence.

Hamid, in his eagerness to be gone from this inexplicably empty and silent place, had already turned and was urging her back to the car. Just past the shadowy gateway, he stopped dead. Virginia narrowly avoided running into him. Staggering in the loose sand, she lost her footing and fell heavily against the lintel. Starting up furiously, she froze on her knees. A terrible whimpering sound was coming from the man ahead of her, and she saw that he had thrown up his hands to shield his face from what he saw.

Peering past him, all she could see was the light. It was at the base of the statue of Osiris, a pulsing presence that was all colors and no color. It had no source, emitted no heat, yet danced off the retina with the overwhelming brightness of the sun. It was not just light, it involved the other senses as well. Its effect was indescribable.

"Hamid, what in God's name—" Her voice sounded far away to her own ears.

But Hamid did not answer. Whatever he had seen and felt in that flaring light had sent him scrambling toward his car.

"Hurry!" he shouted over his shoulder, wrenching open the driver's door and starting the engine at almost the same instant.

Virginia stood up and took a step toward the car. It roared to life and ground through the sand to the road. She never even felt the impact as the bumper caught her and threw her back into the gateway and the muffling blanket of sand.

When she opened her eyes, the shadows in the temple stretched long and black across the ruins. The wind had died down, and there was no sound. It was like being inside an isolation chamber. Virginia wondered for a moment if she had gone deaf, but the sound of her hand scraping along the stones reassured her. She sat up and looked around. Hamid had gone, leaving nothing but some deep depressions where the car had torn furiously through the sand. Escaping from what? She remembered the light and the assault on the senses that had accompanied it. She also remembered H.L.'s words, "Workmen at the Abydos dig have been reporting strange noises, flashing lights, that sort of thing, for several weeks. . . ."

She stood up. The ground bumped and dived for a moment, then resumed its blessed natural stillness. She looked at the Jeep. The keys were in the ignition. It had a stick shift. She had been able to drive one once. There was a concession just on the far side of the Seti I temple, barely three miles away. She could do it. She could climb in, start the engine, and drive away. She could go slowly, just as far as the first straggle of houses and help.

She couldn't. She broke out in a cold sweat just considering getting behind the wheel. She stumbled on a loose rock and steadied herself against the side of the Jeep.

"Well, hell," was all she could find to say.

Twenty minutes later, she was still leaning against the Jeep. A phobia is a phobia. No one who does not suffer from it can possibly understand its obscene power to override reason and will. The conscious mind may argue with it, may plead, may reassure, but the phobia is, at its very heart, irrational. No amount of reassurance affects the blind, sickening fear that possesses the sufferer, or prevents the mindless physical responses that follow. She put her hand on the door handle for perhaps the thousandth time, only to withdraw it an instant later, shaking and weak.

Accepting defeat, she turned and looked up the road.

It was a rough track that served to connect the Old Temple site to the main road to Abydos. It was nearly dark, and the last thing she wanted was to stumble along it alone in the hope of encountering some benevolent soul with a car. Suddenly she was tired, too tired to walk, almost too tired to breathe. What on earth had happened to Hamid? Her mind shied away from his reaction to the light, and from the light itself. A reflection, a mirage, sunstroke, the possibilities ticked by in her mind. Nothing explained the transformation of that pleasant young man into one so terrified, so desperate to get away that he didn't care, perhaps didn't know that he had hit her as he turned to leave her behind.

*Three choices*, Virginia's mind enumerated, *stay here, walk away, drive away*. Well, two and three were not really choices, so that left one. She had slept in the ruins of Abydos before; she could do it again. She stooped and picked up a sleeping bag someone had left rolled tidily against the base of the Osiris statue. The desert was cold at night. A brief search located a strong flashlight in one of the backpacks, as well as a canteen of slightly stale water. Huddled against a fallen column where she had a good view of the courtyard and the gateway, she settled in for the night.

Virginia was profoundly aware of the years that separated her from the girl who had once slept here with only pleased excitement to keep her awake. And Hickson, of course. Even through her exhaustion and the fear she was keeping at bay, she could feel her heart warm at the memory of Hicks that last night in the ruins. He had propped his long body against the statue, drinking coffee out of his Sierra Club cup and looking at her over the rim with his laughing blue eyes.

"Jinn, you engaging ninny, Akhenaten probably killed his beautiful wife to make way for another queen, or had it done, even more likely. You know the evidence suggests that Nefertiti was long gone before they finally killed him."

"And you know the evidence is inconclusive."

He gave an exaggerated sigh. "God, I *hate* sentiment. It petrifies the brain."

She had leaned over then, and kissed him.

"Well, I hate *most* sentiment—" he had begun, preparing to give his full attention to exploring the exceptions when a shout had caused him to raise his head and swear.

"Over here," he answered, glaring at the digger who ran up.

"Sorry, Dr. Hickson, Miss, but Dr. Pierce says will you come quickly, please, up to the small dig and bring the Jeep."

They had driven up the track in the darkness, arguing as always, and she held one of his hands while he drove expertly with the other. They drove out of the precincts, and headed across the desert plain between the river and the mountains, past *Omm El Ga'ab,* the legendary burial site of Osiris himself. The moon was shining, turning all the world to white and black. H.L. was supervising a small dig in the rocky heights above Abydos, at what he believed to be the site of another ancient temple to Osiris. Among the ruins of the Seti I temple was the mysterious structure known as the Osirion.

After years of controversy, scholars had agreed that the Osirion had been built at the same time as the Seti I temple, though some still argued that it was much older. It was a structure like no other, designed to be covered by a mound, apparently to honor the burial place of Osiris. H.L. had never believed that the Osirion was the first such structure. Even as there was an older temple, he believed there was an older Osirion. His theory was that somewhere in the mountains lay the original Osirion, a temple built to simulate Amenti, the dark realm of the Lord of the Underworld. "A labyrinth, I think," he had posited, emulating the labyrinthine progress of Osiris's boat through the Underworld, with twelve chambers representing the twelve hours of the night. "Here, in Abydos, it lies somewhere. The references in *the Book of Gates* and the *Book of What Is in the Underworld* are unmistakable. To me." He had searched for years, opening countless small, barren tombs in the mountains, never giving up. This latest dig would probably turn out to be a storeroom. *Still*, thought Virginia as they careered up the rough road, *he just might find it someday. He was uncanny that way*.

H.L. was dancing with impatience when the Jeep's headlights crawled over the summit and lit up the dig.

"What took so long?" he cried. "Come, come this way."

Excitement seemed to sparkle on his skin as he led the way up the rise to the entrance to the site. Two graduate students waited there in the state of patient exhaustion inseparable from their occupation. Their efforts had cleared a short flight of stairs cut into the rock. H.L. was halfway up before they reached the bottom step, demanding they hurry.

"What did you find?" countered Hickson with a grin, "mummified cats?"

H.L. grinned back, his eyes dancing. He had a large lantern, and proceeded to unlock the gate across the entrance. On the other side of the gate was a room, almost completely choked with fallen stone and rubble. They had to pick their way carefully, over and under columns and wall fragments, until the lantern illuminated another doorway.

"It was here. Among the stones. I just found it." H.L. indicated something at his feet. Hickson squatted and shone the lantern directly on the object. It threw the light from the lantern back into his eyes in a golden dazzle. Wedged among the stones lay a statue, or the top of one, shining through the dust of centuries as only the king of metals can shine. They were looking at the head, and Virginia traced a reverent finger along the curves of the tall Atef crown, the uraeus serpent of royal divinity curling at the brow, the formal serene lines of the face.

"Osiris," she breathed.

"God, it's beautiful," said Hickson prayerfully, in the same breath.

"But what is it doing here? In a storeroom. . . . " she faltered to a stop. Hickson's eyes blazed.

"A tomb?" he asked.

"If so," said H.L., rocking on his heels, "it fits no pattern of tomb ever uncovered. Through this door there is a hallway, and we have been able to penetrate as far as the first intersection."

"The first?" Hickson said sharply.

"Yes. It's clearly a temple of some sort, but again, it fits no pattern we've ever seen. No outer court, no hypostile, no symmetrical courts and sanctuaries. It's all built into the mountain, like a tomb. And I think I could make out doorways along the corridors. A very complex series of rooms and hallways, and no ordinary storeroom, that is for certain. Behind this entrance chamber there lies what I believe to be a maze of hallways . . . a labyrinth."

"Amenti," breathed Virginia, her eyes very bright.

Hickson was edging past the rubble toward the doorway when H.L. stopped him.

"No good. There's been a cave-in just past the second intersection. It's pretty well blocked in all directions from there, except back to the entrance. It's an odd fall; the rock seems almost to have been *fused*. We'll have to bring in much heavier equipment to dig it out. We'll need to apply for an extension, but I think this will convince everyone that it's worth while." He patted the golden crown of Osiris. "Now let's get this fellow out to the Jeep."

It took them several hours to move the stone necessary to free the statue, slightly over three feet tall, and carry it down to the road. Hickson wrapped it in his shirt, and they hoisted it into the back seat of the Jeep. It slipped and came down heavily on Hickson's hand. He gave a yelp and stood up, holding the bruised fingers to his chest.

"It's nothing. Hurts, though," he said.

So Virginia had driven the Jeep, with H.L. in the front,

and Hickson bracing the statue in the back with his good hand. The obsession of archaeology is a strong libation, and they were drunk with joy over their find. They were careering up the desert track, taking the curves too fast as it rose between the hills, singing some bawdy song and laughing, when the tire blew out and the Jeep swerved across the road toward the drop. It was the worst place, where one side of the road fell off into a wadi, a hundred feet of unforgiving stone. Cold panic had sobered her, but not in time. They hit hard against a big boulder, and the Jeep hung at a crazy angle out over the edge. The last thing she remembered was flying through the air, then hitting the ground with a brutal slam, the breath driven out of her body. When she opened her eyes again, H.L. was slumped forward in the Jeep, unconscious against the dash. Hickson, pinned by the heavy gold statue, lay across the back seat, perilously poised above the steep drop. Clenching her teeth against a scream, she got up and ran for the Jeep, but his tiny gesture stopped her.

"Don't touch the car." He barely breathed the words.

She could tell by the sound of his voice that he was hurt. "Hickson. . . . " It was a prayer.

He smiled, and shifted the statue a bit. The Jeep tipped ominously. "Help H.L. Move slow."

She had looked at Hickson and at H.L., both poised above death. When he nodded, she had opened the passenger door with infinite care, inch by interminable inch, her hands slippery with sweat. Dimly conscious, H.L. had tried to help, easing his body out of the car and onto solid ground. She remembered looking back at Hickson, agonized, as H.L.'s feet reached the ground.

"Help H.L. first. It will be all right."

But it hadn't been, of course. Without the elder man's weight, the Jeep swayed violently. There was a moment when she thought that Hickson, struggling out from under the statue, might make it over the side in time. Then the Jeep toppled over the drop, and took the statue, and Hicks, and the future with it.

# Chapter 17

## 1357 B.C.E.
## Abydos

Howard looked up as Roma came into the storeroom where he was cataloging artifacts from the Tibetan gate. He could tell by the ramrod-stiff back that he was in for another prolonged shouting match. Not that Roma ever shouted. But the effect was the same. Howard sighed.

Roma leaned down and rested his hands on the crate in front of Howard, so their faces were uncomfortably close.

"I found Temogen outside the perimeter today. He says you sent him."

"True. I sent him to look at the temple. A discreet survey, that's all. Nothing to get alarmed about."

Roma drew a deep breath and leaned a little closer.

"Dr. Howard. I find it difficult to believe that you really do not understand how serious a breach of security this is. If he had been seen, injured, caught, think for a moment about the consequences."

"Roma, you simply do not understand how to differentiate between the important and the irrelevant. An important document, a very important document, will be found in the ruins of that temple. I want it. It is necessary for the Collection—"

Roma spat a word in his face that brought the blood singing into his ears.

"That is what I think of your precious document, the Collection, and you. Understand something, Howard. I have explained the importance of observing the security regulations on this mission to you before. I have also explained them to Temogen this evening. If you break any of my security safeguards ever again, or cause anyone else to break one, I will send you back to *Traveler One* in a box. A small box."

Rage darkened Howard's mind.

"How dare you speak to me—"

But Roma was gone, leaving him alone in his rage. He brought a fist crashing down on the surface of the crate, for once unconcerned about its fragile contents. God, how he was beset with small minds! It was past enduring. As his anger cooled, he tried to dismiss Roma. *An arrogant young gunslinger, of no importance*. And there was no reason to invest his not-very-veiled threat with any real credence.

Later, when he saw Temogen, he reconsidered this. One side of Temogen's face was black, his eye swollen shut. He moved as if his entire body hurt. The Security Second eyed him sullenly, and Howard could find no words to say.

The others, seeing the physical evidence of Temogen's fall from grace, discussed it only in quiet places, out of Roma's earshot. No one had ever seen Roma display rage; he never even raised his voice. His authority did not depend on violence. Obviously, the same rules did not apply to his second. What had Temogen done or said that had driven Roma to such extreme measures? Over a quiet drink in Vincent's room, Vincent and Lantis debated the correctness of the Chief of Security beating the daylights out of the Security Second.

"It's hard to imagine, somehow," Vincent said, handing Lantis his glass. "I mean, Roma is always so nice."

Lantis laughed and shook his head. "I bet he hasn't been called *nice* by very many people, Vince."

"Don't you like him?"

Lantis thought for a second. "He's a little too distant to like, don't you think? He's a cop, after all. And a bloody tough one. I'm sure Temogen would agree."

"Well, I trust him, and I don't trust Temogen," said Vincent.

"Oh, well, trust is something else. And Temogen isn't exactly among the most likable people I've ever met, come to think of it. I'd say whatever he did, he probably deserved what Roma gave him."

Vincent looked into his glass for a moment. Lantis, his eyes straying around the cluttered room, picked up a piece of paper from the floor. He turned it over casually, and found himself looking at a drawing of Cassandra. The dark eyes and curling hair were instantly recognizable. But somehow, Vincent's pencil had transformed all her nervous energy, all her punishing ambition, into something infinitely softer. The smallest of tender smiles curved her mouth. He looked up and met Vincent's gaze.

"Nice," was all he could find to say.

An explosive sound indicated Vincent's reception of the comment. Then his humor reasserted itself, and he grinned.

"Oh, well, I know it doesn't exactly look like her."

Lantis picked up another drawing. He looked at Vincent for a moment and smiled.

"It's too bad she doesn't ever look like this. Too enraptured with the glories of the past, I suppose. Or the glories of Howard."

Vincent's grin vanished. "She believes in him. In the nobility of the enterprise."

Lantis nodded, understanding in his eyes. "I know. And if it's any comfort, he probably doesn't feel anything more for her than he does for any of us. A pair of hands, a mind to be used. All to further the ends of the Collection. At least, I hope those are the ends."

"Meaning?"

"Well, Roma appears to be even more on the watch than usual. If that's possible. I'd say he suspects the good doctor of something nefarious." The blue eyes sparkled.

Vincent snorted. "Howard never thinks about anything except the Collection."

"I know. But whose collection?"

Vincent's stare sharpened. "You think he's taking things for himself?" He was horrified, but somehow not surprised.

"I think Roma is asking himself that very question. He watches Howard from a distance, the way a hawk watches for a mouse." He made a graceful, swooping motion with his hand, then pounced.

"Hard to think of Howard as a mouse, exactly," said Vincent, unwillingly amused.

Lantis sobered. "Vincent, Roma is *worried*. And that worries me."

"I know. But we're halfway through the recorders. If we can distribute them all, think about the possibility of actually preventing the Cataclysm!"

"I am thinking about it. I'm also thinking about that broken necklace. And then the case of tools disappearing. It feels like something is about to happen. Or rather, that something has already begun to happen, and is going to get worse."

# Chapter 18
## 1357 B.C.E.
## Abydos

Howard, in an effort to reestablish civility with Roma, knocked at his door early the next morning. If Roma felt any surprise at seeing Howard, he gave no sign, merely motioned him in. Howard took the only chair. His eyes wandered around the room for a moment. No rugs, no pictures, nothing but the most spartan necessities occupied the room. This was the room of a soldier in the field. Roma's skin shone with a fine film of sweat. Howard had interrupted the exercises he practiced morning and night. A Persean had to keep his body at peak readiness for whatever demands the constant dangers of his profession might make upon it.

He looked up at Roma, and motioned to the bed.

"Sit down, please, Roma. I want to talk."

Roma sat, his expression noncommittal.

Howard cleared his throat. "Temogen—"

"Is under my direct supervision."

"Yes, of course. But I feel responsible—"

"You are responsible."

Howard shook his head ruefully. "Roma, you really are the most exasperating man. Here I am, trying to apologize

. . . but perhaps I should be apologizing to Temogen. He's the one you nearly beat to death."

Roma raised his brows. "Temogen never came near death, Dr. Howard. And most of what happened to him was not because of the unauthorized trip to the temple."

"Then what. . . . "

"That's between me and Temogen. Let us just say that he questioned my authority in a very direct way. It was . . . unwise."

"I really came here to tell you that I am sorry about sending him out of the labyrinth. It was a mistake. I will not make that mistake again."

"Neither will he," said Roma, with the first gleam of humor Howard had ever seen in his eyes. It chilled him.

"Let us agree," Roma went on, "that it was an unfortunate occurrence and it is over."

Howard's goodwill mission hadn't exactly been a howling success, but perhaps it would serve. He fought against frustration. If Roma's suspicions were not allayed, he would become a serious threat to Howard's plans. The thought of Temogen's bruises sharpened his determination.

"Roma, I know we have had our misunderstandings—"

Roma shook his head, unsmiling. "I have always understood you, Dr. Howard."

A soft chime sounded in the silence. Roma rose and opened his viewscreen. The face of a woman filled it. Her name was Janet, and she was part of the security team stationed at the Greek gate. Her face was starkly controlled.

"Roma," she said, her voice husky, "come as soon as you

can. Ravia—one of our security people—was preparing to come to your gate with some small artifacts from the Delphi sanctuary. Something happened in the gate. She never arrived. She's *disappeared.*"

"Have you told Lantis?" Roma was already shoving equipment into a carryall.

"Yes," she said, the tears breaking through. "He checked the transfer logs. She didn't go anywhere. She's just . . . gone."

"I'm on my way," he said, and switched off the screen.

Howard was on his feet, his face white with shock.

"Good God, Roma! It must be a mistake! She must have gone to one of the other stations, and didn't bother to tell anyone where she was going."

Roma paused in the act of putting on the heavy shoulder harness that held his disrupter.

"I don't suppose the bag of tools told anyone where it was going, either."

"You can't possibly be joking!"

"No. I'm in deadly earnest. I'm on my way to the Greek station. I'll tell Lantis that no one is to use the gate, without my direct authorization. No one."

"Of course," Howard agreed, but he was talking to empty air. Roma had disappeared into the labyrinth at a dead run.

Temogen and Lantis were already in the gate control room when he arrived.

"Stay here and see that no one leaves, for any reason."

Temogen nodded, taking up his stand near the console. Roma took a long look at his bruised face.

"Temogen. Have Daedalus look at that."

"It does not trouble me, Roma," said Temogen.

"But it does trouble the clients," said Roma with a grin.

Lantis was astonished to see Temogen return the grin, and sketch a salute. Then Roma nodded to Lantis, who set the controls and sent him to the Greek station.

Vincent was waiting in the control room with Temogen and Lantis when Roma returned.

"No news," he said, stepping off the gate pad. His face showed the hours of strain. Vincent winced away from the pain he heard in that voice. It was the pain of defeat.

Roma turned to Temogen. "Tomorrow. I want you to go to the Greek station. Find out everything you can about this woman. Who her friends were. Her confidants. Whether she mentioned a destination to anyone."

"And whether someone had a reason to want her gone," continued Temogen equably, preparing to leave.

"Yes. And Temogen?"

Temogen looked around.

"Try not to scare everyone."

"Only a little," replied Temogen with a smile.

Roma turned to Vincent and Lantis.

"No news from the other gates, I suppose."

"None," said Vincent.

"I didn't expect any. I went to every gate myself, and no one admits to having seen her."

He reached into his carryall and took out a small box.

"These are the memory crystals from the Greek station. You and Dr. Daedalus examine these carefully. With an eye to tampering."

"Tampering? Changing the records?"

Roma nodded tiredly. "Currently the visual records show Ravia getting onto the gate pad, holding a small crate. The technician on duty entered the coordinates for the Abydos gate. All absolutely correct. He recalibrated first, and the record shows it took fifty seconds, exactly as it should. She disappeared. And went nowhere."

"We'll start on it tonight," said Vincent, taking the crystals.

"Tomorrow morning will be soon enough. We all need to talk then. Go to bed, Vincent."

"Yes, *Jefe*," said Vincent.

Startled, Roma looked down at him.

"*Jefe*?"

"Yes. It means *chief*. They used to use it on old Earth when addressing generals and dictators, people like that."

Vincent saw with satisfaction the small smile tugging at Roma's mouth.

"Impudent boy. Go to bed now. You, too, Lantis."

Vincent headed for the door. He looked back when he realized Roma was not following.

"What about you?"

"I will stay here tonight."

Lantis was silent for a long moment. Vincent knew he was agonized about the possible malfunction of the gate. If his gate had sent that technician into oblivion, Lantis would be inconsolable.

"It probably was an error, you know," said Vincent. "The

gate has been working perfectly. Or someone may have, well, caused the accident to happen. No one will blame you. Not even Dr. Howard!"

ꙮ ꙮ ꙮ

When they gathered in the control room the next morning, no one looked rested. Roma told the others what he had told Lantis and Vincent the night before. There had been no new developments at the other gates during the night. No one had found Ravia.

"The crate of artifacts," began Howard, "was it found?"

"No," said Roma shortly.

The look of loss on Howard's face brought Roma up short for a moment. Then Howard uttered a frustrated curse and stalked out of the room.

Roma stared after Howard as if he had seen an entirely alien creature. Then he turned to Temogen and jerked his head toward the gate. Without the slightest appearance of uneasiness, Temogen walked over to the gate pad and stood ready. For the first time, Vincent admired the dark and moody Security Second. Lantis entered the code sequence, looking at the console he once had loved as if he hated the sight of it. Then Temogen had gone, and, seconds later, signaled his safe arrival at the Greek station.

Roma glanced around the room with tired eyes. They settled on Daedalus. "I'll be in my quarters," said Roma. "Call me if you need me. Watch the gate."

*It takes a different kind of courage to know when to let go,* thought Vincent. The silence in the room became painful. Cassandra was avoiding everyone's eyes, clearly upset by what had happened, and defensive on Howard's behalf. Daedalus looked old, and very tired.

"Vincent," he said at last, holding up the memory crystals Roma had brought back from the Greek station. "Let us begin. Perhaps the answer to all this is here. Lantis, I believe we need your assistance as well."

Vincent looked at Lantis, and correctly read the bitter smile twisting his lips. Howard had indeed been very annoyed. And not about the lost technician.

# Chapter 19

## 1357 B.C.E.
## Abydos

They never found her. Or the lost artifacts, although no one ever mentioned them again. The memory crystals showed no evidence of tampering, and no one could put forward any evidence that Ravia had an enemy. She had been a pleasant, efficient worker, well liked by her colleagues. Andre, the technician who had entered the transfer coordinates, broke down when they finally declared her lost in time. No efforts could convince him that he was not responsible. Finally, Roma had decreed that he be sent back to *Traveler One*.

"It's new technology," Vincent was saying.

"Yes," Lantis countered, "but you know the theory has been tested thoroughly. I've tested every step of the construction a thousand times. There is just no reason for the gate to malfunction."

"Now we have to talk about our real purpose here," said Daedalus.

They were sitting in Daedalus's room after a long, grueling day of discussions about the gate. Whether to use it, try to finish the mission. Whether to go home. Vincent looked over at Roma, who sat wrapped in apparently very dark thoughts. He had been withdrawn and silent for the past few days, even for him. Vincent got up and went over to him.

"Roma."

The security chief did not even look up. Whatever occupied his mind, it was compelling.

Vincent cleared his throat, and tried again, louder. "Roma."

He looked up then, and a little of the darkness left his face. "Sorry. What is it, Vincent?"

"Are we going to shut down the gate?"

Roma looked at him in silence, as if seeing him from a long way off. Vincent saw him give his head a slight shake, as if to clear it. Alarm began to grow in Vincent's thoughts. He had never seen Roma abstracted before,

"Is something wrong?"

Roma shook his head again, this time a negative.

"Many things. But nothing new."

"Are we going to shut down the gate?" he asked again.

"I have been in touch with the Commander," Roma replied. "She and Howard agree that there is no cause, as yet, for undue alarm."

Vincent was dumbstruck. Lantis found his tongue.

"No cause for alarm!" he said incredulously. "The woman disappears, vanishes, no explanation, nothing but empty air! I'm not surprised that *Howard* is not alarmed, but I'd have thought—"

Roma held up his hand and stopped the tirade.

"It is her view that we should continue here for a while,

with additional safeguards."

"What additional safeguards?" said Lantis bitterly. "We've tried everything we can think of. We can't even reproduce the problem."

Lantis, Vincent, and Daedalus had tried for days, sending inanimate objects back and forth through the gate system, hoping something would disappear and they could observe the circumstances. Hundreds of tests had produced no results.

"Apparently the Commander believes the mission to be worth the risk," said Roma slowly.

"That's Howard's mission," said Daedalus dismissively. "What about ours? Is it worth the risk?"

He looked at his two young co-conspirators, then at Roma.

Roma's deeply shadowed eyes focused on him. "I swore to accompany you on this mission, to protect you and the others, to let no personal considerations come between me and that goal. I can call a halt without your agreement, Daedalus, but I don't want to do that."

"I propose," began Daedalus slowly, "that we send anyone who wants to go back to *Traveler One.* Those of us who choose to stay will do so knowing the risks. We are all aware of the true goal here, and it has nothing to do with the glories of the past, or of saving Earth's pride. We are talking about saving not one life, not even thousands, but billions. We are talking about saving Earth!"

"And those who choose to stay because of Howard and the Collection?"

"That, too, is their decision."

Roma regarded Daedalus in silence. Then he nodded. "As you say. I hope Ravia would agree."

ℳ ℳ ℳ

The next morning as they sat trying to eat, a shadow fell across their table, and Vincent stiffened.

"May I join you?" Howard asked, suiting the action to the word.

Howard's eyes were shadowed, as if from too little sleep. *Probably still grieving over the missing crate of old junk*, thought Lantis savagely.

"I understand your concern. I share it. But nothing is to be gained by acting in haste at this juncture. We are within months, perhaps weeks of completing the first phase of our mission."

Roma stirred, his eyes narrowed. "I am not proposing to shut down the gate, Howard," he said.

Then Howard cleared his throat.

"Well. Good. And we will take all the safety precautions possible, of course. I suggest we complete the Thutmose dig, and perhaps send out the team at the Maya station once more—"

"Just give me a list of the proposed missions still pending," Roma said, his voice sounding tired and distant. "Some of the personnel at other stations want to return to the ship. You'll have to face it that we'll be working with reduced staff. We will not force anyone to stay here."

"You can't mean that!" Howard cried. "They are giving in to panic! You should have reasoned with them, explained—"

"Explained what? That you care more for these relics of death than for their lives?"

"They knew the risks when they came! Nothing is more important than the mission! It is the cornerstone of the new era, it will exalt the entire human family—"

Roma leaned over and looked Howard in the face.

"One more thing, Howard." Roma's voice was bleak. "Spare me any further rhapsodizing about the exalted human family. You'd see us all scattered on the winds of time for one broken statue." His gaze locked with Howard's, and it was Howard who finally broke away. He stood up and left them without a backward look.

Roma turned to Vincent and Lantis. "You two. You're determined to keep planting the time recorders? How much longer?"

"We figure two months to deliver them, another month to collect the data in the matrix," added Vincent.

"We're running out of time. Cut it to one month total. No unnecessary trips. Make sure Daedalus understands. You're taking an enormous risk. I'm not sure I think it's worth it."

"Yes, *Jefe*." Vincent tried to smile. He and Lantis watched the tall figure move slowly away. Puzzled, Vincent tried to decide what was wrong. Lantis was ahead of him.

"Walks like he has to concentrate on it."

ↂ ↂ ↂ

Twenty-two people elected to return to *Traveler One*. The subsidiary gates were down to half staff. Howard digested the news in silence. It would mean a serious shortage of personnel; work would fall behind. He was forced to excise many of the proposed sites from his plans and concentrate on finishing the ones already opened. Howard's answer to the reduced numbers was to double the workload of those who remained. He pushed himself and the others past the limit, and still the objects flowed through the gate and into their protective crates for shipping home.

Vincent and Lantis speeded up their private operations. During the day they dug and packed for Howard. Late at night, when even Howard was asleep, they took turns, following their own maps through time with the recording crystals, delivering each one, tuned to its particular moment. As they went to times with no gates, they wore the transfer suits and set the controls for automatic return. It was riskier, but both were filled with the desire to complete their mission. Only Roma witnessed these forays, standing his lonely vigil in the control room until they were safely back. They did not allow themselves to think about the danger involved in their constant use of the gate system. It was a race against time.

ↂ ↂ ↂ

"I need for you to go," Howard was saying. He looked deep into Cassandra's eyes, his expression worried. "You look so tired. I have been driving you too hard; it is inexcusable. You should have said something."

She shook her head, and gave him a wan smile.

"Not really. I just . . . haven't been sleeping very well."

"It was wrong of me to ask you. It's just that the Greek station is so short-handed, and it is the last shipment. It's the gold Apollo. You remember the one that completed the Charioteer group and was lost? We have to leave the Charioteer, of course, but the Apollo is far more important. A lovely piece, the pinnacle of Greek art, solid gold. But it is not as important as you, my dear." The beautiful voice took on a caressing note.

Instantly her face brightened.

"Of course I'm not too tired! I want to go. I know how important that statue is to the Collection."

He put an arm around her shoulders.

"It is positively the last time you need go there. And when you return, I think you should have a little vacation. Choose someplace you would like to go, and you must take at least a week."

A vacation. She shuddered, and his grip tightened.

"Cassandra! What is it?"

"I know it's silly, but the thought of going anywhere in the gate makes me queasy. Every time I travel through it I have the most miserable sensations. No one else has mentioned them, so it must just be something wrong with me."

"What kind of sensations?" His voice was full of sympathy, of concern.

"Oh, nothing too serious. I mean, of course I can endure

them. Nausea, pain in my head. But the really disturbing thing is that all the while I am in the gate I seem to be experiencing *visions* of some kind. It feels like they last for hours, but of course the transfer is really almost instantaneous. I . . . find it difficult to forget them."

"Have you mentioned this to anyone else? Daedalus? Roma?"

"No, of course not! I really don't want to be thought a prima donna! Everyone else uses the gate without ill effects. I'll just have to get over it."

"Nonsense! Of course you must stop using the gate if it makes you so uncomfortable. I've been insensitive . . . it's just that you are the only one who understands the importance, the only one who shares my feelings . . . I've allowed myself to be selfish."

"I want to go!" she said again, urgently. "You said yourself that it is probably the last time before we all return. And I really do not want to give up. Please, John, don't mention this to Dr. Daedalus, and certainly not to Roma!"

"I quite understand. Of course not. It's very generous of you, my dear Cassandra."

She had her reward in the smile he gave her, promising what she had never even admitted to herself she wanted. The next morning, eager to succeed at her last assignment, she stepped onto the gate pad and gave a gay little wave of good-bye.

But Cassandra never arrived at the Greek station.

# Chapter 20
## 1357 B.C.E.
## Abydos

Daedalus looked up from the schematic he was studying, when Roma and Lantis walked into the common room.

"Where's Howard?" Roma asked.

There was a note in his voice that Daedalus had never heard. He looked at Lantis, and knew instantly that pain was coming. His heart contracted, waiting.

"Here, Mr. Roma. Is there a problem?" said Howard, entering just behind him.

Roma swung around, and stood looking at Howard. Finally, with audible effort, he told him.

"Did you send Cassandra Alda to the Greek station?"

"Why yes, just a few moments ago. Why?"

"You know no one is supposed to use the gate without Temogen or me."

"My good Roma, you weren't there, Temogen wasn't there, and we needed to get on with the work! Lantis *was* there, and he initialized the gate. I hope you don't think our crystallographic engineer incapable of operating the gate system correctly without your guidance!"

"You didn't wait for confirmation from the Greek station

that she arrived."

"No," said Howard, his gaze narrowing. "I was in a hurry. I assume Lantis got it. What is the problem?"

"The problem," said Roma slowly, "is that she did not arrive at the Greek station. She did not arrive anywhere in the system. She is gone, Howard."

"It's . . . not possible. She must have gone to the Greek station. Lantis set the coordinates. I saw him."

Lantis's hands jerked uncontrollably, then he was still.

"She . . . is . . . gone," said Roma deliberately, his voice devoid of all life, all feeling. "Temogen is going through the system. He'll look, but he won't find her. You know that. You sent her out for yet another precious inanimate object, and she is gone. I thought you'd like to know."

"We're shutting down the Greek station, Dr. Howard," said Lantis in a voice devoid of all emotion. "They're going home."

"You can't!" The change in Howard was astonishing. The stunned, frozen figure was galvanized with passion. "You can't shut down anything until we are finished! The collection, my work—"

"Your work," said Roma in that dead voice. Then his eyes, which had been so dull for the past weeks, went bright and cold. "Your work. So much for Cassandra," he made a small, dismissive gesture. "So much for her life, her dreams. So much for all the others who might be sucked into that gate like feathers in the wind. And you are moved to great heights of grief, over your work."

The even voice never changed, never rose. But suddenly

he lunged, and Howard was pinned against the wall, his head held at an impossible angle by Roma's hand.

"Please," Roma was saying softly, imploringly, "please say something else about your work, about the Collection, so I can just twist your head off and be done with you!"

Lantis was frozen, unable to move. He watched in horrified fascination as Howard's face turned from red to purple. Roma's hand tightened, and blood began to stream from Howard's nose.

"Roma," said Daedalus. His voice was old and filled with sorrow. "Violence is failure."

It seemed as if Roma was actually prepared to accept—even welcome—failure, just this once. Then he tore his hands loose and let Howard slump to the floor, gasping and choking for breath.

Roma swung around and pointed a shaking finger at Daedalus and Lantis. "It's over now, you understand. No more."

Daedalus nodded silently in agreement. As Roma moved toward the door, Lantis grasped his arm.

"Does Vincent know?"

Roma shook his head.

"I'll tell him," said Lantis, closing his eyes against the thought. "I'm the one who sent her."

"No," said Roma harshly. "It was Howard who sent her. You just entered the sequence. The correct sequence, Lantis. It was in no way your fault. I'll tell him."

ജ ജ ജ

"Vincent."

Vincent backed away from the door, looking up at Roma's face. He saw a world of information in that stony mask.

"Who?" he asked, bracing himself to hear.

"Cassandra."

Vincent looked down at the drawing he held in one hand. Involuntarily his fingers tightened, crushing the paper. He tried to open his mouth, to ask questions, but his voice failed.

"Are we going home now?" he finally managed to say.

"Yes. Vincent, Lantis set the controls. He blames himself."

"It couldn't have been his fault," said Vincent, his voice dazed with grief.

He looked away, at the floor, the walls, anywhere except into the eyes of Gianni Roma. He could feel tears rising in his eyes, his thin body beginning to shake. Through the haze of pain he was aware of embarrassment that Roma should see him cry.

Then he felt Roma's arms, strong, supporting.

"I know," he was saying huskily. "It will get easier. The pain will get easier. In time."

ഗ ഗ ഗ

The Greek station was a shambles, the people panic-stricken, unable to work. Roma took one look at the team and sent them back to *Traveler One.* The other teams would have to pack up the equipment they had left behind, and remove the traces of their occupancy. He ordered everyone in the other stations not to use their gates for any purpose until they were ready to go home. Everyone started to pack.

The nightmare was upon them. The Tibetan gate reported that one of their people had disappeared. There was a flash, a gate flash, and she was gone. But she was nowhere near the gate. She had been working in her quarters with another archaeologist. No one set the controls; no one opened a gate. It had opened itself and taken her. There was a panic as people realized that they were in jeopardy even when they were not using the gate. The Tibetan gate closed, and then the Mayan station. There was more terror even in leaving, because they all had to go through the gate to get home.

The people came to Abydos, clutching the few personal bits of luggage they had brought with them, dragging hastily packed crates of equipment. Like sleepwalkers, they waited on the pad for the gate to send them to *Traveler One* and safety. Or to oblivion. Each time, the Abydos team held their collective breaths, waiting for the signal that the travelers had arrived safely. They prayed that they would all get out before anyone else was lost. They counted the days until they would go home.

Eastern Europe was abandoned, then China, Oceana, and Africa. The shielding, the disguised plasteel walls that had sheltered them in their various times and locations, the generators and power grids were dismantled and shipped. The crystal matrices would be transferred in a body, once all the other bits and pieces of their occupancy had been removed, once the Abydos team was finished with the work of dissolution, and the great matrix was ready for shutdown.

One by one, the jeweled web of lights on the great time grid in the control room, each indicating the presence of a gate, went dark. Then there was only one left, the Abydos gate with its great master crystal matrix. And then, when they all believed that things could scarcely get worse, communications with *Traveler One* cut off. Roma kept the information from them, trying to discover the source of the problem. Finally, he was forced to tell them. No one could call the ship. They received no messages. Roma and Daedalus did their best to reassure everyone. There was no question of the Commander leaving them behind. No doubt she was simply reserving power. It took an enormous amount of power to communicate across time lines, and they needed to conserve what they had for the final transferal of the matrix and the Abydos team.

Meanwhile, Daedalus and Lantis would examine the communications system to determine if something was malfunctioning. The Commander, they knew, would be doing everything necessary aboard *Traveler One* to ensure their safe return. They all tried to believe these arguments, but one thought was paramount in everyone's mind. They were alone.

Howard had made one more attempt to persuade the travelers to remain and finish the mission. He had been his most eloquent, but his entreaties had fallen on deaf ears. They were all sick with longing to be out of this place. If they could get out of it. As long as they had to wait until the equipment had been packed, the modifications in the labyrinth removed, at least they could continue to work, packing the last of the artifacts. A few more days at most, and they needn't use the gate at all. Howard went on and on, until Vincent had thought he was going to be sick on the floor.

*To increase the nightmare*, thought Vincent as he paced down the empty corridors, *there is the change in Roma*. The Persean, whose movements had been characterized by a dancer's grace, had become clumsy. Occasionally his hand shook. *You can see it in his eyes; he feels he has failed. There is a kind of bruised, puzzled expression. Sometimes, lately, I wonder if he knows who I am*. His response to questions about his health had been met with stony silence. *It was as if*, Vincent thought, *somehow, Roma has died, without ever leaving us.*

Vincent's footsteps made no sound in the darkened halls of the labyrinth. It had become a habit, wandering through the maze at night, as his dreams did not permit him to rest. Endless days spent studying the time theory had produced no answers. As preparations for departure neared completion, the great matrix continued to receive and store the data sent by the hundreds of little recording crystals he and Lantis had strewn through time. They had only managed to plant half the number they had planned to leave, and could only hope they would be enough, that somewhere in those recorded event strings lay the answer to the Cataclysm. He did not know what was destroying Roma. Cassandra had died for a gold statue. Vincent required a better reason.

He realized his absent-minded steps had carried him into a part of the labyrinth that the travelers never used. It was darker, and the air smelled faintly of dry decay. He turned to retrace his steps, and a soft shimmer in the gloom caught his eye. A wooden door stood ajar, and he looked curiously into the room beyond. He caught his breath and stammered a startled apology. Howard was there, packing things into a crate, completely absorbed.

"Vincent!" there was only mild surprise in Howard's voice. "What are you doing here at this time of night?"

"I . . . couldn't sleep."

Vincent's voice trailed off. He was staring at the things in the room. He turned his eyes from one object to the next, bafflement and alarm growing with every new item discovered. A serene and eternally young Virgin cradled the body of the dead Christ, luminous even in the half-light. A young David, full of life and beauty stood negligently beside them. Huge crates waited to receive them. The inlaid gold death mask of a boy king rested on a crate, ready to be packed for shipment.

"But . . . Dr. Howard," his voice was slow, stupid with sorrow and lack of sleep. "You can't mean to take these things." He looked with awe at the works of art filling the room. Rows of crates stretched away into darkness, untold numbers of art treasures and who knew what else.

"You don't think so, Vincent?" asked Howard, quietly.

Vincent looked at him, and tried to gather his thoughts.

"These are famous . . . I mean, they will be famous. The most famous art treasures in their time."

"And they will all perish in the Cataclysm."

"Yes, I know, but they were very important in history before that! Dr. Howard, it will change history! We're not supposed to take anything like that—"

The blow came too suddenly for him to cry out.

ᘓ ᘓ ᘓ

"Has anybody seen Vincent?" asked Lantis the next morning. "He's not in his quarters."

"Have you checked Daedalus's room?" asked Roma absently. "They are working over the theories, looking for—"

"I know where he is supposed to be," Lantis said, his voice ragged. "But he isn't there. He's not anywhere."

Roma was out of his chair before the words were finished. He staggered, and for a moment it looked as if he would fall.

"Look everywhere in the labyrinth. Check the gate system, see if it has been used. Is Temogen back yet?"

Temogen had left the labyrinth, apparently off on another illicit exploration.

"Damn him, I need him now," Roma swore.

They spent the day searching. There was no trace of Vincent. Nor did they find the hidden storeroom, cleverly concealed in the darkened corridors. All that met the desperately searching eyes of the travelers were dusty, unfinished walls. Roma stalked the corridors like a man in a waking nightmare. Only he knew how grave the situation was, how many dark things he was not sharing with the others. The gate records showed it had been used once during the night. There was no visual record, no record to show who had used the gate, or who had entered the coordinates, or the coordinates themselves. No record of who had wiped the records.

The searchers gathered for food and a few moments' rest.

"I can't believe it," Daedalus was saying in a querulous voice, the voice of a very old man. "Vincent. Gone?" It was perhaps the hundredth time that day he had said it.

Howard looked up, unable to mask his impatience. He had joined in the search, but it was clear that he held no hope for success. And, only he knew, with the best of reasons.

"Dr. Daedalus," he said, struggling to keep his tone patient, "I know you are grieved by this. But we need to think of the future—"

"The future?" said Roma, his voice shaking. "What future? What future do any of us have? What about Vincent's future?" He eyed Howard, naked suspicion and hatred flaring in his narrowed stare.

"Vincent is gone. But we have a future, a very bright one. I do not propose to allow you to throw it away at this juncture because you cannot keep things in perspective."

Suddenly, Roma stood up, raising his head like a bull about to charge. Something had taken possession of him; a stranger looked out of his eyes.

"Howard. We are closing down the matrix. It is over."

They all remembered the last time Howard had goaded him past endurance. Daedalus closed his eyes, but Lantis was staring at Roma with a kind of plea on his face, as if he were willing Roma to stop Howard—or kill him.

"I am the leader of this mission, and I will decide when it is over," said Howard pleasantly. A disrupter appeared in his hand, the ready lights pulsing deadly red. Roma's disrupter was out in the same second, but with a difference. He stood, looking down at the weapon.

"You will find that it will not function, but I assure you, this one will. Now, let us be reasonable."

"Reasonable," said Roma, like a man in a dream. He continued to look at the dead disrupter in his hand.

"Yes. We will continue to search for Vincent until you are satisfied that he is not here. We will, of course, repair the gate. Daedalus and Lantis will see to that." He nodded in their direction as if their agreement was beyond question. "Then we will discuss shutting it down."

Daedalus finally raised his head. "Howard, you must understand. We cannot use the gate for your purposes any more. For any purposes, except to try to repair what we have done. We can return to *Traveler One,* I hope, but even that will be risky. If we can put together the correct sequence, when we leave the matrix will seal the breaches between the timelines, repair the membranes. Time will be restored, and there will be no coming back."

Howard waved his hand, dismissing the idea.

"We will, as you say, repair the sequence of time. And as long as we remain in this timeline and do not cross over, there will be no further problem with the gate or with time. Am I correct?"

"Remain here? But to what purpose?" Daedalus's stare

was incredulous.

"To Howard's purpose, Daedalus," said Roma in a deadly quiet voice.

"Exactly," agreed Howard. "Now. I do not wish to be forced to use unpleasant measures that we would all regret. Roma, I am sure you understand what I mean."

Roma nodded, tossing the dead disrupter onto the table. Howard picked it up. "And please understand that none of the others will function either. I have made adequate precautions against any more foolishness. Please don't make me demonstrate any of them to you."

It pleased him, even as it angered his pride, to know how much they had underestimated him. He had known exactly when Roma and Temogen decided to bury their differences and combine forces. Of course, he had been ready.

Roma sat slowly down, watching the disrupter in Howard's hand. "You seem to be in charge," he said evenly.

"Yes. I am."

Lantis glanced at Roma, who nodded, never taking his eyes off Howard. Lantis helped Daedalus to his feet and together they went back to the search.

When they were alone, Howard sat down opposite Roma. His voice maintained its pleasant, even tone.

"Now we are going to come to terms at last. As I have said, I really do not want to have to kill you, Roma. But then again, neither do I want to risk dying at your hands. I fail to take as much comfort in the Persean code as I once did. We have a task to finish, and I need everyone who is left. We can put this unpleasantness behind us, and go forward. It would be a pity, I'm sure you agree, if anyone else were to come to grief."

Roma looked at him for a long moment. Howard could almost see the thoughts chasing themselves behind the tired eyes. He would not risk a confrontation while Howard held the only functioning disrupter. He would wait for Temogen, and together they would find a way to take Howard without putting any of the others at risk. He smiled to himself at the transparency of his would-be opponent.

Roma rose slowly to his feet. "I'm going to help search. We'll talk about this again."

*I'm sure we will*, thought Howard.

When they found Roma's unconscious body in the darkened labyrinth, Lantis and Daedalus carried him to his quarters. Howard was solicitous in his concern.

"Is it serious?" he asked.

Daedalus, shaken out of the stupor of grief, examined him.

"Concussion. Couple of broken ribs. Nothing too serious."

He was preparing a shot when Roma opened his eyes.

"No shots," he ground out.

"It is for the pain," Daedalus said soothingly, and pressed the needle patch against his arm. Alarm flared in Roma's eyes, and then they closed.

"He will be all right in the morning. I can tend to his ribs and the concussion better in his quarters."

ꭥ ꭥ ꭥ

But Roma was not all right in the morning. He was gone.

Soothing their alarm, Howard explained to the assembled group that he had gone through the gate, looking for Vincent.

Daedalus had raised his head then, and his face looked a hundred years old.

"With a concussion?"

Howard smiled thinly.

"I'm sure he considered it no more than a minor inconvenience. I tried to persuade him, but he would go."

"Where? All the gates are closed. Where would he look?"

Howard shrugged. "The great Roma does not condescend to explain his actions. He left, and said he would be back tonight."

Daedalus looked at Howard then, and his eyes accused. The naked grief on his face was painful to look at.

"You sent my boy into the gate, didn't you? You sent Vincent, and now you have sent Roma."

It wasn't until later they realized that Temogen had gone, too. And then there were three.

# Part VII

## A Time for Every Purpose

# Chapter 21

## February 17, 1995 C.E./1357 B.C.E.
## Abydos

Virginia crawled back out of the sleeping bag, her mouth tasting of death and desolation. Even at night, the desert held fewer fears than this place of memory. She picked up her shoulder bag and added the canteen and a small case of tools. The wooden handles, silky to the touch from long use, were so like Hickson's cherished set that her heart contracted painfully. She swung the bag to her shoulder and started out of the ruins.

The Seti I temple lay a little over three miles south, the town a half mile beyond. No doubt there were little trails across the river bank that the local people used, shortening the distance, but it would be suicidal in the dark. A twisted ankle would mean lying in the open on the river bank all night. She paused, looking out at the moon-washed plain. Somewhere in the darkness, a jackal called.

Her heart began to race; her breath sounded loud and harsh in her ears. She felt alternately light and heavy, as though gravity were shifting around her. Pain, nausea, dizziness, her mind cataloged the symptoms with something like surprise. It had been a long time since she had opened the door to the demons of the past. A sound gradually penetrated her ringing ears, and she dragged her head up and opened her eyes. It took a heartbeat for her brain to acknowledge the message her eyes delivered. The light, unnatural and blinding, pulsed at the base of the Osiris statue—a foot from her face. It was growing. She sucked in a breath, smothering the whine she could feel building up in her throat. *Like looking into a window on eternity*, she thought. She closed her eyes against it, every rational, logical brain cell she possessed screaming in terrified protest as she was sucked into the jaws of time.

*Now I know how Jell-O feels . . .* she thought with some small, still-functioning part of her mind. The rest, overloaded with sensory information nature had not designed it to decipher, threatened to shut down in outrage against the onslaught. *Slipping, sliding, congealing . . .* her thoughts continued their inane litany as she fought off the sensations . . . *melting, solidifying, jelling. . . .*

ᘐ ᘐ ᘐ

It was the call of birds, finally, that caused her to open her eyes. *I must have passed out*, she thought, *and stayed out for hours*. The soft predawn light was growing behind the eastern hills. She was lying at the base of the Osiris statue. She put out her hand to steady herself as she rose to her knees, and her hand met polished granite. It took a moment for the thought to take form. *Polished.* It couldn't be polished. The surface of the statue was rough and pitted from centuries of wind and sand, and the thoughtless attentions of countless tourists.

She jerked her hand away and looked up, and a sudden stinging wash of tears blurred her vision. *Mad*, she thought, looking at the polished perfection of the Osiris statue, fresh from the hand of its maker. *Dear God, I've gone mad.* She sat back against the base, and looked around the Osiris Court. There were the twin lily pools, the early morning breeze ruffling the surface of the water and sending the tightly closed buds joy-riding. Beyond the pools the two obelisks rose toward the sky, their incised hieroglyphics sharp and clear. The gods Set and Horus tying together the lotus and papyrus, symbol of the unity of Upper and Lower Egypt, loomed on the walls of the towering pylons. The images were beautifully drawn, twenty feet high. *Perfect. As the day they were painted.*

Her vision darkened, and she felt consciousness slipping away. Everything her senses told her, her mind denied. Beneath her hands she could feel smooth pavement, not a tumble of broken bricks blanketed by sand. She leaned back and tried to quiet her racing heart, to force slow, even breaths. *Hallucinations*, she concluded, *brought on by a blow on the head . . . face*. Her hand went to her mouth and came away sticky with blood. The overwhelming urge to give way to hysteria rose in her throat, the urgent desire to scream, to run.

Gradually, that desire left her. In spite of all the many ills that may prey upon it, there is something intrinsically resilient, or perhaps merely stubborn, about the human mind that denies madness. At least, one's own.

Despite the evidence, Virginia refused to believe she was mad. Admitting to madness would make purposeful action impossible. With no way of distinguishing the real from the delusional, all action would be suspect and, ultimately, meaningless. But Virginia had a long history of purposeful action, of *finding out*, and it was the rigid application of that discipline that had kept her sane and alive after Hickson . . . she sheered away from that thought. *And*, she forced her shaking legs to support her, *I'll be double damned if I'm going to be found running and screaming like a Banshee*. For all she knew, she was totally alone in the universe of her own imagination. But it was necessary to move through that universe with purpose, *to find out*. On which note of reasoning, she started toward the gates of the temple.

A sudden flurry of sound from the other side of the walls indicated that someone was up and around, although not nearly so many as she would have assumed in a temple of this size. *The dig workers*, she thought for a confused moment, then *no, that was then, this is before*. Present and past skidded into each other in her imagination. She fought down the desire to bury her face in her arms and wait until the delusion faded.

Instead, she swung herself up on the base of the statue, keeping the massive figure between her and the gates. Away to the south she could see the curve of the river, the banks green with papyrus, and the huddle of houses that was Abydos. But what interested her most was what was not there. The great bulk of the Seti I temple no longer lifted itself on the banks of the Nile. A mound, dark and featureless, was all that could be seen. A lump caught in her throat. It was the Osirion. Covered by a mound of dirt, the underground temple to Osiris. *The scholars were wrong; Seti I didn't build it,* she thought. *I hope I get to tell someone.* If this was—mentally she swallowed hard, it couldn't possibly be—but if it *was* Thirteenth-Century B.C.E. Egypt, there should be a host of guards and priests about the business of the temple.

She faltered to a halt. What on earth would she say . . . and how? Coptic, which was probably the closest extant language to old Egyptian, would almost certainly be absolutely unintelligible. And then there was the question of what she, an obvious foreigner, was doing violating the sacred precincts of Osiris. The Egyptians had a number of punishments for trespassing and sacrilege—most of them prolonged, all of them fatal. The sound of the gates being unbarred from inside the temple brought her to her knees, scrabbling around behind the statue for cover. She caught a glimpse, a flutter of white, as someone moved inside the gateway. No guards came out to take up their positions. Indecision wracked her. What in God's name was she going to do? Her knees were shaking again, so she crouched, her head bowed.

It was because her face was so close to the ground that she heard it. There, in the little buildup of sand where the base of the statue met the pavement, she could hear a tiny pinging sound. She put out a cautious finger and brushed away the sand. It was square, three and a half inches to a side, unmistakably plastic of some kind. There were several tiny buttons across the bottom. One of them was blinking.

*Plastic*. She touched the button, and the smooth top surface glowed with life. A man's face was projected there, a dark Asiatic face. He appeared to be amused.

Though she recognized the language he spoke as some form of English, she had trouble understanding him at first. Some words seemed to have been shortened, others ran together, and he spoke with a pronounced and, to her, unidentifiable accent. She played the message over, and gradually she was able to make sense of it.

"Roma was right. The guards aren't patrolling the perimeter at night. That should make it easier. Too bad I have to get back to the labyrinth so soon, but if Roma is ready . . ."

Surprise crossed his face, and he appeared to shake something. His own image swung back and forth as if he were shaking a camera aimed at his own face. Then she got it. He was speaking into this little doodad in her hand, a video-recorder of some kind. The surprise on the man's face had turned to fear.

"No—" he was saying. "No, I didn't initialize the gate—" He gagged once, and his features disappeared in a flash of light.

A tiny reproduction of that same searing, unnamed colored light she had seen before. The screen went blank, the button continued to blink. When she pressed it again, she saw the same message. One of the other buttons produced a cryptic message: *Gate initializer disabled*. The third responded with a request for *security code*, followed by an uncompromising blank screen. She sat back again, her hands pressed to her eyes. Okay. *Okay*. A small, very fancy little recording device, whose designer wouldn't be born for over three thousand years. So what was it doing here? And the man had mentioned the labyrinth. He had to mean the Amenti temple found by H.L. six years ago. *Or*, she corrected herself mentally, *three thousand three hundred fifty years from now, give or take a decade. If what I think but don't believe is true*. Three miles' walk through the desert mountains. It had been impossible to consider in the middle of the night. Could she do it at dawn? On the whole, Virginia considered that talking to someone who spoke English, however odd it sounded, was preferable to trying to make herself understood in Coptic. And now was the time, before anyone was up and around. At least she knew the way.

Slipping cautiously along the walls and keeping to the shadows, Virginia circled the courtyard until she found a gate giving onto a path on the western side of the temple. It led across the rising ground to the mountains.

She went lightly at first, as noiselessly as possible among the loose rock and sand. The air was still cool, perfumed by the blend of river and desert as it is nowhere else in the world. She made good time, anxious to be out of sight of the temple by full light. Action—even insane action—was energizing. An hour brought her to the top of the first rise of the cliffs. *Even now, it is not a well-traveled road*, she thought. *No throngs of worshippers visit this temple. No one maintains the road. During Akhenaten's reign it would not have been abandoned. Wouldn't they have redirected it to serve the Aten?*

*But then*, she went on with her inner discussion with herself, *where are the wheel marks, the ruts of traffic? No chariots carrying dignitaries, no wagons of offerings or supplies had been up this road for a long time. Had the Amenti temple been abandoned? Or could it have been lost? Hidden so well, so secretly, that the priests of Aten could not find it? Did not even know of its existence? Some part of an inner cult, perhaps.* As the track made its first bend, she turned and looked back across the plain to the Old Temple. The sun was above the eastern cliffs, turning the low-lying haze at the river's edge into a veil of gold. A finger of light dazzled off the golden obelisks in front of the temple. The colors of the great wall paintings glowed in the new light. Perhaps it was worth madness to have seen this, after all.

The next hour Virginia climbed with the sun racing her to the summit. The cool of early morning vanished in a blaze of growing heat. In her own time, modern equipment and dogged determination had forced a negotiable track up to the tombs hidden in these mountains. Now there was only an all-but-invisible path, narrow and frequently disappearing among huge boulders, almost as if it were hiding itself. Virginia threw all her formidable powers of concentration into negotiating that path, aware that if she was wrong she would find herself a very long distance from any sort of help. One more mile.

# Chapter 22
## 1357 B.C.E.
## Abydos

He could not see, and there was nothing to hear. In the absolute darkness, and the absolute silence, Roma sat up, cursing the dizziness, the sickness that coursed through him. When he was able to focus his eyes, he realized that the darkness was not quite absolute, after all. The tiny light near his feet told him his transcomp was miraculously still with him. Howard couldn't have overlooked it, so he must have left it intentionally. He picked it up and entered his security code. The transport function had been disabled, the matrix-linked crystal removed from the casing. But the screen lit up, providing enough light for him to see a few feet around him.

An hour later, he had made a complete circuit of the room. Probably thirty feet square, the room was a cell in the living rock of the mountains. It was unfinished. Mounds of rubble camouflaged pits and loose piles of paving stones. There was no sign of an opening in the walls, although he knew there must be one. He would find it. He had nothing else to do.

Three hours later, he had crawled over a good part of the floor. He had found a canteen of water and some dry rations, but no way out.

Twenty-four hours later, he had examined every square inch of the walls with his fingertips as high as he could reach. If there was a way out, he could not find it.

When at last he did find it, Roma had lost track of the amount of time he had spent in the sealed room. He drifted out of the edge of unconsciousness when light suddenly bloomed in the darkness. Howard, holding a lantern, stood looking down at him.

He dragged himself to his feet, using the wall for support, and confronted his enemy.

"Well, well. Come to finish your work, Dr. Howard?"

Howard smiled. "I am a long way from finished. I will need more time, much more."

"Howard, there *is* no more time. Surely you must have realized by now that the gate has become deadly?"

"The trouble with you, Roma, is that you have no imagination. What is broken may be fixed. The real issue is, what to do with you now? It had me puzzled for a while but I think I have hit on an . . . elegant solution."

Roma glanced at his transcomp, a few inches from his hand. Something hard, anything to distract Howard for a moment. He made a sudden movement. Howard had seen the direction of his glance, and his hand reached the transcomp seconds before Roma's.

"Ah ah. I think not." His voice was pleasant as he pocketed the transcomp. "It was thoughtful of me to leave it with you, don't you think? Solitude can be so . . . boring. It should make interesting listening. I look forward to it.

"You'll have noticed that I disabled the transport function."

Roma nodded, moistening his cracked lips. "I noticed."

Howard threw out his hands, almost in a gesture of entreaty.

"If only you would be reasonable, Roma. But you can't be, can you? So much the good little soldier. Out of all the others, I could have used your help. It's a pity but there it is. And, of course, there is no one else, now. They are all gone."

Roma saw the truth of it in Howard's deep, dark gaze. But he couldn't stop himself from making a gesture of denial.

"Gone?"

"Yes. All of them. Now it's your turn."

Howard took another transcomp out of his breast pocket. Roma knew the transport function on this one would be working.

"Wait—listen, Howard. Just for a moment, forget the Collection, the Reconstruction . . . forget the *gold*, Howard."

Howard smiled again, and shook his head.

"Roma, you still manage to amaze me. Do you really think that is the end of it, the gold? That *that* is what this has all been about? The *gold*?"

He laughed in genuine amusement.

"I knew your vision was small, but I did expect more than this. Still, at least you're consistent. How I have laughed, over these months, at all of you with your superior ethics, your secret mission, your concern that we not take too many, or the wrong things. Oh, they're pleasant, these lovely things, and I admit I do intend to keep all my favorites. But they are, in the end, a very small part of my plans."

"Plans?"

"Yes, you foolish, narrow-minded little hero. Did you think I really wouldn't find out about Daedalus's absurd little plot? Did you really think I didn't know that the mission was a blind for the Director's own plans for power and glory? Naturally I watched, from the beginning, the comings and goings of all your little minions. I've known from the beginning about the time recorders, so helpfully scattered throughout time by your two faithful puppies. And more important, I understand their significance as even Daedalus failed to do."

Roma stared at him, trying to gather his thoughts.

"Don't bother trying to figure it out," said Howard, and his scorn was palpable. "It's so simple, though, I would have supposed even you would not have found it beyond your powers. I'm reasonably certain Daedalus would have, if he hadn't allowed himself to become distracted by all that emotional wallowing. A few techs!"

He snapped his fingers, and Roma felt the mist of rage gathering before his eyes.

"Think, Roma. If we can record time, not just the events that do happen in one event string, but in all the event string possibilities as well. Don't you see? We can control time. Not just the big events, like the Cataclysm. The real power lies in the small events. Which child will survive infancy and live to start a war, or find a cure for a plague. Which business deal will topple an economy, or found one.

Which line of reasoning will yield a great discovery, for creation, or destruction. There's power to be had from either. We can select whichever advantageous string of events to allow in our time . . . in my time, if you will. You worried that I wanted to own too much of history's treasure. Stupid man, I will own *history*!"

"Howard, you can't tamper with history. Daedalus explained about the time shifts between tracks. You are compromising the fabric of time as it is. If we don't shut down the gate, initiate the reconstruct sequence, and restore time to its original configuration as much as possible—"

"And you really imagine I would permit that? Give up the results of all this effort? Not likely. Of course I can tamper with history. I have done so, several times, and I enjoyed it immensely."

"The Library."

"Yes, of course! I thought you were suspicious. The Romans didn't burn the Library. I did. A little incendiary device flicked out at the last minute and poof!"

"But why do it if it was going to burn anyway?"

"Why, to see if I could, of course. To see if time could be changed. Oh, the Romans will still get the blame, but I —and you, of course, for a short time—will know the truth. I was worried that you might catch on, but I shouldn't have wasted my concern. The drug was too strong, even for a Persean."

Howard's voice rang in Roma's ears. Drug? Howard saw the question, the dawning comprehension on his face.

"A small quantity of a psychotropic interferon, judiciously

administered every day, and you were manageable. A delightful drug for those who find real life burdensome and stressful. They call it *crystal*, an old-fashioned name, and a delicious irony when you come to think of it. Of course, if you use it too often it builds up in the muscle tissue and the nerves. The body grows lax, the mind unable to concentrate. And, of course, the user is made more and more susceptible to suggestion. Easier to control. It slowed you down, made it possible for me to delay you in taking control, shutting down the gate system too early. Of course I couldn't permit that. I need all that information so cleverly stored there by Daedalus and Lantis. I admit, the malfunction of the gate was a setback. Unfortunately, they became one with the elements," he made an oddly beautiful gesture with his hand, "before Daedalus and Lantis could be persuaded to provide me with the means to repair the gate. But I will find it. It will take time, but then I have time. All the time in the universe."

Seeing Howard's fingers moving toward the transfer control, Roma gathered his last effort.

"Howard, Daedalus and Lantis may find a solution. We may be able to find our missing people, Vincent, Cassandra perhaps . . . if we return—"

"You waste your time . . . and mine, worrying about very unimportant matters. They are gone. And so are you."

Roma launched himself through the air with almost his old speed and control. The transfer beam hit him a fraction of a second before his fingers could close on Howard's wrist.

The gate effect was somewhat longer than usual, and the shock wave nearly threw Howard to the ground. Roma had vanished, but the transcomp warning lights indicated that the transfer had been incomplete. He shrugged. It really didn't matter to him whether Roma went somewhere, or nowhere. So long as he went.

# Chapter 23

## 1357 B.C.E.
## Abydos

The viewscreen emitted a small beeping sound. Someone was approaching the outer perimeter. Howard sighed and reached for the control. No doubt some witless peasant wandering up the road looking for a lost goat. The dark eyes widened slightly at what he saw. "Well, well," he said aloud, "who are you and where . . . or should I say *when* do you belong?" The woman shown on the viewscreen stopped and sat down on a boulder near the edge of the path. Two feet above her head, the silent and invisible sentinel stood watch, recording her every gesture. She reached into her bag and pulled out a canteen of water. The sentinel picked up the sound of her swallows, the slight cough that followed. It faithfully recorded the tangle of fine red hair bundled back with a scarf, even the beads of moisture gathered along the edges of brow and cheek. The slight tan did not disguise that this was no Egyptian. The clothes, though torn and dirty, did not belong in this century. Not in this millennium. The man who watched the viewscreen frowned slightly. That this woman had arrived through the malfunctioning gate he had no doubt. But she had walked over the top of the crest in the road with something very like purpose. She did not hesitate. She showed no sign of being lost. She walked like a person who knew exactly where she was going. "Damn," he said without rancor. Turning, he ran.

If she got to the entrance before he increased the security force field she might very well get inside. He raced through the hallways, his footsteps muted and dead-sounding. The very stones drank up sound in this place. "Three, four," he counted the turnings, cursing his failure to reset the security system after Temogen went out. He had never believed the force field was necessary in the first place. And then, after all, there was no one left to threaten his safety. So he had thought. Tiresome of Roma to have been right about something. Still, he could not have foreseen this particular eventuality. Where had this woman come from?

At the next intersection, four columns carved like bundles of papyrus distinguished the corridor where Roma had his room. Turning left, he barely stopped himself in time. The eerie light crept and crawled along the hallway toward him, the walls and floor shifting uneasily as if to a silent, unfelt earthquake. Nausea reached for his stomach, and he gagged. Falling back, he dragged his transcomp from his pocket and began to enter the sequence for the gate. With a sense of incredulity he realized that he was going to be the merest second too late. The approaching collision between being and nonbeing reached him just as he disappeared.

ꙅ ꙅ ꙅ

Virginia replaced the nearly empty canteen in her bag and stood up. The entrance should be just around the next curve of the cliff. She looked across the broken and tumbled land, throwing back the unbearable brightness of the sun. It came to her suddenly that she had passed the place where Hickson had gone to his death. She had walked right past it and never thought of him or of that night. Disbelieving, she looked back down the track. No vision came to torment her, no sound of steel and gold and flesh slamming into the cliff side. The air carried only the whisper of the desert wind, the tiny sounds of small life scraping in the sand, the eternal flies. She turned and went on toward Amenti.

Virginia had been so certain she would find the opening easily. The mountainside remained stubbornly empty of signs. A tiny dry desert plant clinging to life, a tumble of rock and sand, and a sheer wall of limestone. She ran a hand across the rock, unable to believe the temple wasn't here. Desperate disappointment and a kind of unfocused anger rose in her breast. Resisting the urge to throw herself against the unmarked rock face and howl, she sat down and stared inward. How had it looked before H.L. had opened the Amenti temple? The road had wound along the side of the mountain, rounded a sharp bend, and swept inward in a semicircular curve against the cliff before going on around the next fold of mountain.

Here in this little inward curve two great faces of rock

met, one slightly in front of the other. It was here, among the piles of stone and debris, that H.L. had discerned the signs of ancient workmanship. He had dug away the outer drifts of stone and dirt, exposing the beginning of the entrance. Cut into the stone of the mountain itself, a flight of shallow steps led up to the entrance of Amenti, the stairwell filled with earth and stones to simulate the side of the mountain. No pile of stones or slope of piled dirt rested against the cliff face now. Two outcrops of rock stood together near the tall vertical seam between the two slabs of limestone.

Her hand twitched, and she looked down at her fingers. She had run her hand across the cliff face and it had been smooth. Featureless. And completely clean. Her fingers tingled slightly and she wiped them against her trousers before running her hand over the stone again. No dust, no sand, no particles of earth. As if the stone somehow *repelled* all natural accretions? Standing up, Virginia walked over to the two boulders near the joint in the rock, and stepped between them.

She looked back at the wall. The illusion was almost perfect. If viewed from anywhere except this one angle, the rocks seemed solid. Only by squeezing between these two rocks could one see that the outer slab rested two feet in front of the inner, leaving a narrow opening that led to the Amenti temple. Sometime in the future, after the death of Akhenaten, workers would cut away that limestone facade and create an imposing entrance for later workers to fill in and bury again. For now, she had merely to draw a breath and slip between the two faces of rock to enter the underworld of Osiris.

It wasn't quite that easy. Virginia took a breath and one step forward. A stinging slap of energy hit her, knocking her flat on the floor of the tunnel. The air crackled with something that smelled like ozone. She also smelled singed cloth. Little lights danced in the air before her nose. She pushed herself up on her knees and waited. Nothing more happened. She climbed to her feet, and extended one hand in front of her. Nothing. Moving like a blind woman, Virginia edged up the tunnel with her hand in front of her, testing the air with every step. She finally looked back, and saw the slight shimmer that distorted the air near the entrance. *Some front doorbell.*

The tunnel behind the cliff ran up at a steep angle into the mountainside, before it ended at the foot of a short flight of stairs. Light from the opening soon faded away, and Virginia turned on her flashlight. At the top of the stairs was a massive double door. She looked at the tall leaves of heavy cedar, and blessed every god in Egypt that one of the doors stood ajar. Pausing on the threshold, she shone the flashlight around the room beyond. Though not nearly so immense as many of the great temple halls in Egypt, this one was sufficiently large to swallow the beam of light.

Slowly Virginia moved past the doors, pausing to listen. As her eyes adjusted she became aware of another source of light seeping into the hall from the far side. Her flashlight picked out great columns painted in sienna and red and black, a smooth painted pavement, and overhead, nearly lost in the lofty shadows, the glimmer of carefully placed gold stars. And the god was here too. Enthroned in the center of the columned hall, Osiris stared at her, gleaming in the darkness. Virginia swallowed against memory. "God it's beautiful . . . " Hickson's voice whispered from the past. She lowered her gaze and walked around the edges of the room where the columns made deeper shadows in the gloom. The absence of sound made her breath and heartbeat seem loud in her ears, the slight scuff of her boots on the floor magnified unbearably. On the far side of the hall stood another great doorway, closed. She laid her hand on the smooth, sweet-smelling wood, and was almost unsurprised when it swung open soundlessly, admitting her to Amenti, the Hidden Land.

She half expected another shock, perhaps a lethal one. She squinted into the corridor, looking for that tell-tale shimmer. She saw only, with jolt of surprise, that it was light. What had seemed merely a slight lifting of the darkness in the outer hall was steadily growing illumination inside the labyrinth. The temperature was pleasant—and, unless she was dreaming, slightly humidified. She stood beyond the doors to the hall, with the corridor stretching away on either side of her. Bas-relief carvings covered the walls, beautiful and fresh. She resisted the desire to run a reverent hand over the carvings depicting Isis in the papyrus swamps nursing the infant Horus. She turned to her right, walking slowly down the corridor that seemed to stretch endlessly in both directions.

As she moved into the labyrinth, the light grew until it

was possible to turn off the flashlight. Aheaa on her left she could see a glow from a wall sconce high on the wall. It was a pretty thing, a copper sconce holding a shell carved from alabaster. Moving toward it, she found no fire behind the alabaster shell. A glowing globe of glass or translucent material, perhaps crystal, lay concealed behind the Egyptian torch holder. The globe had no connection to anything at all, so presumably it contained its own power source. The wall sconces appeared at regular intervals along the corridors, bathing the labyrinth in gentle, unchanging light. *Curiouser and curiouser.*

The size of the place astonished her. She had passed four intersections from the entrance, and the end of the hallway was not in sight. When H.L.'s team had managed to open the Amenti temple, they had been successful in excavating only the front portion of what had clearly once been—or had once been intended to be—a much larger complex of rooms and hallways. The central portion of the labyrinth was impenetrable. In this time, however, the hallways continued into the shadowy distance, mysterious but passable. Virginia recognized the importance of keeping track of where she was, so she jotted down the turnings in her notebook.

There was something different about this intersection. A column stood on either side of each of the four ways, carved in the familiar bundle of papyrus reeds. Perhaps marking an important location? She took the turn to her right and had gone a few steps when she stopped, paralyzed. The indescribable light was oozing up the hallway toward her, threatening reason and reality with its terrible sense of *otherness*. She bit back a scream, jerking around and running back down the corridor toward the columns at the intersection. Looking over her shoulder, she saw the corridor of solid stone had turned to quicksand, the carvings shifting and moving and somehow overlaying themselves as if they existed on a hundred, a thousand walls simultaneously. And it was getting closer.

Knowing with terrible certainty that she must not come in contact with that luminous otherness, she threw herself down the first branching corridor and ran as if all the hounds of hell were at her heels. She stumbled once, and looked back. It seemed the boiling light lapped at her feet like an onrushing tide, threatening to sweep over her the next second. With leaden legs and burning lungs she ran on, careering off the corridor walls, brushing too close to a pillar and receiving a jarring blow, but still running, her prayers a wild invocation of all the gods of Egypt and childhood and myth rolled into one subvocal plea. Too much had happened in the last day, too many hours of shock and fear and old loss relived.

Another turn loomed up and she forced herself around it. Tired legs betrayed her and she lost her balance, pitching forward and banging her chin on the stone floor. She could feel blood filling her mouth, and again little points of light danced before her eyes. Fearing that if she stayed there, gave in to the rising unconsciousness, the otherness would be upon her, she dragged herself up and stumbled forward a few feet, only to fall again. She felt rather than saw the upheaval of light and space roar past the intersection behind her. This time when she hit the wall it gave against her weight, and she fell sideways into darkness.

*God, I'm getting really tired of this.* The thought came out of the dark as Virginia opened her eyes. She rolled over and let her face rest against the cool polished floor. It seemed solid enough to risk sitting up. Her head swam, but the whirling sparks had gone. She groped and felt the lump of her shoulder bag spilled on the floor beside her. The darkness was absolute. Her fingers swept the floor in widening circles, searching with increasing desperation for the heavy flashlight. The darkness pressed down upon her like the thousands of tons of heavy stone over her head, closing off hope and breath. Once, when she was a child, Virginia had visited a cave famous for its limestone formations. At one point the tour guide had turned off all the lights, including his flashlight, and told them that it was one of the few places on earth where people could experience absolute darkness. But only briefly. People went mad in absolute darkness. Panic was gibbering in the darkness when her hand finally hit the plastic cylinder and she found the switch. "Let there be light," she whispered prayerfully. And there was light.

The light did not, however, come from the flashlight. At least, most of it flooded around her from globes set in the walls, similar to those in the outer labyrinth. She was in a small room, perhaps fourteen feet square. The walls were painted with scenes of fowlers casting their nets in the papyrus marshes. Each carefully delineated frond of the papyrus plants showed clear and bright, fish swam among the stylized wavelets in the water, and a charming flock of birds erupted out of the waving fronds in the face of the placid fowler. The cool blues and greens soothed her eyes and the last mutterings of panic receded.

The room had been occupied recently. There was a rather hard-looking bed against one wall. Opposite the bed was a shelf of some smooth shining substance, holding a neat arrangement of small objects that took the light like jewels. Above the shelf, a rectangular slab of black glass marked with a faint grid hung on the wall. In the corner near the glass slab was a chair, hard and uncompromising. *No ease for the weary to be had there*, she mused, and continued her survey. There was a chest at the foot of the bed, and two more beside the door. And nothing else whatsoever. Belatedly Virginia shut off the flashlight, and picked up the litter of things that had spilled from her bag. Holding onto the bed for support, she climbed to her feet and sat down on the edge. For a while it was enough, just to sit there and wait to see if anything else was going to happen.

Virginia's eyes roamed across those azure papyrus swamps covering the walls. Near the head of the bed there was a discernible line running from floor to ceiling. Adrenaline began to flow again. She walked over to the wall, thinking that if anything happened, anything at all, she would quite possibly die from shock, and it would probably be better to let well enough alone. She put out a cautious hand and pressed the wall beside the crack. Nothing happened. Her fingers glided over the smooth plaster, and finally found a button concealed among the whorls of painted water. A soft shushing sound sent her back a step, and the section of wall opened inward. The prosaic nature of the hidden offices would have been amusing under other circumstances. Her reflection in the wall mirror was enough to stifle amusement. "All the major plumbing groups are represented," she said reverently, preparing with deep gratitude to make use of them all.

Someday, Virginia promised herself later, some hour soon she would find out who had moved into the Amenti temple and made it comfortable with light, air-conditioning, and hot water. A European colleague had once complained to her that Americans were obsessed with plumbing. She remembered admitting the truth of that accusation, because, as she had said, Americans are *used* to plumbing. Primitive conditions prevailed at the digs in many of the most interesting parts of the world, but her attempts at camaraderie in those places had never eradicated her conviction that ultimately hot water and decent sanitation encouraged true progress.

This was turning out to be the most interesting part of the world she had yet visited. Meanwhile, she had managed to wash the blood and dirt out of her mouth and hair and she was clean. The archeologist in her might argue that someone had profaned the Osirion, but she had drunk a quart of fresh cold water and could feel only gratitude to whatever progressive mind was behind the homely comforts installed in this most ancient place. The trunk at the foot of the bed proved to hold clothing. Wrapped in a black robe clearly made for someone much taller, she lay down on the bed. She had held exhaustion at bay for hours and could ignore it no longer. "Now," she said aloud, "if I just knew how to turn off the lights. . . . " The lights went out. "Thank you," she whispered, and was asleep.

Her watch told her she had been asleep for four hours when she again opened her eyes. "Light," she said, unable to restrain the slight jumping of her heart in case it didn't work this time and she was left in the dark. The lights came on. She sat up stiffly, her muscles complaining. After a quick glance at her dirty and torn clothes, she inspected the contents of the trunks again. One of them yielded a jumpsuit of some lightweight neutral fabric. Though much too large, it was clean. She hoped the owner wouldn't mind when she explained. She hoped she got to explain.

Another trunk held a number of small plastic trays sealed with a thin film of some sort. There was a tab at the corner that, when pulled off, revealed a reddish paste and a small spoon tucked into the tray. "Doesn't this look yummy," she thought, rather horrified. The spoon clearly indicated that it was food. Of some kind. She turned to her bag and pulled out the sad remains of the candy bar she had brought with her from Cairo. It had melted in yesterday's heat and reformed itself in the cool, turning slightly gray in the process. Nevertheless, it had started out as chocolate, so she ate it, eyeing the red paste with a distinct lack of confidence.

Having looted her host's room of clothes and comfort, Virginia decided to pursue her search for his identity. The trunks had yielded only clothing, which had told her he was tall, over six feet. There were no pictures or papers of any kind, none of the small personal clutter that accompanies most people on a long journey. *This one travels light.* She looked over the items on the shelf. There was a small plastic or perhaps ceramic object, rounded on the top, with a hole in the center. Arranged around the bottom edge were a series of small, narrow red crystals. The relationship seemed obvious enough. She picked up one of the crystals and stuck it into the opening. From somewhere in the innards of the glass slab came a tiny electronic chirp, and then letters marched across the grid on the black screen. They informed her that this was the personal journal of someone called Gianni Roma. There was a list of entries by date. Virginia suppressed the sensation of violating his privacy, and picked one at random. "I'm sorry, Gianni," she whispered, "but I have to know what is going on."

And then he was just there, in front of her, seated in a chair, the twin of the one in the corner. Virginia found herself backed up against the bed, her hands over her mouth as if to force back all the yelling she had wanted to give vent to since arriving at Abydos. She sat down rather harder than she intended, never taking her eyes off the man in the chair. He was sitting at a slight angle to the screen on the wall, looking down from time to time at the small black instrument in his lap—a twin of the one in her bag. He began to speak, reciting the events of the day for the benefit of the viewscreen. After a long pause she stood up and circled him, still expecting him to look up and see her. There was no sign from him. He went on talking in a soft voice, oblivious of her presence. She stepped between him and the screen. He looked through her, clearly concentrating on his report. Finally, she stretched out her hand and allowed it to pass through his body. It seemed like a horribly invasive act, for though she now knew that the man had no substance, was only an image of life and not life itself, he seemed very *present*. He was easier to understand than the man on the recording device. She leaned against the shelf, watching his face and listened to his voice.

*Day 1: . . . Well, it was a pretty good joke on us. The inhabitants here have contrived some very inventive security devices of their own, and I have been having fun with them. Howard wanted me to deactivate them but I think we'll leave them right where they are. Extra security never hurts. . . .*

His face had a kind of quiet strength she liked. His reserve, which she guessed was integral to his character, had permitted only a small twinkle as he described the Egyptian security devices. They would have been simple, she knew, and deadly. Pits with sharpened stakes or poisonous vipers at the bottom that spanned darkened hallways, or hid under light reed coverings that fell beneath the first unwary step. Walls that would collapse when touched, dropping a ton of stone on top of the intruder. Poisonous vipers in harmless-looking spaces. . . . Those were just a few of the deathtraps with which the Egyptians had invited the uninvited to a lingering death in the tombs and temples they had violated. None of them struck her as funny, but clearly the man called Roma had found them genuinely amusing. Sarcasm had touched the even timbre of his voice only when he mentioned Howard, and then the bright eyes had gone cold. Then he was gone, leaving only empty air where man and chair had been. Virginia drew a deep breath, and picked up another crystal. She sat down in the chair, and prepared to listen to the rest of the journals of Gianni Roma.

# Part VIII

## Time and Time Again

# Chapter 24

## 1357 B.C.E.
## Gianni Roma

*Day 2: Howard is impossible. All he can think of is his precious Collection. He has no grasp of security. I insisted on some extra measures to protect the Gate. Easy for any of us to get past, but a serious deterrent for any outsider. Howard keeps yapping about this being sacred ground, and no Egyptian venturing in anyway. But I want to dissuade any unannounced visitors. I have set up temporary security measures to protect the installation of the gate, and am proceeding with more permanent safeguards. Temogen did an adequate job of intelligence gathering, and it does look like a secure site. When I found out about that peasant I nearly sent him back in pieces, but he assures me it was an accident. No other incidents since the force field was installed. . . .*

*Day 3: I took Vincent on a tour of the gate systems, making certain the security procedures are all in place. He was very excited, and I must admit it is amazing to travel back and forth through time. Lantis is satisfied that the physical functioning of the gate system is at top efficiency.*

Back and forth through time? Somehow she knew he didn't mean time zones. She felt cold. This man was talking about time travel. The journal was a complete, day-by-day account of Gianni Roma and his efforts to provide security for the as yet unnamed mission. Many entries were brief and, for her purposes, uninformative. Others, however, began almost at once to form a pattern, one she hoped would answer her increasingly desperate questions.

*Day 5: All the gate systems are ready. Cassandra and Howard could hardly wait to go to the Minoan gate. . . .*

*Day 9: Cassandra and Howard returned from Knossos with the first shipment. They were ecstatic. You'd think those crates held the keys to existence, instead of lumps of metal and stone.*

*Day 20: The China gate is secure. I have copies of their memory crystals for Lantis to review, but their procedures are correct.*

*Day 21: I returned from the China gate to discover that Vincent had gone to the European station to look into the matter of the broken necklace. Howard sent him. In fact, I arrived back only a few minutes before he did. I was furious with Howard for sending him. We had words. . . .*

*Regarding Vincent's mission, he is finicky about detail, so I trust him to bring me a complete report. Probably the thing was broken before it was sent, but it would be incorrect not to check out every possibility. Naturally I expect a full description of everything relating to the gate, however small, that might indicate a problem. . . .*

*Day 22: I have reviewed Vincent's report on the European station. Everyone there swears the necklace was in perfect condition, packed in shock-absorbent gel, and sent through all according to prescribed procedure. They were shocked when I described its condition when it arrived here. Howard was not so casual about this mishap, of course, since it involved one of his precious art treasures. . . .*

*Day 70: I have been studying the information sent to Cassandra from the Greek station. Some piece of luggage got sent through the gate but did not go to its proper destination. Howard dismissed the whole thing as unimportant. How can a man so brilliant as he be so stupid? I am preparing to go to the Greek station to begin an investigation of this latest incident. Too many little things have been happening lately. It's only a matter of time until it is something so big even Howard cannot ignore it. I am ordering everyone to stay out of the gate until I complete my investigation. . . .*

*Day 73: I have been to each of the gates and reviewed their procedures. No one admits to any breach of security measures, or any shortcutting in setting coordinates. Not that I expected any such admission. It doesn't make sense and I hate things that don't make sense. Daedalus is reviewing the theory, of course, and Lantis is touring around checking the physical functioning of the gates. But somehow, I doubt the problem is with the technology. . . .*

*Day 110: I found Temogen outside the perimeter again. Howard had actually sent him across the river to search the temple. Howard! I can't believe the arrogant stupidity of the man. It is a serious breach of security for any of us to go out in potentially populated areas without proper cover. I explained it to him again. I explained it to Temogen, too, but a little more . . forcefully. . . .*

*Day 111: Well, it's finally happened. Ravia, one of the*

*technicians at the Greek station, disappeared in the gate. I went to every gate in the system, and no one had seen or heard anything. Lantis is examining the gate for the thirtieth time. Temogen is prowling around looking for some evidence of tampering or personal spite. I spent all day at the Greek station with them, trying to make sense of this. I intend to recommend that one of the other technicians go back to the ship; he is so upset he's a walking disaster. That will leave the Greek station two short, and Howard is, of course, concerned about the diminished number of artifacts that can be processed through their gate. He actually suggested sending Cassandra to fill in. Nothing matters to him except his precious artifacts. I think perhaps a little investigation into his personal effects is in order. It would be too bad if some of the more important objects didn't actually end up in the Collection at all, but in some place smaller, more private—like Howard's estate. . . .*

*Day 113: Howard had a close brush with a necropolis guard last night. He used the tranquilizer gun correctly, so no harm has been done. But it can't happen too often. He must show more caution. All he can do is gloat over the loot. Strange how it has stopped being cultural reconstruction for me and become just that, loot. Are we so certain about what we are doing? If it weren't for Daedalus and his mission, I would call this to a halt right now. . . .*

*Day 114: I went to the Atlantean site today. Lantis has begun construction on the gate there. Due to its isolation, security is easy enough. It's unlikely the place will ever be found, much less tampered with. Still, procedure is procedure. Cassandra is longing to go, but I am not ready to let any of the team go there until I am certain that it is safe. . . .*

*Day 130: I can't believe it. I can't bloody believe it. Cassandra got sucked into that gate like a moth into a flame. Howard had asked her to go to the Greek station to supervise the removal of a statue—gold, of course. I objected but she would go. I found her difficult, obsessive, and unbelievably blind, but—she was very young. . . .*

*Temogen and I went to the Greek station, and on to all the others, but there was no sign of her. From now on, one of the security team must be present when the gate is in use. Howard may have been personally selected by the Director to lead this expedition, but I think I'll just step up my surveillance. Howard is a man obsessed, and such men are dangerous. It is becoming obvious that we will have to shut down now. We're trying to hold on a little longer, for the sake of Daedalus's crusade against the Cataclysm. No mention of this to Howard, of course. For him, it remains business as usual. . . .*

*I came . . . very close to killing Howard. Daedalus stopped me, fortunately. Or not. . . .*

*Day 132: Maeva, an archaeologist, disappeared from the Tibetan gate today. I knew her, and her son. Same story as before. She didn't go to any of the other gates. But there was one difference. She wasn't even in the gate. She disappeared from her quarters. This thing can just reach out and take people . . . wherever it takes them.*

*Panic has set in, and we are shutting down the gate. Work has ceased at every station, the people too terrified to sleep. No one is willing to use the gate except to return to Traveler One—or try to. . . .*

Virginia leaned back and stared at the image of the man who seemed so real. The picture building up was not a pretty one. There was disaffection apparent in the entries. The high hopes and energy of the earliest recordings were growing darker, more moody and withdrawn. The man's face, probably grave at its best, had become positively grim. No hint of a smile in the bright hazel eyes, no curve to the stern mouth. He must, she thought, have been a difficult person to know. He spoke with real feeling about the loss of the people who had disappeared. Then again, he had spoken with a complete absence of feeling about nearly killing Howard. The pensive yet deadened tone had chilled her.

*Day 140: The Mayan station closed today, and the people returned. Those that were left. Most of the artifacts had been recovered, so it is not too serious a loss for the almighty Collection. The missing may feel differently, of course, assuming they still feel anything. And even one gold idol is a serious loss for Howard the mad. Where? Where are they going? And why doesn't he go there, too?*

*Day 145: Abydos is alone. The others have all returned, the gates abandoned. All that is left is for Lantis and me to pack up the matrices and bring them back to Abydos for the final transfer home.*

*Since the last transfer of personnel, I have been unable to contact the Commander. I have no idea whether they arrived safely on* Traveler One *. . . or went . . . somewhere else. Or went anywhere. I have not told the others. . . .*

She looked at the man before her, and was shocked at

the change in him. The muscles of the face were slack, the eyes sunken and glazed. His speech, once crisp and decisive, was slurred and halting. Exhaustion and grief would certainly take a toll, but did that adequately explain this disintegration?

*Day 148: Today it was Vincent. Poor boy. All he ever wanted was to be left alone with his everlasting scribbling and drawing. I wonder where he went? The others are numb. I doubt Daedalus will ever recover. I'm searching the labyrinth for some sign of what happened to him. Of one thing I am certain—I know Howard is behind this. But I need proof. Howard is the enemy, and it is always fatal to underestimate the enemy. . . .*

Virginia became aware that she was shaking. It was all there, entry after entry, describing the day-to-day efforts of these travelers from the future. Efforts that involved going to other times, other civilizations and—stealing? Artifacts and records, art treasures? Roma had mentioned archaeologists, so they were apparently not just thieves out for personal gain. But on such a scale, to take from the past *in* the past . . . wasn't that more than the scholarly pursuit of knowledge? It was a terrible story, filled with suggestions of sacrifice and betrayal. But it was a story told from the point of view of one person. There had been others. And there was no clue as to what had happened to Roma. That was the last of the entries, although there was space in the holder for several more crystals. Had Roma not lived to make more entries?

Her mouth felt dry as she considered the alternative. Or had someone else removed them? Virginia sat back and stretched. She had become completely absorbed in the story related by this compelling echo of Gianni Roma. She reviewed what she knew. Travelers from somewhere, *somewhen*, she corrected herself, had gone back in time, reaching Egypt through a time gate. They had set up a whole network of gates in Europe, Asia, Oceana, Atlantis—her mind shivered away from that thought—and proceeded to, what should she call it? Rob the past?

How did the man Roma and his disdain for gold and loot fit into that picture? Roma was the security officer of this band of travelers. He had done his best to protect the people who were entrusted to him, but malfunctioning technology had eroded the morale and discipline of the group. Then people began to disappear in the time gates, gone who knew where, or perhaps their atoms were just disassembled and scattered in time. Dead, then, all of them? That was bad news for someone who wanted very much to travel through time—and soon.

It sounded as if this site was the main one, the control center for the entire operation. Cassandra and someone called Vincent had been lost, but the others—Temogen, Roma, Howard, Lantis and, was it possible, Daedalus? Wouldn't they have finally done what Roma had suggested he wanted to do, stop using the gate until they got it fixed? Well, it wasn't fixed. She was the living proof of that. Surely they had not all disappeared? Surely one of them must be left? That, she reflected, could be good or bad, depending on which one it was. Based on Roma's journal, Howard was suspicious and so was Temogen. Again, she argued, just because Howard was obsessed with loot and Temogen sounded somewhat questionable, that didn't make them villains.

Feeling as though her head was going to explode, Virginia stood up and realized she was starving. She went over to the red paste and picked it up. *They were human, after all; it must be edible.* She tasted it cautiously. Space food, she decided, probably packed with vitamins and electrolytes and whatnot, and it tasted like a cross between beef jerky and library paste. "Delicious." She ate it all.

# Chapter 25

## 1357 B.C.E.
## Cassandra Alda

Virginia decided to begin her investigation with the first person to disappear from Abydos, according to Roma's journal. Cassandra Alda, Howard's assistant. She consulted the map on Roma's viewscreen. The halls appeared in different colors. A block of passages between the entrance to the labyrinth and its center were green, and the travelers' quarters were on these hallways. On either side and beyond this block were passages in purple. No identification of what rooms lay in these areas. In the center, at the far edge of the area occupied by the travelers, was a room marked in blue, and identified cryptically as the Matrix. She had no desire to wander around in those halls without a guide, so she spent quite a time with her map, trying to copy the computer's version accurately. Many of the notations did not make sense to her, employing either a language or a code she did not recognize.

She felt a strong reluctance to leave this little refuge. Picking up her bag, she gave a last look around the room. It had become almost hers, almost friendly. Based on the journal entries, she decided she wouldn't want to get on the wrong side of Gianni Roma, but she wasn't afraid of him, either. Besides, she thought wryly, he smelled right, whatever that meant. Smiling a little grimly, she pushed the button beside the door and stepped through the opening and out into the labyrinth.

Keeping a wary eye for the light effect, Virginia made her way down the halls, counting the intersections. The hallways were no more welcoming or threatening than before. They were just there, cool, seemingly immense, and full of shadows. Occasionally she would see a corridor that was dark, and would sense a dusty, disused smell in the air. These were obviously parts of the labyrinth unused by the travelers. The feeling of overwhelming immensity was partly an illusion, she discovered, due to the unrelenting sameness of the corridors. Still, the labyrinth was large enough to discourage casual exploring.

Her map included some markings that the computer had colored red. Something about that color, the universal code for stop, danger, emergency, made her circle those markings with extra care. Egyptian "security devices"? Or a little something planted by Gianni Roma to "discourage unannounced visitors"? Either way, she definitely did not want to stumble into them by surprise. She was relieved to see that most of those red markings lay in the unused portion of the labyrinth. Cassandra Alda's room was marked on the third corridor parallel to Roma's, and down four intersections to the right. On silent feet, Virginia went down the quiet halls, restraining the urge to swivel her head constantly on the alert for that terrible engulfing light to come boiling up the corridor at her.

Finding the door was another matter. Roma's door had, upon close inspection, been marked by a small crystal embedded in the wall. Its red color was easy to find, once you knew where to look. Either she was in the wrong hallway or Cassandra's door crystal was a different color. Pacing the stretch of hallway she shone her flashlight across the walls, until a glint of light disclosed the almost colorless crystal's location. When she touched the crystal it brightened, and the hidden doorway slid soundlessly upward. Taking a deep breath, she stepped inside, politely requesting "lights" and half expecting an outraged exclamation from its former inhabitant.

Unlike Roma, Cassandra Alda had left behind ample evidence of her occupancy. She had the same narrow bed, several chests of some sort of plastic, and a viewscreen with a crystal reader on a shelf below. Here the resemblance ended. The tile floor was warmed by a beautiful Kirman rug, the price of which in Virginia's time would have paid her salary for a year. The chair, inlaid with ivory and gold, would have done honor to Queen Nefertiti herself. Exquisite red naiads danced across a black Greek amphora, meriting pride of place in any museum. A scatter of jewelry lay on the shelf and spilled from an inlaid gold casket, beaten gold leaves forming a necklace, bracelets inlaid with carnelian, turquoise, and obsidian, and one stunning scarab amulet of lapis lazuli inlaid into heavy gold. The sensuous blue color was like a magnet, and Virginia could not keep from picking it up. Suspended on a gold chain from which fell hundreds of tiny golden balls, the scarab lay across her hand, mysterious and quite unbelievably beautiful. It was made to lie around a woman's throat, taking warmth from her skin and pulse. It would require a strong and resolute soul to find such a piece and virtuously lay it aside for a museum to entomb in a glass case. Had Cassandra Alda intended to do that, retaining possession only temporarily, until time to ship it—wherever they were shipping their finds?

Reverently and reluctantly, Virginia laid the necklace down and turned to the crystal reader. Suppressing a sense of sacrilege, she sat down in the lovely, royal chair, and picked up a memory crystal. "How do you do, Miss Alda," she said. "My name is Virginia. So—anything interesting been happening lately?"

*Day 1: I can't believe it. We are actually here. The gate works, and we are ready to begin our assembly of artifacts for the Collection. Dr. Howard predicts that we shall make the largest single addition to the ancient artifact division, and I am certain he is correct. I am particularly eager to go to the Greek station and oversee the work there. They are good people, but I have never really believed that Carter fully understands the pre-classical periods.*

*Day 4: Tomorrow, God and the great Roma willing, Dr. Howard and I will go to the Minoan station on Crete. Assuming Roma's final check of the gate system satisfies him. I appreciate the need for safety, but I think Roma absolutely delights in creating obstacles to our work.*

*Day 7: We finished packing the Minoan pieces late this evening. Lovely things, but I am convinced that previous theories about Atlantis are incorrect. Daedalus agrees, and he is still searching for it. What a tremendous triumph that would be! Howard would be transported!*

Virginia leaned back in her chair and considered the woman who had materialized in front of her. Cassandra Alda had been young, young and idealistic. She had possessed lovely dark eyes, a classical profile, and a wealth of springy dark curling hair. When she mentioned Howard's name, her eyes had glowed and her entire face quickened into beauty. It was hard to believe that she was dead, or lost somewhere in time. She seemed—present. It was a trick of the imaging system, Virginia knew, but it was difficult to remember in the face of what appeared to be a breathing, living person. She could hear the softest intake of breath. Her eyes stung, and when she reached out to replace the crystal her hand trembled.

*Day 9: I have gone back and forth several times. It is a bit enervating, but nothing to seriously trouble me. The work at the Greek station is progressing well. A pity the Asia Minor station came to nothing. I can't really understand Daedalus when he tries to explain. I am not all that certain he understands himself. But whatever the reason, it appears there will be no Asia Minor station for the time being. The crystal matrix simply rejects the coordinates until a time far too late for our interests.*

*Day 20: What a tragedy. That gold necklace was really special. An important addition to the Eastern European collection. Howard feels the loss as if it had been his own. The Collection is everything to him, and we all know that the work here could not possibly have been half so fruitful without him.*

*He knows so much, he has studied these ancient cultures for so long, what would we do without his guidance and encouragement? No wonder he was so furious. I can't imagine what those fools at the European station were about. Clearly they must have failed in proper packing procedures. Howard had a right to be angry.*

It was strange, hearing the same story from such a different viewpoint. Clearly Cassandra's views about Howard were quite the opposite from those of Gianni Roma. It was obvious she had felt more than idealistic admiration for the leader of the expedition. Her enthusiasm for the "Collection" had seemed equally strong. Was she something more than a soulless looter? There had been an unpleasant twist to her lips when she mentioned the "fools" who had failed to send the necklace through intact. The fine eyes had flashed when she defended Howard's anger over the loss.

Shrewdly, Virginia wondered at what point the Collection had become Howard's Collection, and whether Cassandra was as oblivious to it as she seemed in her journal. Was it hindsight that made Virginia wonder why no one had felt alarm at discovering something that had left whole and had arrived broken? Or was it the usual assumption of "operator error"? Or, worse yet, had they been so taken with the loss of the artifact, the significance of its loss was overlooked?

*Day 29: Daedalus told us all today about Atlantis. Howard was thrilled, we all were, for the good of the Collection is always primary with him. He cannot wait until the gate is finished. Pity it's to be under water, because I am not much fond of that idea, but he assures us it is a case like Asia Minor. The matrix got cranky so we have to build the gate where it will allow us to. Funny to think that we are being directed by a hunk of crystal technology. I wonder if even Lantis and Daedalus really understand it?*

*Day 70: Someone in the Greek station told me something strange today. It seems she was trying to go to the China gate and there was some unexplained surge in the transport gate. She barely got out in time. Her luggage disappeared, and it didn't arrive in China. Funny to think of her tools and such arriving somewhere far ahead or back in the earliest days. What would the people then think? Fortunately she didn't have much with her. And, of course, no one has a clue what happened. Roma overreacted, as usual, but I feel certain that she didn't enter the correct coordinates. We have had no other reports like this, so likely it was her own fault. Howard says she'll no doubt be more careful in future unless she wants to learn to speak Neanderthal!*

*Day 82: I helped Howard polish some of the gold objects from the Seti I tomb. They are unbelievably beautiful. I felt so privileged, just to touch them. Howard feels the same. Once he mentioned "his collection," but then he corrected himself—a slip of the tongue. In spite of Roma and the others, and their suspicions, I know he only thinks about enriching the cultural base.*

Her voice had faltered a little there, when she described Howard's "slip of the tongue."

*Day 111: More incompetence in the Greek station. One of the technicians apparently set the coordinates incorrectly and disappeared. They deny it, of course, and the other technician who was there says she did everything correctly. If so, where did she go? He has no answer. Some people have an amazing ability to hide from the truth! It's terrible, of course. I know that Howard is deeply disturbed by this. And, of course, he is annoyed because he says people will get hysterical. Poor man, he struggles so with the responsibility for us all and for the Collection, it makes me furious to see people adding to his burdens this way. Inexcusable. . . .*

Virginia noted the tell-tale rigidity around the mouth, the strained look in the bright, dark eyes. Cassandra was not finding it easy to dismiss obviously growing qualms about the gate.

*Day 114: The Atlantis gate is almost finished. I wanted to go right away, but Daedalus and Lantis both fussed about it. Something about anomalies. And Roma is more impossible every day. I have an idea—I get these premonitions—that something is going to happen. Perhaps it's because using the gate affects me so oddly, makes me queasy and frightened. I haven't mentioned this to anyone, of course; they would only fuss. And I wouldn't want Dr. Howard to lose confidence in me.*

*Day 129: Tomorrow I will go through to the Greek station. Lantis and Daedalus objected, of course, but Howard personally asked me to go and check on the packing. There is an Apollo statue, pure gold and standing in a chariot, too lovely to be believed, that we found hidden in the Delphi sanctuary. Naturally he wants me to supervise its transfer. I feel uneasy, as if something is about to happen. I hate these feelings; they interfere with my work. Howard says I need a short vacation when I return. So thoughtful, so very kind. I think I shall go to . . . well, almost anywhere is possible, isn't it?*

Virginia looked at the girl seated so near, and possibly a million miles and a million years away from her. The dark eyes looked sunken and haunted, the lips dry and pale. She had spoken her last entry in a voice filled with uncertainty. "So thoughtful, so very kind," she had said. And her lips had tried to smile. Where was she now? Virginia knew the significance of the date. Cassandra Alda had stepped into the time gate the next day and disappeared, the elements of her youth and passion sent somewhere in time, perhaps, or perhaps just spread through time like a scattering of tears. Roma had raged, and she had seen grief in his face when spoke of it. Had Howard mourned?

Her thoughts brought her up short. She felt a strong sympathy for her counterpart from the future, and a sense of deep recognition. Virginia herself had once gone to Abydos with exactly that glow of inner fire, that reckless devotion to her work that shone from the remembered images of Cassandra Alda. She too had felt the unbearable sense of purpose, driving her, pushing her to succeed and stand out and conquer. No rest for her spirit, no admission of emotion or frailty could play a part in her world. She, Virginia, had her way to make in the world of archaeology. She had to find out, to know, to discover the previously unknown secrets of her chosen obsession.

She knew beyond a shadow of a doubt that, like Cassandra, she would have gone into that gate, no matter what private furies shadowed her head. No amount of warning from Roma or Lantis would have dissuaded her. *The Sanctuary at Delphi*, and a *gold statue of Apollo*, one of the fabled thousands of precious statues melted down by the barbarians, not one of which survived in her own time—her thoughts took wing at the thought of it. Of course she would go. As she sat there, knowing the danger, she *longed* to go.

Like Virginia herself, Cassandra had been a woman possessed by the past. She had also been obsessed by a man who was a visionary, or perhaps a madman. *Which shall we call you, Dr. Howard*? All through Cassandra's journals that shining loyalty had remained undimmed—except, just for a moment, when she spoke of "his collection." That had shaken her. Had Howard been unable to bear the relinquishing of the treasures he had risked so much to find? Whatever the Collection was, it was something even Roma referred to with respect, though grudging. Both he and Cassandra had referred to "rebuilding the Cultural Base." That had a weighty sound. When had *the* Collection become *Howard's* collection? And when had Virginia decided that Roma's view of Howard, and not Cassandra's, was the one to be trusted?

Virginia stood up and began to search the room. Besides the jewelry there were clothes and a few personal items, including a comb. She stood looking down at it. It was made of beautifully carved jade, set with pearls. The comb of a Chinese princess, or perhaps an emperor's concubine. Had Howard given it to Cassandra? If so, he was a generous mentor, to put it no higher. She swallowed, and put it resolutely in her pocket. When you were lost in time, a comb was just a comb. She had five other travel diaries to find and listen to. Unless she found one of the travelers first. She consulted her map. Vincent had been the next one to go. She went in search of his room. It took a little longer, as she had to circumvent several corridors marked with red.

# Chapter 26
## 1357 B.C.E.
## Vincent Ginevra

She looked at the sensitive face, the dark eyes so full of dreams, and her heart bled a little. He was so young. She had found his room without trouble, with a growing sense of confidence. But her head continued to ache and she felt the way she often felt before a thunderstorm. Every surface was covered with a litter of papers, loosely bundled together. Drawings—charging horses, studies of the human body, men in armor and women with soft cheeks and secretive smiles danced across the pages with an eloquence so beautiful her heart ached. She would have no need to skip through the journal entries as she had with Roma and Cassandra. Vincent had left only a pathetically small number of crystals. Though she had to force herself to listen in the beginning, the boyish, enthusiastic voice soon captivated her.

*Day 12: I had to listen to a lot of yelling today, one way and another. Howard yelled because I was drawing some of the artifacts instead of packing them. Daedalus yelled (a) because of ditto and (b) because I had not finished working on the corollary for his newest interpretation of the theory. I like the theoretical work, but it seems somehow dry compared with what we're learning here. Finally, Roma yelled because I do not make regular journal entries. On the whole, not a restful day. A few more hours, and I will have finished my sketches on this series, however. . . .*

*Day 20: Howard was beside himself when that gold and emerald necklace came through broken. It was a beautiful thing. He wants me to go to the European station and write a report on what went amiss. . . .*

*Day 22: Well, I finished the report and there was enough detail even to satisfy both Howard and Roma. Not that it told us anything. No one admits anything, and I must admit I was impressed with their methods and record keeping at the European station. It seems unlikely that there was any real carelessness on their part. I am at a loss to explain it. Still, I had an idea about improving our packing procedure. I'm going to sketch it out tonight and give it to Howard tomorrow. . . .*

*Day 82: Worked all day in the Seti I tomb. There are certainly some magnificent things there for the Collection. I am particularly drawn to the European objects, however. Especially the painting, though some of the embryonic science is very interesting as well. Sometimes I think Howard only cares for gold. . . .*

There it was again, the reference to Howard and his obsession with gold, with beautiful things gathered from the vaults of history. It was very clear from the beginning that Vincent did not share Cassandra's belief in the leader of the expedition.

*Day 90: I had a nice chat with Cassandra tonight. We compared notes on the new packing system—she says I have a very inventive mind for a scientist! She'd better not let old Daedalus hear her say that! Still, she meant well. She admired some of the drawings I did while at the European station. It was kind of her, I think. . . .*

It was equally clear, in his shining gaze and shy smile, that he had loved her. Had she been gentle with the boy, careful of his feelings? Probably not, Virginia admitted to herself. There would have been very little room in Cassandra's mind for his naïve devotion. Archaeology is an all-consuming passion. Only someone like Howard, one of its shining lights in their time, Virginia gathered, would have stood a chance against it.

She had been kind, Vincent had said. She had admired his drawings. Slowly Virginia lifted one and looked at it again. Then she reached into her bag and took out the drawing she had found in the ruins at Abydos. They were by the same hand. They were of the same face. Cassandra's face.

She put in the next crystal and gasped as it showed a different Vincent. His eyes were sunken, his face looked pinched with shock. She had to strain to hear the dragging voice.

*Day 130: I can't believe it. Cassandra Alda disappeared today. It was horrible. She was so excited about going back to the Greek station, and so full of plans for Asia Minor. I can't take it in. What is happening here?*

The last entry was unbearable.

*Day 158: I want to go home.*

That was the end. Seven little entries to account for the life of such a gifted young man from the future. All that charm and unspent affection, gone in the gate. The tormented eyes, the shaking voice would haunt her for a long time to come.

Enough, she said to herself. Enough for today. She went back to the labyrinth, heading for the room she was already starting to consider her own.

ꝏ ꝏ ꝏ

Absorbed in her thoughts, Virginia turned a corner and halted midstride so suddenly she staggered for balance. Then she stood paralyzed while her heart thudded painfully, trying to force air into suddenly breathless lungs. She was no longer alone in the labyrinth. If she had ever been alone. He was standing at the end of the first corridor. For a moment she believed she had found her traveler.

"Shit!"

It was not the best opening remark to make to a person whose help she hoped to enlist.

The man did not appear to be offended. Or perhaps he was, on second thought, because he disappeared on the next breath. Disappointment blended with shock, and the corridor seemed to grow suddenly darker.

*I won't scream*, she thought. *I will not scream. It is nothing but disordered imagination. Or another projection, like from the memory crystals*. It didn't help that he had looked a lot like Gianni Roma.

She stumbled down the corridor, past the spot where she had seen the apparition, and forced herself to follow the map back to Roma's room. Once there, she sat in the chair, hugging her bag to her chest, concentrating on breathing. Too many shocks. Too many people seeming to be there and not being there. What was real and what was not? Would she ever know the difference again?

She jerked her watch up in front of her face and forced her eyes to focus. She had entered the Amenti temple just before noon. After she passed out in Roma's room (she fought down a bubble of hysterical laughter at how that sounded), her watch had said three. Assuming she had not been unconscious for twenty-six hours, it must have been three in the afternoon of the same day. She continued to calculate, deciding finally that it was now probably about four in the morning. Why couldn't she have worn a digital watch, one of those fancy ones that told A.M. and P.M. and stored addresses? Time to sleep. She went over to the bed and made herself lie down on it. She kept the lights on, and fell asleep wishing deeply that she knew how to lock the door.

She spent what was left of the night dreaming that she was walking, running up and down the corridors of the labyrinth. It was filled with shadows. Sometimes the shadows would resolve themselves into the person of Roma, reaching out his hand, trying to speak. It was maddening, almost hearing his voice. Occasionally the shadows took the form of another man, one whose face remained in darkness. In her dream she was trying to get somewhere. It was desperately important that she get there, but her destination kept eluding her. Sometimes she would think she was almost there, and then she would be back at the beginning of the maze, knowing with the devastating clarity of dreams that she was running in circles. She rounded a corner and found herself face to face with Roma. He shouted, and the sound of his voice brought her up wide awake, bolt upright with her back pressed into the corner, shaking and soaking wet from her own sweat.

Slowly she slid down the wall and folded her arms around her knees, drawing them up to her chin. She closed her eyes until the shivering stopped. She had no way of knowing what she knew. No rational way. She tried to clarify in her mind what it was that kept nagging at her awareness. There was a growing sense of *wrongness* about this place, and about herself. It ran up and down her skin like ants. Something had been set in motion, and she had to stop it. And she also knew that there wasn't much time left.

ꙮ ꙮ ꙮ

Virginia looked at the black object she had picked up in the ruins. Then she looked at the viewscreen. How hard could it be? You probably still picked what kind of information you wanted and the computer told you. She went over to the viewscreen. She drew her fingers across the shining black surface, and a number of small lights and symbols came on. Wherever she touched, a symbol lighted up. She pressed one.

After what seemed like hours, she had found a file of information about the little black box. They called it a transcomp. As she had suspected, it was an audiovisual recording device, and all the travelers must have carried one. They would have used it to take notes, to record their journals in the field, to take pictures of events and discoveries. It also had computer capability, storing and processing basic information. Each of its many functions was held in a tiny crystal. In fact, the transcomp itself was little else but a holding and playback device for these crystals.

One of the most interesting set of functions involved the gate. The gate interface crystals were the blue ones, and they allowed the user to access the gate for local transfer. They could not be used safely, the academic prose informed her, for transferring between gates. Their power was limited as they were tuned to one matrix, designed to be used for small transfers from place to place within one time period. Except in emergencies. The effect would be unpredictable, the prose warned, and users were cautioned strongly.

Her transcomp, formerly the property of the questionable Temogen, had no blue crystal. Having opened the back, she saw ranks of crystals, most of them red like the memory crystals in the readers. But no blue ones, although there was an empty space. She shut it and dropped it back in her bag. Then she went out into the labyrinth to look for more ghosts.

# Chapter 27

## 1357 B.C.E.

## Nikko Lantis

The ghostly figure appeared again just as she was entering the corridor that promised to hold the room that Nikko Lantis had used. At the far end he flickered into existence as before, and just as quickly vanished. She passed Lantis's door and went on down the corridor. As she approached the spot where she had seen Roma, she realized that he had stood at the edge of the dark, unused-looking part of the labyrinth. It had been the same corridor, but seen from a different angle yesterday.

She walked a short way down the hall. The walls had an unfinished quality, with only a few hieroglyphic signs and drawings roughly sketched in. She hesitated at the edge of the light. Ahead of her the hall appeared completely dark and empty. There was a flashlight in her bag. She dismissed the half-formed idea of exploring there even as it crossed her mind.

She turned around and went back to Lantis's door. *The engineer*, she thought, looking around the room. It looked like an engineer's room. Technical drawings, schematics, and weird-looking devices and components lay in the sort of chaos that makes perfect sense to its creator. None of it made any sense to her. Bypassing the clutter, she went straight to the reader and picked up the first crystal.

An altogether handsome young man appeared before her, and she looked straight into the second-most beautiful pair of blue eyes she had ever seen. She could not suppress the thought that had she been Cassandra and Vincent's sensitive charm had failed to capture her attention, surely Lantis's male beauty would have. Howard must really have been something special.

*Day 1: It was a smooth transition. The gate is operating at maximum efficiency. We have made a good start, as Roma has done such a good job at finding a suitable site. I congratulated him. The labyrinth should be most suitable for our base. I will begin immediately assembling the force field for the entrance. . . .*

*Day 2: Everyone reported in today, and all the sites are ready to begin work. Roma insisted on checking the installations personally, and I agreed with his caution. But Howard and Cassandra could hardly stand any further delay. . . .*

*Day 20: Small emergency today. One of the artifacts came through the gate broken. Howard nearly went berserk. Jewelry from a barrow in what was Eastern Europe. I must say, I should not have expected such damage—European station insists it was mint condition when it left. . . .*

*Day 30: One month anniversary. To celebrate, Howard sent his first shipment home. Actually, it looked like Howard couldn't decide whether to celebrate or go into mourning. He could hardly stand seeing his beloved artifacts vanish in the gate. I saw Roma watching him. He looked . . . curious. But the curators should be satisfied. This was an unbelievably rich selection for the*

*Collection. Howard thinks we shall all be heroes! The man is an egomaniac, but a brilliant one.*

*Oh, yes, additional note: Daedalus has cracked the Atlantis barrier and located the TS coordinates for it. Gate construction will commence as soon as we decide on the time. Howard was very pleased, of course. Smells fresh meat. . . .*

So far Lantis's version had tallied with Roma's and Vincent's journals. The early enthusiasm; the onset of small accidents, disturbing at first but not yet alarming. The sarcastic twist of his lips as he mentioned Howard's excitement over the Atlantis gate indicated he also shared their dislike and distrust of Howard. The great Dr. Howard certainly seemed to have had a way with people. So far, Cassandra was the only dissenter in this *Roshamon's* collection of testimony.

*Day 80: Howard is in ecstasy. The Seti I tomb proved to be richer than even he imagined. He wanted everyone to drop their work and help ferry the artifacts. . . .*

*Day 120: More reports. I approached Howard about shutting down the gate for a while, until we understand what is happening. I've been over the system thoroughly. Everything functioning normally according to the design documents. Which would be reassuring, except the engineer at the Greek station says the same. I asked Daedalus if he is sure he understands the theory. He says he can't have made a mistake; he understands it perfectly. I asked him then why are people disappearing. No answer. Howard is only worried about any possible delay in shipping. I have insisted that no one travel through the gate until we sort it out. Roma backed me up. I thought Howard would have a stroke. . . .*

*Day 129: Daedalus is working on a theory to explain malfunctioning gates at other stations. Howard is furious at any suggestion of slowing down. He plans to send Cassandra through to the Greek station. I warned him—we both did—that this may not be advised. Howard insists. Since the Greek shipment came in half missing, he is convinced they are stealing stuff, or breaking it themselves through carelessness. The man has tunnel vision. I told Cassandra she should refuse, but she is totally under the man's sway. Half mad herself, when it comes to it. . . .*

*Day 130: Yesterday, we lost Cassandra. She didn't arrive at any of the other stations—Roma and Temogen went through to each gate—and no one had seen her. The Greek station is in chaos—people are terrified. Then, today, Roma ordered them to shut it down, as perhaps it is the source of the problem. Howard nearly had apoplexy. Cassandra . . . she didn't matter to him at all. I thought for a moment that Roma was going to kill him. Pity. . . .*

The progression continued. The handsome young man aged, the beautiful eyes developed a staring quality, the mouth became bitter. His recollection of Howard's reaction to Cassandra's death—or whatever it had been—chilled her.

*Day 150: Since Vincent went, Daedalus is growing more despondent. He asks if the gate is malfunctioning . . . over and over. But it isn't. Every test says it is working perfectly. Except that people and things are disappearing—now, people not even in the gate. I insist it must be theoretical. . . .*

*Day 151: I record this, but I do not believe it. Temogen and Roma, both gone. Temogen apparently walked out of here two nights ago. Roma was looking for him, waiting for him. He never came back. Then Roma just disappeared. He was hurt after that . . . very convenient accident. No one saw him go. Howard says he is off at other stations—but how is that possible? The other gates are closed. We have not been able to contact the Commander. We are all alone. Daedalus is growing weaker—doesn't eat or sleep—just pores over his notes and journals, looking, looking. . . .*

*Day 156: Daedalus told us. He has aged a hundred years; looks like death. The problem is not the mechanism, or the theory. It is in the application of the theory we have used—it is in the very fabric of time. We know, now, where the others have gone—that is, we know what happened to them. There is no way to know where—or when—they are without months of study. Perhaps years. And then we would have to use the gate to reach them. And we can't do that. If the others are alive somewhere in time, they will survive. They have the advantage of knowing more about history than do the makers of it. Daedalus agrees that the only possible solution is to close the gate—permanently. Daedalus is making preparations, secretly. Howard would kill us if he knew. . . .*

*Day 158: I have approached Daedalus. He is ready. We will leave Howard, if necessary. Daedalus is preparing for the final dissolution. He has worked out a two-part sequence that should not only shut down the gate but restore time to its original configuration in the lines we have disrupted. There is one grave result, of course. The artifacts. Those that have already been shipped across the timeline will be saved, but the rest will be lost to us. A terrible blow to the Collection. Daedalus believes they will be restored to their own time. As we will be. I wish I could believe that. . . .*

*Day 159: He has won. The madman controls time, or the destruction of it. We went to the matrix to shut down the gate and two of the crystals were gone. Howard has hidden them. Without them, we cannot reset the matrix and try to reestablish time in its original configuration. And . . . the schematics for the gate, all the data, have been . . . taken. Small comfort that it will do him no good without the repair sequence. If only we could get through to him—it means the end of everything!*

*Day 162: Howard claims to have discovered something . . . promises to give us the power crystals. He insists that Daedalus and I check the gate first—as if that will do any good. I am . . . almost too tired. It's hard to think about going back . . . without the others. Even harder to believe that we are responsible for destroying the very thing we came here to save. We came here with such high hopes. Vincent always said all the truest answers were to be found in art. . . .*

He smiled, and she could see tears standing in the sapphire depths of his eyes, before his image faded. Terror and sorrow threatened to overwhelm her. Sick, Virginia took the last crystal out of the reader and laid it down. She would see those blue eyes in her dreams tonight, if she had another night. He had gone to the gate with the look of a man facing oblivion, praying it would be nothing worse.

The sensation of *wrongness* was growing intolerable. *As if I were a piece of a jigsaw puzzle pushed into the wrong space.* She almost fit, but not quite, and the difference was agony. Her head ached until she thought she would give in and sob. Had Howard given them the crystals, and had they all gone back to the ship that would take them home?

Somehow, she didn't think so.

She looked around the room again. *This is alien technology*, she thought, *just as alien as if they had been another species*. Her eyes were drawn to a box near the bed. Slowly she approached it, as if something outside herself directed her movements. It was not a box, it was a rack, and it held ranks of crystals. Yellow, clear, pink, violet, red. No blue ones.

Methodically, Virginia began a search of Lantis's quarters. She found, as with the others, clothes and very little else in the chests. There were some of the food packages, and she took one out and broke the seal. This one was smooth and dark, and had the consistency of . . . unbelievable. Trust an engineer. It was chocolate. *I'm glad to have my theory verified*, she thought. *Time passes and times change, but chocolate is a constant.*

# Chapter 28

## 1357 B.C.E.

## Temogen

*Day 1: I told Roma the stupid peasant just appeared and saw me. I had no choice. He didn't agree, of course. Roma doesn't always understand . . . expediency. I also told him I thought keeping journal entries was a waste of time. I have better, more enjoyable things to do, even in this backwater rathole. . . .*

*Day 21: The only enjoyable thing that happened today was listening to Roma chew out Howard for ignoring security. One has to admire his nerve. Howard is a powerful man. . . .*

*Day 35: I have been reviewing the literature of these people. What a valiant concept of warfare! Some of the strategies—clumsy, of course, and crude weapons, but still, there is something about meeting the enemy with a sword in your hand, behind a charging horse—the heat, the dust, the clamor of battle—it sounds glorious!*

*Day 72: This traveling to other gates, looking to explain stupid mistakes by incompetent teckies, is becoming a bore. And making these entries is a bore, too. But the procedure must be followed . . . .*

*Day 109: Had an interesting little chat with the big man today. It seems that Howard believes some little trinkets may be lying around the temple across the river. He wants me to go over and, I believe his exact words were, "spy out the land." Where does he get this stuff? Naturally I will have to wait until Roma is otherwise occupied. The man has so little imagination. . . .*

*Day 111: One of the diggers disappeared today from the Greek station. Roma wants me to go there and look around. Perhaps someone there wanted her to disappear. Or not. But it is something to do. . . .*

*Day 112: I Found nothing at the Greek station. And if there had been something to find, I would have found it. I questioned everyone . . . most thoroughly. This is an interminable assignment. Grubbing in the dirt, making reports, and talk, talk, talk. At least there are some important military files to transfer to the Collection. Much more interesting than all these art treasures Howard is so besotted with. Gold is gold, to buy things with. But might, power . . . these are the things worth fighting for. . . .*

Virginia shivered, thinking, *Well, this one is different.* If Vincent was a dreamer and Lantis the answer to a maiden's prayer, Temogen was the stuff that nightmares are made of. She looked at the dark face. He had been exasperated by the scholars and their pedantic process, uninterested in the splendor of the finds. The only flicker of interest had come at the mention of the military records, the stories of death and suffering and violence. Had Roma known what kind of man Temogen's journal entries revealed him to be? Why was she so certain that Roma had been any different?

The next entry showed an exhausted Temogen, fiddling

with an inlaid flail she could not help cataloging mentally as to date and dynasty.

*Day 130: I've been through every gate. I looked everywhere. She wasn't there. Even Roma admitted it was a thorough search. She was just . . . gone. . . .*

The flail snapped under the restless fingers, and she saw something more than violence in the oblique gaze. She saw the beginnings of fear.

*Day 132: Tibetan gate reported a loss yesterday. We checked it out, but there was nothing to be done. I am . . . uneasy with this. Surely we have enough trinkets for the Collection. I am not unwilling to fight . . . but we do not know the name of the enemy.*

*Roma talked to me about closing the gate. He is wary. He knows I haven't forgotten . . . certain things. But on this we agree: we must take command and get the civilians out of here. This precious gate . . . it has been nothing but disaster since we came here. Roma must be planning to take Howard soon. . . .*

*Day 148: This is madness! Vincent gone in the night! None of us are safe now, and those fools pore over their diagrams and theories until I want to push all of them into the gate. Except Howard . . . for him I would reserve a sword!*

*Day 149: I missed the big showdown between Howard and Roma. Apparently our Dr. Howard faced down the great Roma and subdued him. Of course, the disrupter helped. Roma won't take this for long. We are to talk tonight. . . .*

*I have been remembering something from that time I went across the river, to the temple. Howard is absorbed in dreams of gold and paranoia, so I believe I'll slip over there for another look while I wait for Roma to become again a man of action, not words. . . .*

He had gone, she knew. He had gone to the temple, and he had left his transcomp there for her to find. The man who had considered journal entries a bore unworthy of his time—something drove him to record his final adventure. She considered the few new pieces of information she had received. Roma had attacked or at least confronted Howard, and Howard had bested him with the aid of a disrupter. She didn't need to wonder what that was; the name was brilliantly descriptive. She had sensed Temogen's grudging respect for Roma, and growing hatred for Howard. Temogen might be a savage in a civilized man's skin, but as such he had admired courage.

Could he have come back from the temple? It didn't seem possible, remembering his choked scream and the flash of light that followed his message on the transcomp. If she had to choose between Howard and Temogen as the last surviving traveler, why on earth would she have preferred it to be Temogen? Was it too much to hope that Temogen, before he had gone, had found a sword?

*Daedalus and Howard*, she named them silently. *You are the only ones who have yet to speak from the grave, or the great beyond, or wherever you are. Which one of you is still here?* Beyond reason, her mind held tenaciously to the belief that someone was still here with her. But if so, why didn't he show himself? Whichever one it was, he had to know she was here.

Daedalus was next on the map. Virginia walked out into the labyrinth, half expecting her spectral companion to be waiting at the door. Instead, he was a few feet down the corridor, a tall and enigmatic presence that was somehow more than shadow but less than substance. She had almost gotten over the convulsive jerk of muscles and heart. It's only an image, like an echo, she thought resolutely. He was between her and Daedalus's corridor. Then he was gone. Resolutely she walked forward, wondering if she were a sleepwalker and these visions somehow part of walking dreams. Her foot sent something skipping along the hallway. Stooping, she picked up a small round disk, heavy for its size. She turned it over and saw the image of Medusa, her head a writhing mass of snakes. She had seen this emblem before, she realized. She had noticed it in his journal entries, pinned to the front of the black jumpsuit he wore. It belonged to Gianni Roma. Her fingers closed convulsively around the disk. It was warm.

# Chapter 29

## 1357 B.C.E.

## Arthur Daedalus

*Day 1: We successfully entered Eighteenth Dynasty Egypt. Howard would not have tolerated delay, and I am satisfied that the gate operates as it should. Lantis is a good engineer, the best. He built it as I specified.*

*Day 5: Glorious day. I am grateful for the opportunity to test the theory. All seems unquestionably correct. I have been busy helping Howard locate the finds. The equipment is adequate, but opening tons of rock is still a dusty business.*

*Day 20: I must check with Lantis about the broken trinket that came through today. That shouldn't have happened—if it was complete when the European station sent it. Early days for a malfunction! I am rapidly completing calculations for the location of Atlantis. I have been following obscure references in Plato. Once I disregarded the Santorini theory I have been getting closer. I have been having difficulty defining parameters in the crystal matrix. It is curiously resistant. Nothing in the base theory explains it. However, precise TS coordinates should clarify the problem. It is beautiful technology. I am proud of my contribution to it, however small.*

*Day 29: At last! A major breakthrough on Atlantean problem. I believe I have located the correct coordinates, but the crystal matrix only accepts those that locate it post-Cataclysm. No line can be opened to predevastation Atlantis. It is similar to the problem with the Asia Minor attempt. Retrieving artifacts from the ocean floor will be more difficult than from dry land, but if it is the only way to get at them, Howard will be satisfied. I am looking forward to the look on his face when he contemplates artifacts from the Royal City of Atlantis. They will be an absolutely unique contribution to the Collection—the only existing creations of a vanished civilization.*

*Day 30: Howard was jubilant! His reaction was everything I could have hoped for—and as predictable. He sent a team from the Greek station to begin the gate. I don't envy them that task! However, Howard is determined to begin the operation without delay, and I really cannot blame him. No one has ever provided the Collection with such artifacts as these!*

*Day 112: The situation is puzzling—no, more than that—alarming. I am examining my notes on the testing of the gate. I can find nothing amiss. I will recreate, step by step, the development of the theory. I need more data. Howard is furious—wants everyone to dig and carry. I am beginning to hate all this talk of artifacts. The Reconstruction is of supreme importance, but the Collection is after all only one part of that great enterprise. And not to be compared with our real purpose here. Howard will always remain a mystery to me, I suspect. I am working almost all the time now, as it is impossible to sleep with Howard obsessing and all these strange happenings.*

Virginia paused, her hand hovering over the crystals remaining in the reader. Here was something new. *Our real purpose. . . .* So there had been another purpose in this vast raiding through time, the *real* purpose, though no one else had mentioned it. What had it been?

*Day 140: The evacuation has become a rout. People in desperate haste to get back to* Traveler One. *The gate is working almost constantly, day and night, people, equipment. How long until something goes wrong again? And Howard—he feels no concern for all those unfortunate people. Only cares about his collection, these relics of death. I am beginning to wonder if this technology, which we all believed to be such a cultural advance, is in fact accursed.*

*Day 145: Vincent and I have been working over the theories and formulae for days and have found nothing. He is a good boy but his heart is not in it! I was so certain I understood every nuance of the theories . . . what could possibly have gone wrong?*

*Day 149: It . . . seems so quiet here, now. Cassandra, and now Vincent . . . so very young.*

The same sad, frightening progression had been apparent in the face of Dr. Arthur Daedalus. He had begun the mission with a kind of restrained joy illuminating an ageless, compassionate face. And then he had begun to disintegrate. She closed her eyes against the pain in the face suddenly old, intolerably grieved. *Vincent.* The skin on his face shrank when he mentioned his name.

*Day 151: Temogen gone. Now . . . Roma. No one saw them go. At least . . . no one admits it.*

*Day 152: I can't eat or sleep. I revolve the time theory over and over, but cannot see the answer. I can see nothing amiss with our application of the theory. Something terrible has been let loose. Perhaps I have lost my sanity. Howard certainly has lost his. At least, now I am too weak to dig!*

*Day 156: I can't face the truth. I know now what happened to Vincent and all the others. Time travel works . . . the theory works, because all times coexist, all possibilities that may happen do happen. Einstein vindicated. Its very viability has been our undoing. Must tell Lantis. But we must be careful. I do not know how Howard will react. Without Roma, we are . . . all alone with him.*

*I told Lantis. I explained what has happened. I told him to prepare the final destruction of the gate system. It must not be used, must never be used. All because Howard insisted we go to other times of possibility, never our own! Howard would not risk going back in our own track—too afraid his own present would be altered. So he insisted on going back to different tracks—that's the problem. Each shift tore the membrane between tracks—disrupted the fabric of time that separates one track from the infinity of others—the very substance of the universe. Each small disruption added to the others—we have compromised all existence. People have been sucked into other tracks, lost in time somewhere—this track, that track, who knows? Can't even try to explain it to Howard.*

*Day 157: I have prepared the formula for dissolution and set the crystal matrix. I have also written instructions for use—not a fool. Howard may suspect. Too weak to fight him off now. But Lantis knows what to do—one of us must make it . . . must repair time. If we fail, we must at least destroy the gate.*

*Day 158: I have been thinking about our time recorders, sending their data back to the matrix. We thought of them as grain, promising a harvest of hope for Earth's salvation. We didn't realize they were . . . dragon's teeth. I wonder if the creators of this technology, those vanished people of Agate, knew what was killing them? Did they suspect, when their world was smashed, the irony of the truth? Please, God, let us destroy the matrix in time.*

Here it was, the answer she had searched for through all the recordings of these people's private hopes and fears. And she was in no way equipped to believe it, much less take any sort of action against it. *The fabric of time was breaking down. The membrane between this track, that track, the substance of the universe*. What could anyone do with such knowledge. What could she possibly do?

A strange lassitude struck her. She could do nothing. Obviously there was no point in continuing this struggle. Time was breaking down because of the malfunction of a time-travel device. She was helpless, as helpless as she had ever been, helpless as when she stood on that mountain road and watched Hickson plunge to his death. He had died, and she would die, and perhaps everyone and everything in the universe would die. Or she would wake up.

She had listened to all the travelers' journal entries except for Howard's, and nothing she had heard would help her in the slightest. Could she muster her strength and resolve enough to listen to this terrible story one more time, from the perspective of the man who was perhaps the architect of the tragedy? Numbly, she stood up. She did not even look to see if the ghost of Roma still waited for her. She was in the grip of a strange calm that admitted no emotion, called for no action. There was nothing to do.

A dull roaring sound penetrated her abstraction. She raised her head and looked straight into the window of eternity. *Let it take you*, some part of her mind argued. *As well now as later*. But even as the core of her mind would not admit to madness, it also refused to admit to mortality. Whatever reserves of strength that had lain buried in nerves and muscles spun her around and sent her running back down the corridor, turning this way and that at random, the skin on her back shrinking away from the edge of oblivion. And then it was gone. Just as suddenly as it had appeared, the window closed. *Not a window*, she thought, *the gate*. She ran into a wall and yelled with pain.

Her legs, suddenly turned to pillars of cotton, folded and let her slide down onto the floor. She buried her face in her arms and waited. If that terrible tide of displacement had come roaring up the corridor, she would have been helpless to move. There was no safety anywhere here, she realized. It was time itself that chased her up and down the hallways. Eventually it would find her in Roma's room as well as here. How could you lock the door against time?

ᘐ ᘐ ᘐ

Gradually the worst of the terror faded. She began to think again, to be aware. She could open her eyes and not see the terrible miasma of displaced time. Her body cried out for food, for rest. Pain began gathering in various parts of her body. She was bruised and shaken, but all she needed was to open her eyes and go back to Roma's room. Only one more traveler remained missing and unaccounted for in this dark wilderness of hallways. She would find her way back and rest before going in search of the last journal. Only she would have to open her eyes. Something that lives inside all sentient beings made her put off that simple act until her mind screamed at her. Because she knew, in spite of tightly closed eyelids, what she was going to see when she opened her eyes. Or rather, what she would not see. The hallway in which she lay was totally dark.

She understood part of what had happened. Her terrified flight had carried her away from the well-lighted corridors in which the travelers had made their temporary homes. She had penetrated into the shadowy part of the labyrinth that smelled of dust and disuse. But surely . . . surely it had not been totally dark? She couldn't be that far from one of the main hallways. . . . Yet the darkness was absolute.

Virginia dragged herself up and reached into her bag for the flashlight. Her fingers found the casing, the batteries, and the glass. In pieces. Impossibly bad really could get worse. She closed her eyes and imagined the map. She located Daedalus's room in her mind and tried desperately to imagine what turns she had taken in her mad flight through the labyrinth. She had not bothered to map the unused corridors of the maze. Tears of frustration rose but she refused to let them fall. She propped herself against the wall and studied her mental map. It wasn't a true labyrinth, as she had already discovered. A true labyrinth began and ended in the same place, its seemingly endless single corridor winding around and around, back and forth to the center and back again. This map showed the Amenti labyrinth was really a series of corridors that crossed one another at regular intervals, rather like a net. She had only to remember how many turns she had made. Impossible. There was nothing for it but to retrace as many of her steps as she could, and hope it would bring her in sight of one of the lighted corridors. If she followed one corridor all the way to its end, she should find one of the cross corridors giving onto the light. It might take time, but then . . . she did not follow that thought to its obvious conclusion.

She had been facing the other way . . . hadn't she? . . . when she dropped down here. Slowly she turned and faced the opposite direction. It was equally dark. She remembered the red marks on the computer's map, indicating danger. *I could walk right into a pit full of sharpened stakes. Or start a rockfall.* Shaken, she stopped. *Or*, her mind went on relentlessly, *I could just stay here until I die of thirst or starvation, or the gate opens and sucks me in*. She started moving forward, eyes wide open against the darkness, hands held in front of her for balance.

Each shaking footstep was followed by a pause as she registered that she was not dead yet. Forward, a few feet, then a rest when she could not force herself to take one more step. Her neck ached from constantly swiveling her head. There were no doubt cross corridors, and she was terrified she might pass one that gave onto the light. "Virginia, you utter fool," she said aloud. Of course there were cross corridors, openings in the walls. She moved sideways until her reaching hand touched the stone. It was a little easier then, close to the wall, moving forward with one hand brushing the stone. She passed several breaks in the corridor wall, but could perceive no break in the darkness. *If anyone shows up here, anyone at all, I'll go mad and start to run*, her mind gibbered; then, *don't be silly, you are already mad.*

She lost contact with the wall then, and the suddenness startled her. She took the expected number of steps forward, but did not find the wall. The darkness had assumed mass, like a smothering blanket cutting off oxygen from the air. There was smell, somehow a different quality to the air. Could black become blacker? She stopped, disoriented, in the act of lifting her foot for the next step. Shakily she lowered herself to the floor. One hand met dusty stone. The other met nothing at all. The hair lifted along her arms and at the back of her neck. Her taught muscles jerked her convulsively backward. Lifting her hand she slid it along the floor until she found the edge. She had been within inches—no, centimeters—of walking off into one of those ancient Egyptian security devices so amusing to Gianni Roma.

It was several minutes before she could do anything but shake. Her mind fluttered around all the things that might be at the bottom of the pit—sharpened stakes, scorpions, poisonous vipers. Then she shut off the imaginings. *It's irrelevant*, her mind told her, *because the fall would have killed you.* She could feel the whimper building up, and backed slowly away from the edge, her hand dragging across the wall back to the last opening. She turned down it, still on hands and knees, and crawled for what seemed like hours. But then, far in the distance, she could see . . . couldn't she? . . . a slight diminishing of the darkness.

Restraining a desire to run forward, to get away from this smothering darkness, she got to her feet and felt her way down the corridor. It was because she was moving slowly, walking carefully that she saw the wink of a crystal on the wall ahead. She had successfully penetrated the heart of darkness and had found the missing explorer.

# Chapter 30

## 1357 B.C.E.

## John Howard

She dropped the first crystal into the reader. *Dr. Howard, I presume?*

*Day 1: We have successfully entered Old Egypt, New Kingdom, Eighteenth Dynasty. Dr. Lantis assures me the gate is stable. My assessment of the suitability of the site for our main gate was correct. The Labyrinthine Temple is perfect for our base of operations. The* Ban of Akhenaten *has worked in our favor; the place is deserted. Subsidiary gates are being established. I have great hopes for several, the Mayan site in particular. It is a nuisance, having to choose a virtually uninhabited or abandoned site for the major gates, but it cannot be helped, according to Daedalus. . . .*

*Day 20: Terrible! I abhor carelessness. The gold necklace from Europe arrived in pieces. A lovely piece—hundreds of beaten-gold leaves in a circle—inlays of amethyst and emerald . . . it would have nearly completed my Ancient European collection. Vincent will go to the European station and investigate as I cannot spare Roma just now. . . .*

*Day 21: Naturally, the fools at the station denied responsibility! Vincent's report seems complete, but perhaps it was an error not to send Roma. He is much more intimidating than Vincent. He had better make it clear to those fools at the European station that nothing else had better come through in pieces—unless it's themselves! Ha!*

*Day 30: Daedalus has convinced himself he has located coordinates for Atlantis. What a coup that will be! An absolutely unique source, no known artifacts in existence . . . I hope he knows what he's talking about. . . .*

Virginia thought, *I've met you before, oh, yes. I've seen that passionate glow many times. Not a few times in my own eyes.* She was well acquainted with the top men and women in her field, and many others who were not so near the top. The most successful ones, she had observed, often had more than knowledge. They had style. They had the ability to persuade, to captivate, to will stubborn fingers to loosen tight purse strings, always with the same end in mind: to keep the cash, the life's blood of any archaeologist with a penchant for digging, flowing into the bottomless maw of the past.

They could be devastatingly attractive. She remembered them, lean and sun-weathered, with eyes like sailors', always seeming to see a little farther than ordinary eyes. Only they did not see the horizon. They looked with steadfast devotion only into the past. Virginia was intimately connected with the strange, obsessive love affair archaeologists all share for, as Daedalus so pointedly put it, *the relics of death*. But of the many ruthless, charming men she had met, worked with, and even liked, none had had Howard's magnetism. He had made no effort to disguise the scorn he felt for his fellow travelers. He had not been trying to impress anyone in his entries. He was stating his experience exactly as he had felt it. And even through the absolutely heartless obsession, his charm and personal power had tugged like a magnet. No wonder Cassandra, loving archaeology as passionately as had the god of her idolatry, had worshipped at his shrine.

*Day 76: We went forward and opened the Seti I tomb today. Wonderful things! We have to be careful, but it is worth the risk. It is maddening to have to watch and wait while they filled up the tomb and sealed it. The guards of the tombs are not proof against tranquilizer darts, and, of course, they will not dare tell anyone that they woke up in the morning with no idea of what happened. I feel sure of success.*

*Day 85: We cleared the last of the Seti I tomb and will begin on Thutmose II tomorrow. It is not so rich a find, but still it is filled with wonders.*

*Roma's interference continues to drive me to distraction. He actually insists that we put some artifacts back, both the Seti I find and the scrolls he was so incensed about. Talking to me about their importance to Western thought and theological development! As if his opinion of such matters is of any interest whatsoever.*

He held in his hands a gold statue, probably Isis, she thought. She watched the long fingers caress the smooth curves of the goddess. There was a softening of the mobile mouth as if he touched the flesh of a living woman. She shuddered.

*Day 90: Although the artifacts continue to come through on schedule, we have received some reports of strange happenings at some of the other gates. Hysterical reports of people disappearing. I must find time to investigate. Nothing must interrupt the work!*

*Day 114: Daedalus and Lantis are still worrying and tinkering over the Atlantis gate. I told them to get on with it. Their caution is overdone. If they are successful, we shall have something to take forward that will surpass every other contribution to the Collection. Think of it, to bring Atlantis into the cultural base! Nothing since the beginning of the Reconstruction can compare with it! Nothing must stop us! Nothing!*

*Day 115: It is a triumph! The Atlantis gate has been established! Lantis is still whining about anomalies. He and Daedalus were unable to establish a gate prior to the devastation.*

The next entry showed something had happened to disrupt the smiling calm, the controlled satisfaction of the man. Eyes, hands, mouth all betrayed him.

*Day 130: I can't believe it . . . something has happened to Cassandra. She was ready to go through to the Greek outpost. Lantis sent her through. Greek station reports she never arrived, and there was no trace of her. She will be a serious loss, especially as she is . . . was most knowledgeable on the Greek and Macedonian collection.*

*Day 132: This is intolerable! They have shut down the gate at the Greek station! The Commander is harassing me to do the same here. She demands to speak to Roma and Daedalus . . . not at all likely! Fortunately, I was prepared for the mindless fear of fools confronted with a little . . . insecurity. I control all communications and nothing gets through, except to me. I have also removed the privacy locks from their computers, Roma's insistence on journals will serve me well. The irony is very sweet. I will not be turned aside from my goal! Nothing will stop me, and when I return with the richest addition to the Collection since the Reconstruction began, I will be vindicated!*

*Day 148: Roma thinks he has only to brandish his weapons at me and I will cede my authority. I have seen him with Temogen, planning quietly. He is a fool, and I am prepared.*

*Day 149: It was childishly easy. With Temogen out of the way, I had only to let him continue his eternal prowling and prying. I had a place chosen to send him, an exquisitely appropriate place. But the gate chose that moment to misbehave, and the sequence was incomplete. I have no idea where he went. I could probably get him back if I wanted to. But, of course, I don't want to.*

He held up a small, sparkling object that she recognized as a gate initiator crystal, casually tossing it in one hand as he spoke.

*Day 162: I heard them talking, Daedalus and Lantis. They are the only ones left. They were planning to take down the gate. Daedalus was going to trick me, leave me here alone, stranded. But I fooled them. I took the power crystals and hid them. Without the crystals, they cannot shut down the gate. And they will never find them. I lured them into the gate, pretending that I was going to show them something I had discovered. I neither know nor care where they went. They were traitors. A way must be found to solve the problem of the fragmentation in time, and continue the work. Daedalus must have left sufficient information to repair the gate. He hid it, of course. Even in face of all that happened, he still thought he could outwit me. I will find it, of course. All in good time.*

Virginia stirred in the great gold chair. It had come as no surprise that Howard's room was furnished like the tomb of a pharaoh. Precious objects gleamed from every corner. She put down the little box, exquisitely carved of Chinese cinnabar and beyond price, that held his memory crystals.

He had murdered them all, or sent each one alone and unprepared into the past. All the ones left after Roma. But Howard did not mention what he had done to the security chief. Had he murdered him? Or merely sent him through the gate with the massive indifference he had shown the others. And how had he succeeded against a man so formidable, so hostile?

With reluctance approaching loathing, she looked though the inlaid and carved chests. They contained a hundred items of fabulous price, but nothing of value. Then, at the bottom of one, neatly wrapped in a spangled Egyptian robe, she found another transcomp. She pressed what she knew was the playback button. She sat back to listen to Roma's almost unrecognizable voice as he told his tale of defeat.

*Day 152: I tried—and failed. Howard is smarter than I knew, or more cunning. I was hurt in that convenient rockfall in the labyrinth, and Daedalus gave me something for the pain before I could stop him. It made me sleepy, as if nights without sleep weren't enough. But there is no excuse. I woke up here, wherever this is. Truly, I underestimated Howard. He was waiting for me to try it!*

*Temogen is not here. I need him now. Although we've had our differences, surely he will see the situation and do the right thing. Together we will be able to overpower this madman and shut down the crystal matrix. I know Daedalus and Lantis are working on it secretly. But they will need help.*

*Day 162: I've searched every crack of this rathole he's locked me in, and there is no way out. He's keeping me alive, for some reason, but why has Temogen not found a way to let me out? Howard must have won him over—or killed him. I find myself wishing the gate would take me, too. Anything to get out of here.*

She looked at the bruised and bleeding face, lighted only by the transcomp. Roma's last entries, from wherever Howard had imprisoned him. Hurt, dying . . . maybe he would have been easy for Howard to finish off. She had found all the pieces, and they were of no use whatever. She felt an overwhelming sense of loss.

# PART IX

## In the Nick of Time

# Chapter 31

## 1357 B.C.E.
## Abydos

Habit took Virginia back to Roma's room. Unthinkable to wait, to spend an unnecessary moment in Howard's opulent quarters. Pointless to listen any more to the dead voices, search any further through shining, glorious, valueless treasures for which far too high a price had already been paid. For which an unthinkably high price was yet to be paid. The spare, spartan room welcomed her. Soon, she knew, she would have to decide what to do. She could leave Amenti. Go out into Akhenaten's Egypt and try to find some kindly people who would help her, the strangest of strangers in a strange land. Such people had existed throughout time; there would be some here. She would find them. Or not. Or she could stay here, companioned by the holographic images of the lost travelers, eating their space rations until they ran out, or until the gate took her to join them. *It didn't really matter much,* she thought idly. The malfunctioning time gate was not restricting its effects to Amenti. It had attacked her in the temple. Even now it was spreading throughout the world. All the worlds everywhere, everywhen. She imagined the mindless panic that would afflict humanity, in this age and every other, as time caved in and that obscene light, the opposite of creation, swept over them. *Let there be darkness*. On the whole, she preferred to meet it here, with the shades of people who, if not exactly friends, were at least familiar. Somehow it became possible to close her eyes.

It came as she was hovering on the edge of sleep. *I could probably get him back, if I wanted to*. The resonant voice, so smooth and soft, talking about the man he had removed so cleverly. Virginia sat up, wide awake. *How?* Her mind demanded, *how could he get him back? Why was he different from the others who had disappeared in the gate?* There had been no equivocation about the others; once gone they were unrecoverable. But not Roma. *I could get him back*. . . . She went to the viewscreen and ran her fingers over the surface. There had to be a way to access this. Her head ached in the glare. "Dim the lights," she said to the invisible genie of the lamps. As the light obediently dimmed, she got it. Could it possibly be that easy?

"Computer, tell me about transcomps and initiating the gate."

After an hour or so of patiently rephrasing her questions, she found what she wanted. *If*, the voice of Arthur Daedalus informed her, *the user tried to transfer too great a distance using the transcomp interface with the gate, there was the danger that the transfer would be incomplete. The user could be trapped in between times. It might, theoretically, be possible to recall such a person, provided the sequence of transfer was known, and the transfer crystal placed in the gate control sequencer.* Users were again cautioned against using transcomp initiators to transfer between times except in the case of direst need.

Virginia picked up the bronze emblem she had found in the tunnels. Howard had imprisoned Roma somewhere in the Amenti labyrinth. If he had dragged him, unconscious or hurt, to the main gate, then there was no hope. But she didn't think Howard had done that. Howard would not want to risk the others seeing him carrying the unconscious man through the labyrinth. No, if she had been Howard, she would have used the transcomp to transfer him to his prison. When he decided what to do with him, the same reasoning would have applied. Unless Roma was unconscious, Howard would have been confronting a desperate, angry man. And a dangerous one. Her springing hope would not allow it.

He would have confronted Roma and sent him into time on the spot, again using a transcomp. Not Roma's transcomp—Howard would not have left it with him if there was the slightest possibility of his using it to transfer out of his prison. Howard's transcomp, with a live gate initiator crystal. The crystal that would have recorded the transfer coordinates. Her mind shied away from the very real possibility that she would fail to find the crystal, to find the gate . . . *dear Heaven*, was she seriously considering going to the source of this madness? She could not consider failure. She would find the crystal if she had to take this labyrinth apart a brick at a time, even if it took her the rest of eternity. What other use had she for eternity?

ꙮ ꙮ ꙮ

It was not so difficult, after all. She found it in the first place she looked, the lovely cinnabar box with the other crystals, a crystal drop of azure glowing with promise. Now, she thought, holding it tightly in her hand, now for the hard part. Now for the gate.

"Show me the gate," she said to Howard's viewscreen. "No, not the schematic, the location." The map on the viewscreen obediently increased to show the required information. The gate was several corridors away, in a section of the labyrinth she had not yet visited. The direction, she slowly realized, from which that boiling fog of nonbeing always came.

*I'm going to succeed, I'm going to . . . I think I can, I know I can . . .* Virginia chanted, running in the direction of the gate. *Maybe it's not at home right now.* The gate complex resided in the center of the labyrinth, at the far edge of the block occupied by the travelers. The heart of Amenti, she thought, the place where Osiris, Lord of Forever, was enthroned. Gateway to the Fields of the Blessed. Or, in this case, obliteration. She ran, but her flesh seemed to shrink inward, away from the possibility of the assault of nonbeing. The sense of *wrongness* was overpowering. The air felt glutinous, slowing her, holding her back. Her gorge rose, and she swallowed hard, pushing forward. As she turned the last corner, she sank to her heels in the middle of the corridor, unable to move.

The solid stone walls of the labyrinth had vanished. In their place were dozens, no hundreds . . . thousands of *non*walls. Walls with no substance, no reality, yet somehow there. The floor, the ceiling, all swam and dove and undulated, floor upon floor into an infinity of floors, ceiling over ceiling in the same mind-numbing dance. It lacked the violence, the hurricane sense of motion of whatever had chased her through the labyrinth, had sucked her into this time in the first place. But she had no doubt that this was the source of that other, terrifying effect. It was still an affront to the mind and senses. Slowly Virginia put out a hand and touched the shifting floor inches from her feet. Her hand signaled it had touched a floor, but it was now one of a thousand hands. She jerked back as a wave of nausea swept through her. *Osiris*, she prayed, *how do I walk through forever? That, only the gods dare to do*. She rested her forehead on her knees for a moment, but it was no use. She would have to go on.

She clutched the bronze emblem of Medusa in her hand like a talisman, and started forward. Almost immediately she was on her hands and knees, crawling. She tried closing her eyes, but the sensations intensified in the self-imposed darkness. Slowly, desperately, she dragged herself along the corridor, hearing the voices of a million lost souls whispering and wailing all around her. She could see . . . not people; the shadows of people . . . like that flicker of movement seen sometimes at dusk at the edge of sight that leaves the mind confused. She crawled past, around, through throngs of people. Her experience, her life was reduced to just one tiny window of sanity, to get through that ghastly afflicted corridor to the door of the gate control room. She had no idea how close she was to it until she banged her face against it. It slid up and she was through.

It was no better inside. She had looked at the images of the gate control console until her eyes ached, memorized everything necessary for this task. She could no more have operated the controls than she could fly, but she could plug the transfer crystal into the control sequencer. If Roma's transfer coordinates were the last ones in the crystal, then the gate might stabilize him and bring him back. She tried not to look around at the wavering, shifting images. *Time*, she thought. *I'm looking at time writhing and whipping through the air like some monster's tentacles.* She dragged her face across the console, trying to focus on finding the sequencer panel. Her fingers, guided by some mysterious facility, found it. A thousand fingers pressed, an infinity of panels opened. *Is it possible that I will put it into the wrong slot in time? The console presumably exists in an infinity of times, as do the crystals, as do I.* Her eyes blurred, and she shoved the crystal into its snug little slot.

The disappointment would probably have killed her, had she been able to feel it. A million blue crystals brightened, a few million lights flickered across the consoles, and nothing else whatever happened. Virginia crawled back to the door. What kept her going she couldn't imagine, then or ever. She only knew that she had forced a thousand suffering bodies back down those terrible corridors where time had become unstuck, and one of her had made it to the end. When she dragged herself onto a stable patch of floor, she longed to lie there, face down, eyes shut, and scream. Every atom in her being wanted to scream.

# Chapter 32

## 1357 B.C.E.
## Abydos

Not *yet*, something warned her. *If you give in now you'll never stop*. She got up and began walking. As she turned the corner she saw her familiar specter lying across her path, mocking her failure. Too tired, too defeated to accord it her usual courtesy, she walked through it. Or tried to. Her foot caught against solid flesh and sent her sprawling. He gave a grunt of surprise, and she scrambled sideways to the other side of the corridor. She considered him for a moment. The lean face was marred by bruises and half-healed wounds, the crisp hair matted with dried blood. He looked very like a man who had tried to dig his way out of a tomb with his bare hands. Finally, she found her voice. "Hello, Perseus," she said. "Andromeda here. What kept you?"

In the end, Virginia had to half carry him back to his room. She could feel his body trembling with effort as she lowered him to the side of the bed. He was gasping like a landed fish. She fetched him water, and sat down in the chair to watch him drink it. He gulped, hardly waiting to swallow, the water splashing over his mouth and onto his shirt. She handed him a package of food, which he ate in the same desperate, impatient manner. Her heart warmed a little as she looked at him. Solid. Real. Alive. Her mind kept adding to its happy litany. When she thought the silence was going to kill her, he finally looked up and focused his eyes on her.

"Would you look in that chest? A small white box."

She opened the chest and handed him the box. The lid folded back, displaying a medical kit. It might come from a distant future, but the paraphernalia had a familiar look. After a brief search, he pulled something out and pressed it to the inside of his arm.

"What is that?"

"It's . . . an antidote. To a drug." Then, "Andromeda?" he said finally.

She smiled. "I saw the medallion. It is yours, isn't it?" She reached into her pocket and pulled it out, dropping it in his palm. "Perseus and Andromeda and the gorgon."

He looked at her in stony silence, for an instant. Then his eyes closed, and he went down sideways onto the bed.

ꝏ ꝏ ꝏ

When he opened his eyes again, several hours later, she had not moved.

"Feeling better?" she asked.

"Yes. Better than I have in months."

"Then you really must have felt like hell on the highway," she said.

He smiled humorlessly. "I've been drugged. What I just

took will clear it out of my system, whatever is left. It's been a while since he—"

"Howard?"

He froze. Virginia would later swear she could see every nerve ending in his body come to attention.

"Well, now. What do you know about Howard?"

"The journal entries are protected by privacy locks. You couldn't have accessed them."

She sighed. "Well, I did."

"Only what the journal entries told me. I've been through them all. Yours, Howard's, all of them. It's how I guessed that using the transfer crystal might bring you back."

His eyes narrowed. "You're telling me that you stabilized the transfer."

"Yes. You're welcome, by the way."

"Did the gate pull you in?" he said at last.

"Yes. I suppose so. I was in the ruins at Abydos and—"

"When?"

"1995."

"How did you find this place?"

So she told him about herself, about H.L. Pierce and the ancient Amenti temple he had discovered in the mountains above Abydos. She told him about the strange sightings in the ruins, the disappearances, the reason for her coming.

He shook his head. "You'll forgive me if I find all this a little hard to believe. You just accidentally got sucked into the gate, just happened to know that the labyrinth was here and how to find it, and just put your time here to good use familiarizing yourself with advanced technology from the future. Such good use that you could take this knowledge and stabilize an unstable transfer."

"The computer told me how to do it. I use a computer every day in my work. It's one of an archaeologist's most important tools. The only trick was figuring out how to access the correct data. I can show you the file."

"You're an archaeologist," he said softly, not quite masking his loathing of the word.

"Yes. An Egyptologist, in fact. So tell me, what exactly were you doing here? Why was it necessary to rob the past? Or was it just very lucrative?"

He visibly controlled an angry gesture, and replied in a cold voice.

"Being lucrative did not enter into it, not that I expect you to understand that. No, this was all about saving the glories of past civilizations, recapturing our human traditions of creativity and artistry." He sounded as if the words tasted bad in his mouth. "In about four hundred years from your time, Earth will be destroyed. There will be very few survivors from the human population—none of the monuments, art, and antiquities at all. Except for a few remnants in off-world collections. Howard and a few other historians and dirt-grubbers got the idea of coming back in time to save them. Are we any more guilty of robbing the past than you are? Or just more successful?"

"Well, I suppose if you're going to all the trouble of time travel, it makes more sense to go back when the things were new. After all, why take home a beat-up old relic when you can have one in mint condition? Although I'm not sure I would call all this . . . successful." She kept her tone even. "What destroyed—or will destroy—Earth?"

"We call it the Cataclysm. We don't know what caused it."

"It didn't occur to anybody to try and do something about the disaster? Forgive me if that seems to me to be a far more important use of all this time-travel effort."

"I don't have to explain our mission to you—"

"You know, I think you do," she said mildly. "I'm finding it really hard to believe that you would do all this for a bunch of what I'm sure you regard as useless old relics."

"You know nothing of what I think."

"Quite the contrary," she gestured to the memory crystals. His gaze became glacial.

"I'm sorry," her voice was sincere, "but I was desperate to find out what had happened here. What was happening to me."

After a moment, he nodded. "Yes. Well, as it happens you are right. I didn't come because of the Collection."

"Daedalus mentioned the *real* mission in his journal."

"Did he? We'd agreed not to put it in any of our reports, personal or public. But all our efforts meant nothing in the end. Howard always knew."

He responded to the questions in her eyes. "Dr. Daedalus's plan was to sow recorder crystals throughout time, or as much of it as we could get to on the first mission. The scientists and computers back home could then analyze all that data, and try to find the cause of the Cataclysm."

"And prevent it?"

"Yes." His eyes were bleak. "You can have no conception of the devastation it will cause Earth in the future."

"Really," said the dirt-grubber sitting opposite him. "Well, I expect I'll have a pretty good grasp of the idea by the time this gate affair of yours is quite finished destroying the current one."

A faint red flush crept up his neck, but he made no answer. In fact, she thought as she regarded him closely, he looked better by the second.

"Your antidote seems to be helping."

"Yes. It was thoughtful of Howard to tell me what he had been giving me, just before he pulled the trigger. It helps to know what to look for. Speaking of which, you apparently know what happened here after I left. Perhaps you will tell me what you have found out."

So she told him everything she knew about Howard, and Lantis and Daedalus, and their last desperate struggle to repair the ravages of the gate.

"So. Lantis and Daedalus devised a program to shut down the gate and re-form history. I knew they were close. And Howard hid the crystals necessary to initiate the sequence. Where is he, do you know?"

He said it so smoothly, so casually, she knew it was the heart of his suspicion. What did he imagine, she wondered. That she and Howard were somehow in league? That she was the enemy?

"No, I don't know where he is. What an inane question."

"Why?"

"Because if I had met him he would have shoved me

into your bloody gate and I would also now be 'one with the elements.'"

"Not necessarily."

"Don't be ridiculous. Even if I could be deemed to have a motive to help Howard mangle time, what reason could he possibly have for making me an accomplice? What would he get out of it?"

He eyed her speculatively for a moment. "Well, you're an archaeologist, for one thing. Howard is used to the adulation and assistance of devoted acolytes. He thrives on it. He lost his last devotee in the gate. And then, you're decorative. I'm not sure how much that would mean to Howard, but it probably wouldn't *diminish* your appeal."

She felt the scarlet rush of color rising to the roots of her hair. Before she could stop herself, her hand flashed out to deliver a stinging slap. He caught her wrist an inch from his face and regarded her calmly.

"Has anyone ever told you that you have a filthy temper?"

"Yes," she responded through gritted teeth. "Has anyone ever told you that you have a filthy mind?"

"No," he said, and his surprise seemed genuine.

Her hand started to tingle from restricted blood flow.

"Have you discovered what happened to Howard?"

"No," she hissed. "I haven't seen him . . . or, at least. . . ." She stopped.

"Yes?" He tightened his grip on her wrist just enough to make her fingers go completely numb.

"I saw you . . . and several times I saw what I took to be someone else, like a shadow, but never clearly. It could have been him, I suppose. All I can really say is that it wasn't you."

"Did he react at all?"

"No. I could barely see it, just an impression, and somehow it wasn't really there."

It sounded lame, and he clearly did not believe her.

"Look at it from my perspective," he said after a moment. "You just appear here, where you have no right to be, knowing things you shouldn't know. You claim to know nothing about Howard or his whereabouts, and you'll have to forgive me if I do not feel able to just take your word for that. I can't afford to."

"Then there is my perspective to consider," Virginia said, her voice shaking. "I find myself here, through no fault of my own, because you and a bunch of your fellow looters have been using technology you don't understand and can't control to pillage the past. Not only have you stripped this world of humanity's most important artistic accomplishments, you have probably changed the flow of history beyond all recognition. You haven't just endangered my life, you have endangered all existence. Not bad for one little expedition into the past. In my efforts to understand what has happened here I thought it might be a good idea to try to bring you back. For my trouble I have nearly fallen into a pit lined with stakes, or snakes, or both, been chased through the corridors of this horrible labyrinth by time itself, and had a suspicious lout cut off all circulation in my hand."

To her surprise, he relaxed his hold. "All right. I have no choice but to accept at least part of your story. Howard would certainly have no reason for bringing me back. We'll leave it for now."

He took some food out of one of the chests, and they ate. Virginia felt as if she was having a picnic sitting on top of an active volcano. But she was starved, and still shaken from her crawl through the time displacement field. Watching him force food into his mouth and swallow it, she followed his example. When they were finished, he gestured toward the bed.

"Go to sleep," Roma said abruptly.

"Impossible. The whole place . . . the whole universe could go up any minute."

"Staying awake won't keep that from happening. I need sleep even if you don't. Tomorrow will be busy enough."

He turned to the viewscreen and flicked his fingers across the lighted grid in a complex pattern. He opened an undiscovered panel in the wall near the bed and took out a large, wicked-looking handgun of some kind. It looked exactly the way something called a disrupter ought to look. He opened something on it and, after looking inside, made a small sound she chose to interpret as satisfaction. She remembered his journal entry about his disrupter not functioning when Howard jumped him. She derived sudden comfort from the knowledge that he had a spare. Then he took the top blanket from the bed, soiled now with dirt and blood, and stretched out across the doorway.

"Lights dim," he said.

She was left no alternative but to lie down or remain standing in the near darkness.

"What were you doing just now?"
"Locking the door."
"Then why are you sleeping across the threshold?"
"Extra security never hurts."

# Chapter 33

## 1357 B.C.E.
## Abydos

When Virginia opened her eyes the next morning, he was already at work on the computer, silently accessing files by moving his fingers across the screen in some complex, lightning-fast pattern. He had employed hot water and soap, and was wearing clean clothes, another jumpsuit identical to the one she had taken. His hair was still wet. It gave him a boyish, vulnerable look. When she stirred he turned slowly and looked at her, and she revised this thought. Gianni Roma had probably never looked vulnerable in his life, and if he had ever looked boyish, it must have been when he was very, very young. The livid bruises on his face and arms were already beginning to heal. He looked worlds better than he had the night before. But his expression had not softened.

Sighing inwardly, Virginia set about making herself ready for another day of trying to outrun time. When she too had enjoyed the benison of hot water, she sat down, determined to maintain a professional, polite demeanor.

She adopted an impersonal tone. "What do we do first?"

Her professional demeanor was slightly compromised by her efforts to drag Cassandra's priceless jade comb through her hair. The effort brought tears to her eyes. Long hair was impractical on a dig, she reminded herself. In the security of her job in San Francisco, she had let it grow, certain that she would never be on another dig. Did rooting through time count as a dig?

"Here," Roma said absently, handing her something that looked like a pocket knife and never taking his eyes off the viewscreen. "The third button."

She pressed, and a small series of wires sprang out.

"And what is this?" she asked warily.

"A comb."

Seeing her look of disbelief, he took it back and drew it through her hair. Her head tingled. The tangles disappeared.

"I'm glad to see some things have improved in the future," she laughed.

Virginia was only minimally ashamed that she was employing one of the oldest of ploys to win, if not his trust, at least a less hostile truce. But her professional demeanor was clearly not getting her anywhere. After a long moment, he folded his arms and regarded her with something that could have been amusement flickering about his mouth.

"Andromeda?"

"Only on special occasions. Dr. Virginia Alexander, for every day. As we're sharing your room, you can call me Virginia. I already know your name. Does anyone call you Gianni?"

He ignored her question. "You understand I can't send

you home."

"That's not the real issue here, is it? Going home just means waiting for time to unravel all around me unless we can fix this thing here and now. Well, unless you can. It doesn't seem likely that I would be able to do much about it."

"You seem to have done quite a lot so far. Perhaps I should thank you for stabilizing the transfer crystal. How did you come up with that idea?" The suspicion was sharp and alert behind the pleasant tone.

"Howard told me." She watched suspicion flower behind his eyes.

"The journal entries. I told you, I listened to them. Howard said he could get you back if he wanted to. So I asked the computer about it. That's all."

He digested that in silence for a moment. "Begin by telling me everything that has happened since you came through the gate."

She obeyed, stopping only when he asked for more information, or to clarify a point.

"Can you remember exactly when you experienced the gate effect?"

Skillfully he drew from her a reconstruction of events, with the times of the terrible onslaughts of nonbeing identified far more precisely than she had believed possible.

He entered the times in the computer and waited as the lighted symbols marched across the viewscreen.

"There is the beginning of a pattern here. Toward the end, the gate was stabilized by being recalibrated before each use. It's possible that opening and closing by itself, without the palliative effect of recalibration every time, it becomes more unstable with each occurrence. I might be able to stabilize it somewhat and buy time."

"Time to find Daedalus's repair sequence?"

He nodded. "And then I will have to go after the two missing crystals."

"I notice you said *I*. I think you mean *we*." His scarcely concealed antagonism was grating on her nerves.

He took a deep breath, and she prepared herself for argument. His answer both relieved and alarmed her.

"If there were any other way, I would keep you out of it," he said.

Again that tinge of dislike, of disdain. And of deep mistrust.

She felt her temper rising. "It's my world, too, you know. In fact, if I understand it correctly, it's my world, period. You come from somewhere else entirely."

He shook his head. "In fact, if *I* understand it correctly," he mimicked her tone, "so do you. Come from somewhere else entirely."

She felt the blood drain out of her face, and sat down abruptly on the bed.

"What are you saying?"

"According to Daedalus, the fabric of time is like a crystal lattice. Know anything about geology?"

She shook her head. "Very little."

"According to his theory, the structure of time is like an unbounded crystal—a lattice, but with an infinite number of planes intersecting another infinite number of planes at various angles. The individual timelines are the lines of intersection where planes cross. They are connected to each other via the shared points, forming a network of intersecting metalines known as event strings. So everything that can happen does happen, in some timeline. And all event possibilities for each timeline are held together by these intersecting event strings. With me so far?"

She nodded as if she were.

"Around our timeline and intersecting it are an infinite number of other timelines, each with an infinite number of variations connected by event strings. We have been removing artifacts centuries before you were born. Yet you say that you came to Abydos because things, important art treasures, were disappearing out of museums and collections in your own time."

She nodded, frowning. "But if the things had been stolen in the past. . . . " she began hesitantly.

"Exactly. If we had taken them in the past of your timeline they wouldn't just disappear in your time, right in front of you. They would never have been there. Time would have been altered in the past, and the objects would not have been there to disappear."

"But they did disappear."

"Yes. Because the fabric of time is breaking down. Daedalus explained it to us. My guess is, and it's only a guess, you come from an adjacent timeline, most probably my own. We are connected to this timeline through the event strings at synchronous points programmed into the crystal matrix. But the strings, the connections, are breaking down between the timelines and they are folding in on each other. So if a moment of our timeline touches a moment in this other timeline, then the event strings could become enmeshed. We took the objects in this timeline in the past, but when the two timelines collided, that disappearance took place in the other at the point of collision. The objects would disappear at the instant in time the two lines met.

"If we aren't successful in repairing the gate, my world and my time will not be any better off. We're talking about the fabric of time everywhere, in every timeline. The breakdown will continue, growing more and more dangerous, until none of the timelines maintain any integrity. Everything, everywhere will die. Menelaus—my home world—will die, too. In my timeline, and in every other. Do you understand?"

Understand? Was it possible to understand the enormity of what he was saying?

"Certainly. You think he hid the crystals somewhere in time?"

"Yes. I think he used the gate."

"And the repair sequence?"

He thought for a moment. "If I were Howard, I would do anything to find it. He needs the repair sequence so he can continue to use the gate for his own purposes without endangering his own precious existence. As for the second half, the dissolution sequence, I would be doing my damnedest to destroy it to prevent someone from doing what we are planning. To restore time to its original configuration and send all this back where it belongs. And to shut down the crystal matrix, permanently. I think Daedalus and Lantis would have left a backup copy somewhere against that very eventuality. I have to believe that. And, having found it, we still have to find the crystals."

*Find them* . . . she let the thought trail off. *Somewhere in time. Somewhere in all the vastness of time two little crystals were hidden. Lord of Forever, help us.*

"There's one thing more."

"Yes?"

The keen eyes narrowed. "We can improve the situation somewhat. Lessen the risk. But you know—"

"What happened to the others could happen to me? Yes."

"Good. Now, with the help of Lantis's notes, I have put together what I think is a sequence that will stabilize the gate."

"Does that mean the gate effect will stop boiling up and down the corridors?"

"For a time."

"If we're going to try doing something about stabilizing this gate, let's do it now," she said finally. "If it goes berserk again, I don't think I could outrun it. I'm too tired."

He nodded and stood up. They walked through the hallways in silence, until she felt the time displacement effect crawling along her skin. Roma's intimate knowledge of the labyrinth and the location of dangers made their progress easy, and the trip was all too short. One more turn and they would be there. Her footsteps halted. He turned and looked at her questioningly.

"What's wrong?"

"We're getting close to it. The gate."

He turned and continued on, and she forced her unwilling feet to follow.

It wasn't until they turned the corner and confronted what she thought of as the time corridor that he understood the dread that filled her voice when she mentioned the gate. The damage stretched farther up the hallway now, almost to the intersection. Soon, this entire section of the labyrinth would be caught in the displacement effect. Roma stared at the crawling, shifting tunnel and took an involuntary step backward. He uttered what sounded like an oath under his breath.

"You got through that?" was all he could find to say.

There was something about the way he said *you* that finally pushed Virginia's ragged temper over the edge.

"Yes, you arrogant . . . yes, I did. I crawled through it. I shoved the transfer crystal into your bloody gate, and I crawled through it again on the way back. I. Me. Myself. The dirt grubber. And you are here because I did. I can't tell you how thrilled I am with the results."

Virginia sat down, her back to the wall and hung her head, nauseated at the very thought of setting foot in that obscene corridor through time.

Roma, after a heartbeat, squatted on his heels on the opposite side. He regarded her, a mixture of emotions moving across his face.

"I don't know you. You can't expect me to be able to assess your abilities. . . . "

"I expect nothing at all from you. I'm sorry I'm an archaeologist, since you have such reason to hate them, but there it is. And you wouldn't be here if I were something else." Neither would she, of course, and she was grateful under the circumstances that he refrained from pointing that out.

"True. I'm sorry." He smiled then, the first genuine smile she had seen on his face. It transformed the stern features. Her heart missed a beat, and she answered it.

"And I'm sorry," she added hastily, "if I said anything to hurt you, about—well, about any of this being your fault. I know it wasn't. I know you did everything that could have been done to try to stop Howard."

"*Trying* is a word that has no meaning for me," he said quietly.

"You were drugged; you said so yourself. Would he have succeeded if you hadn't been?"

"Possibly not," he said, with a glimmer of the smile lingering about his lips, "but that is something we shall never know."

"I'd say that what is really important is not, if you will excuse the expression, what is in the past. If you can defeat Howard now, that is what will ultimately count."

He ignored her attempt at palliating what he was determined to regard as failure. "When we get to the console, we have to enter a sequence that will recalibrate the gate. We'll be incapacitated in minutes inside that." He indicated the chaos lapping at their feet. "You were phenomenally lucky you made it out again the last time. We stand a better chance of success if we each do half."

He explained the sequence necessary to stabilize the gate. Virginia repeated it over for him until her tongue began to stumble. Finally he nodded and stood up, extending his hand, intending to pull her to her feet. She shook her head.

"No. This way. It makes up in stability what it lacks in dignity." She drew in a deep breath and crawled into the time corridor.

She did not try to look at him as they made their way on hands and knees up that corridor through eternity. She knew he was there, struggling as she was against the madness. When she reached the gate console, the maelstrom howling around her had permeated every nerve ending she possessed. She was paralyzed until she felt his hand on her wrist, hauling her up and over the console. She forced her fingers, all tens of thousands of them, to locate what she could only pray were the right buttons. She did not look at them, for vision only communicated madness. In her mind's eye she saw the console, the rows of buttons and touch pads. She heard Roma's voice, *the top row, left to right, in this order*, and she entered the sequence with shaking fingers. She had fallen before the hurricane of sound around her began to die, leaving behind a silence so profound she could hear her own heartbeat. She opened her eyes.

He was leaning over the console, his eyes closed. She wondered if her own face was as white as his. No, she corrected herself, *green.*

Roma cleared his throat slightly. "Thank you, Dr. Alexander."

"Anytime."

He was surprised into a laugh, and she joined him, although a little shakily. She drew in a deep breath, cringing a little at the renewed pain in her head.

He looked around the room. The time grid showed twenty gate lights active, where there had been only one. Howard had reactivated the gates. He leaned against the console, and tried to think. That crawling journey through displaced time drained energy from the body like water through a sieve. Then he pushed himself upright.

"With just a little luck, that will last a while. Perhaps time enough to find the dissolution sequence."

The console lights flashed, and he looked at it, frowning and shaking his head.

She looked curiously at the pad, bathed in light shining down from a large opening in the ceiling.

"What's up there?"

"The crystal matrix."

"Could I see it?"

He shrugged.

He stood up and walked to the wall behind the console. At a touch of his hand, a panel slid back. He motioned her inside.

The sudden smooth movement upward should not have startled her, but it did. When the door opened, she found she could not move.

The room curved over her head in a smooth black dome. Like the face of heaven, it was jeweled by a million stars, points of light that sent beams cutting through space at every angle and into the heart of the thing that lay suspended in the center. Great spars of opalescent crystal crossed and recrossed, forming an intricate web that drew the light from its own overhead galaxy into itself. Pulses of light shot through the crystal like trails of fire. The air rang.

She swallowed, looking at the impossible, beautiful, terrible artifact from the future.

There was an intricate series of catwalks and ladders running through the matrix. Eyeing the narrow walkways, she followed him, gritting her teeth against the crystal vibration that sang along her nerves.

Roma was climbing up one of the ladders, edging his way out on a catwalk overhanging the matrix. The air seemed alive.

"What would happen if you touched the crystal?" she asked.

He looked around, amused. "Nothing."

She ran a hand along the side of one of the crystal spars, half expecting it to feel hot, or give off a shock. It was cool, satin-smooth to the touch. Something nagged at her memory. It was hard to think, with the subsonic ring in her teeth and bones and muscles, and most of all in her head. *This is a time machine*, she thought, catching her breath on the thought. And Roma, crawling across that arching bridge of bright crystal, is actually crawling across the fabric of time.

In the center of the matrix a circular railing enclosed an open space, probably thirty feet across. Looking down into this well she felt her stomach roil. Indescribable colors and forms and sounds all writhed together. Below the shifting of being and nonbeing she could see the gate pad, looking small and insignificant under a canopy of eternity.

"It's time, isn't it?" she asked, awed. "You can *see* time."

"Yes. It's the formation and dissolution of event strings."

"What would happen if you fell into that?"

He shook his head. "You don't even want to think about it."

She imagined stepping off, dropping down into that place where time shifted and dissolved and was never fully realized. Vertigo drove her back from the edge.

"Roma," she said slowly, an idea forming just beyond her consciousness.

He looked down at her.

Several things happened at once. In one quick, fluid movement Roma slid off his perch and dropped down beside her, his hand sweeping across her mouth. Her head snapped backward against the unforgiving crystal spar, and she went down, pain exploding behind her eyes. Roma, crouched beside her, had his disrupter leveled at something on the other side of the matrix. *Not something*, she thought hazily. Someone. She squinted in the direction the disrupter pointed, but could see nothing.

Finally he lowered his hand and looked down at her.

"Sorry," he said.

She sat up, clutching her ringing head. "You nearly exploded my head," she said furiously. "What did you think you were doing?"

"I saw . . . thought I saw something." He was scanning the shimmering web around them with narrowed eyes.

"What did you think you saw?" she demanded, but he ignored her.

"Roma," she said quietly, "what did you think you saw?"

He looked up and made a dismissive gesture. "Nothing. A shadow. You said you've seen them yourself. I'm sorry I startled you."

Startled her. The anger she felt was almost as painful as the lump on her head.

"We don't have time to debate shadows," he said impatiently. "We have to find the power crystals. Time is running out."

"Is the gate stable enough to use? To find the crystals, I mean?"

"It depends. We've stabilized it somewhat, and stopped it from throwing out waves of time displacement. It would probably accept coordinates for one of the gates, because the link on the other side would also stabilize the transfer. But if he hid the crystals somewhere without a gate, we'd never make it. We'd need at least one of the power crystals for that, and both of them to begin the dissolution sequence."

# Chapter 34

## 1357 B.C.E.
## Abydos

They went back to the control room. He was eyeing the gate, his expression unreadable. Suddenly he opened a panel in the console and pulled out a square black casing about eleven inches square.

"What is that?" she asked curiously.

"This," he said, tucking it under his arm, "is the coordinate interface module."

"And that means?"

"It means that no one can enter coordinates into the console and use the gate."

She digested this in silence. Gradually her face began to burn.

"But we are the only ones here."

"Perhaps. Or not. Either way, no one is using the gate."

She spun on her heel, intent on stalking out into the corridor. But he caught her arm, not ungently, before she could reach the door.

"I'm sorry. We have to stay together."

"So you can watch me? So I won't steal that coordinates thing and use the gate to go God knows where to do God knows what?"

"I wasn't thinking that."

"What then? That I'm in league with Howard and will give him the module? After I overpower you, of course."

His mouth lifted a trifle. "I really wasn't thinking that. Security is what I do, Dr. Alexander. It's who I am."

She felt, suddenly, that she would do almost anything to wipe that lurking suspicion out of his eyes.

"Fine. Have it your way."

He looked at her speculatively.

"You listened to all the journal entries?"

The sudden change of subject made her stammer. "All I could find," she said cautiously.

"Tell me about Lantis's last few entries."

She settled down to remember. "He said that Howard had promised to give Lantis and Daedalus the power crystals to shut down the gate. He said Howard insisted they check the gate once more before he would give them the crystals. Rather a transparent ruse, I thought, to get them there so he could . . . But they were so . . . terribly tired," she finished gently.

Roma was silent for a moment. "If it seemed transparent to you, it would also have seemed so to Daedalus and Lantis. I think they knew what he would do, or try to do."

"Perhaps they hoped to be able to persuade him, or stop him, or something."

He shook his head. "Not likely. I'll have to listen to the journals myself. Starting with Howard. Then we'll move on to Lantis. It's somewhere. We'll find it."

He did not sound terribly hopeful, in spite of his words,

but she made no comment.

They were in Howard's quarters, looking for any clues that would tell them where to look for the missing crystals, or the dissolution sequence. With a quick glance at her face, he put one of the memory crystals into Howard's reader. When Howard's recorded self appeared it was clear from the look on Roma's face that he had not, until this moment, accepted her story that she had accessed the journal entries.

"He must have found a way to disable the privacy locks," he said finally.

"Why did he leave his own entries open?"

He shook his head. "It's an interlinked system. If he disabled the lock function, he may not have been able to protect his own journals. Or, whatever happened to him may have caught him by surprise. Something permanent, I hope."

Roma, his mouth set in a very tight line, listened to all of Howard's journal entries. Virginia had tried to occupy her mind with searching through the chests of treasure, shutting out the beautiful, compelling voice and its tale of obsession and betrayal. Hours passed, and Roma went through the computer files, all the data crystals. Finally he jerked his chair around in frustration.

"Nothing. There is nothing here that shouldn't be here. No odd little notes, no strange additions to the files. I've even read his treatises on archaeology. My intelligence program can discern no pattern that might denote a cipher or code. As if I haven't heard enough about the glories of the past to last me several lifetimes."

Virginia was looking at a small chest she had found. It was Egyptian, a cedar box inlaid with gold and semiprecious stones. The top portrayed the Aten, the sun disk elevated by Akhenaten to supremacy, supplanting all the other gods of Egypt.

She opened the box and gasped.

Roma looked up, surprised.

"The *Ban of Akhenaten*," she said, her voice such a mixture of emotions it was unrecognizable. She held up a small papyrus scroll.

He waited.

"I found it. That is, I will find this scroll, here at Abydos. In the old temple. It will be the most important find of my career."

His gaze grew intent. "He mentions that particular scroll, here in his notes."

She got up then, and read the entry over his shoulder. In addition to Howard's notes there was a visual replica of the scroll's hieroglyphic text.

"Except," she said after a moment, "it's wrong."

"Wrong?"

"The text. It is incorrect."

"Howard is the most famous archaeologist of our time. You're saying he made a mistake translating this document?"

"I don't see how he could have made a mistake, either. There are several lines here that don't exist in the original. He must have added them deliberately."

She took the papyrus over to the screen and smoothed

it beside the replica.

"See, here it says *Thou art lovely, great, glittering high above every land, thy rays encompass the lands unto the extent of all that thou hast made! Thou art Ra, thou reachest unto their end, and subjectest them to thy beloved son Akhenaten. Thou art afar off, yet thy rays are upon earth.* All correct. But these columns," she indicated a vertical series of characters on the viewscreen, "do not exist in the original."

He peered at the two documents, and she sensed a stirring of interest.

"You're certain."

"I lived with this text for four years. I'm certain."

She began to read the insertion.

*What then didst thou do with the flame of fire and with the tablet of crystal after thou didst bury them? I uttered words over it, I adjured it, and I extinguished the fire.*

To this point, the text is an accurate transcription of a passage out of the *Book of the Dead*. Accurate, but bearing no relationship to the *Ban of Akhenaten*. But *this*," her finger indicated another row, "occurs in no text I am aware of."

"Couldn't he have found a text that had not been discovered in your time?"

"Certainly. No doubt Howard had a truckload of such texts." She tried to keep the bitterness out of her voice. "This one doesn't make sense. *The arrow delivered by the outstretched arm of my brother shall be nothing. Before the Ennead who have bolted the door over his hand, he shall be nothing. Though he has strength like an eagle, a bull (or perhaps maleness, or again phallus) like strong cord binding the offerings, he shall be received like an asp, held above his hand. Like a star residing in emptiness.*

"What does it mean?"

"Nothing."

She saw hope fading, and frustration growing in the hazel eyes.

"I thought you said—"

"Oh, I can tell you what it *says*," she said with emphasis, "But it doesn't *mean* anything. It's written in the style of *A Tale of Two Brothers*, but I suspect it is not a genuine text. It's a jumble of phrases. The whole thing just sounds . . . wrong."

The interest flickered and died. "You are suggesting," he began, disbelief clear in his voice, "that because this text is not familiar to you that it is some kind of code? You can't even fathom the possibility that they may come from some Egyptian text you have never heard of."

"Mr. Roma," she said haughtily, never realizing she was echoing Howard's own exasperated form of address, "I do not question your expertise in your field. I am prepared to take your word on security devices and martial arts and getting the drop on the bad guys. Even under the circumstances," she could not resist adding nastily, and had the satisfaction of seeing him flush. "On the other hand, I am a very good Egyptologist. Perhaps you should consider according me the same respect. This text does not belong here. It *must* mean something."

"This can have no relevance. Even if you are right and this is not a genuine text, Howard would have no reason to write down the location of the crystals disguised as an

Egyptian document. He *knows* where he put them. We're looking for something else."

A further exhaustive search produced no further evidence, no clue to the location of the missing crystals. It seemed they had reached an impasse.

As the afternoon wore on, Virginia became aware that the sense of *wrongness* was creeping over her, shadowing her thoughts. She became more edgy. The headache was back, worse than before. It made thinking even more difficult.

"I'm going to Lantis's quarters," Roma said, abandoning the search through Howard's notes. He barely glanced at her in his desire to be out of Howard's room.

ᘛ ᘛ ᘛ

"Empty out that chest. We're looking for anything that might be a message." He sat down to listen to the last entries in Lantis's journal.

Virginia took items first out of the chest Roma indicated, and then the others. There were no crystals at all, except for the ones in the box Roma was exploring. He went methodically through the journal, without finding anything. Except, she thought, seeing the expression in his eyes, deepening pain. He had, after all, known these people, even cared about them. If these messages had the power to haunt her dreams, what must it be like for him?

*It's hard to think about going back . . . without the others. Even harder to believe that we are responsible for destroying the very thing we came here to save. We came here with such high hopes. Vincent always said all the truest answers were to be found not in science, but in art. . . .*

Roma looked away from the image of Lantis, sitting so close to him yet separated by the unbridgeable gap between reality and simulation. He took the memory crystal out of the reader, and drew a deep breath as Lantis faded away.

"If there is a message here I can't find it. There's nothing on any of these crystals that could contain a complex series of matrix settings. Howard would hardly have left them if they did. I've scanned for a crystal signature hidden in the room. All the rooms. Nothing. This is pointless."

"Perhaps Daedalus?"

He brought his fist crashing suddenly down onto the shelf, and the holder of crystals jumped and spilled. After a second, his control reasserted itself and he stood up.

"Yes. Perhaps Daedalus."

He turned away, then abruptly squatted down, gathering the scattered crystals and putting them back in the rack.

Something that had been nagging at the back of her mind suddenly came together.

"Roma."

He looked up, the crystals in his hands.

"Not Daedalus. Vincent."

"Vincent was gone before Lantis and Daedalus put together the sequence."

"And so Howard would not think to look in his room. Lantis mentions Vincent in the last line of the entry. It has to be there."

ᘛ ᘛ ᘛ

In minutes they were in Vincent's room. Roma's face looked as if it had been carved out of stone as he looked at the room, so cluttered yet somehow so empty.

"There aren't many journal entries," she remarked, looking at the few crystals near the viewer.

"No," his expression softened a little. "I was always after him to make more regular reports." He picked up a drawing, fallen onto the floor, and laid it on the shelf.

"I was thinking," she began, "the drawings are all he really cared about. The others, they all had art objects created by others, or weapons, or scientific tools, whatever. Vincent had nothing much except his drawings. They're quite lovely." She was looking down at a drawing of a fantastic machine, with whimsical winged creatures surrounding it. Vincent had amused himself by adding longhand notes to it, written backwards. She felt a sudden, intolerable stinging in her eyes and she put the drawing gently back on the pile.

"His room's a mess," she said, laughing shakily to cover her emotion.

Roma was looking at the bed. It hadn't been made. Unlike all the others. Even in the midst of the disasters, the terror, each of the travelers had left their rooms with things in order, and the beds made. Except Vincent. It spoke so poignantly of a life cut short, taken by surprise.

"He got up," he said slowly, and she heard a note in his voice that made her take a step backward. "He got up in the night, and went out. He expected to come back. But he didn't. That bloody bastard found him and sent him through the gate!"

For a moment he literally shook with rage. Gradually, he got himself under control again.

"Let's get on with it," he said curtly, turning to the small collection of memory crystals. He played the few journal entries, and Virginia avoided looking at Roma's face, busying herself with searching Vincent's storage chests. Drawing materials, paper, a few data crystals Roma identified as reference materials. Nothing that resembled a clue to the missing power crystals or the dissolution sequence. When she had looked at Vincent's few possessions, she cradled her aching head in her hands.

Roma reached the end of the journal entries, and Vincent's image faded for the last time.

"That's all. There are no more crystals." He looked at her, then looked again.

"You look terrible."

"Thank you," she said caustically.

A fraction of a smile touched his lips. "Why is it that women, sitting on the edge of disaster, can still care how they look?"

"It's a gene pool thing," she replied with dignity.

He snorted, and stood up. "Maybe I'll find something that we've overlooked. I'll check Daedalus's quarters, too. We know they were working together, at the end. Perhaps Howard missed something when he was cleaning up. You look like you should try to get some rest."

She looked around at the haunted room. "Not here. I'll go back to . . . back." Back to that austere soldier's cell, uncluttered by possessions or obsessions. At least, she amended silently with regard to the latter, none she recognized or understood.

He made no comment, merely motioning her to the door. Together they walked through the labyrinth as though he were seeing her home. When they reached his room he scanned it closely, set the security system, and left. She felt no indignation over his locking her in. Whether he did it to protect her or himself, she didn't care. Without hesitation she lay down on the hard bed and closed her eyes. The dangers here would come, awake or asleep. The two states were not all that different of late.

# Part X

## All in Good Time

# Chapter 35

## 1357 B.C.E.
## Abydos

Images of destruction darkened Virginia's dreams—boiling light and crawling walls and moaning ghosts flitting through the shadows that lurked around the edges. Howard's face, dark and handsome as he contemplated his treasures, illumined from within by his own fires, smiled raptly at her and mouthed the nonsense phrase he had added to the *Ban*. A man stood at the edge of the sea, counting the waves as they crashed on the shore. He had paper and pen in his hand, and was drawing furiously, throwing the papers over his shoulder as soon as they were finished. He turned then, and looked at her accusingly out of Lantis's luminous blue eyes.

"You see," he was saying bitterly, "time will die now, ages without number, and the art of truth with it."

Then the sky darkened and a woman's face shone against the clouds. Her mouth was open, screaming in intolerable pain, her eyes bright and cold and deadly, and her head was a mass of writhing serpents. It was her own face.

She sat up, wide awake, trembling with excitement. She heard soft breathing in the darkness, and relief washed over her.

"Roma, thank God! I think I've figured out . . . lights!"

Before her eyes could adjust to the sudden blaze of light, a brutal hand clamped over her mouth with such force it nearly snapped her neck. She clawed at it, until his other hand came up behind her head, and his grip tightened warningly. She found herself looking into the eyes of Dr. John Howard, who smiled down at her. If she moved again, those fathomless dark eyes promised, he would crush her jaw without regret. He read acknowledgment in her face, and released her. Drawing the chair up to the bedside, he sat down.

"Dr. Alexander, I presume," he said in his beautiful voice.

"How do you know who I am?" she asked, furious that her voice came out a shaken whisper.

"I know because I have been in the labyrinth, watching you and your irritating friend ever since Roma so obligingly recalibrated the gate. I, too, was caught in time. But I had a functioning transcomp with me when you performed that service. All I needed was just that little moment of stability to finish the transfer. And there I was. And there you were. So very . . . busy. In fact, Roma nearly saw me, in the matrix.

"And now," he continued, "we come to the crux of the matter. You'll understand that I can't do with your interference. It's a pity, certainly, because you have been quite entertaining so far. But all good things come to an end."

*He's going to kill me.* The thought streaked through her mind like lightening. *Dear God, he is going to kill me.* Nothing comes as quite such a shock as the realization of mortality.

"What possible harm can I do you?" she asked, trying to keep her voice steady and reasonable.

"Ultimately, none at all. In the interim, however, you are becoming a serious nuisance, one I do not have time for. Now I propose to take you for a little walk, to a place where you will be quite safe if you do what I tell you. And while we walk, you will tell me about the dissolution sequence."

She drew back against the wall, praying that Roma would come soon. "I know nothing about it," she began.

"I think you do," he replied, and the look in his eyes was anything but pleasant.

"But I don't! We couldn't find it. If you've been watching, then you know that."

"As you say, I have been watching you. In the room just now when you woke up with Roma's name on your lips. Very touching. Since he's not here to tell just what it is that you've figured out, I think you shall have to make do with me."

"But it wasn't about that," she began.

He jerked her roughly to her feet, and pulled a disrupter out of his belt. He brought the muzzle to her cheek, and she flinched away from the touch of cold death on her face. "Now, if you make any noise out there, or try to run, or do anything at all except what I tell you, I will kill you. Do you understand?"

She nodded, unable to trust her voice.

"Good. Then I think we will continue this conversation elsewhere."

He pressed the disrupter against the side of her head,

warning her to silence. They were in the corridor now, heading away from Daedalus's room, away from Roma, toward the dark center of the labyrinth. Their footsteps were muffled in the dead air. Virginia dismissed any idea of struggling, and concentrated on counting the turns.

She had arrived at twenty when Howard produced a powerful handlight. They had left the light behind. The hallways grew rougher, narrower, and the air much warmer. Soon she was breathless. They must be deep in the mountain. Once she caught a glimpse of a shadowy opening across the floor of a corridor crossing the one they traveled. A pit, waiting for the unwary, the unbeliever. She wondered idly what was in bottom of this one. They turned into a large open space, so large the far side was untouched by the powerful light he carried. Something about the space made her uneasy.

Howard did not share her discomfort. "This is better. It would be unfortunate if Roma interrupted us before we finish our talk. For both of you."

"He's not drugged anymore, you know," she poured scorn into her voice. "You think you'd be a match for him now?"

His expression was one of genuine astonishment.

"Tell me, Dr. Alexander," he said, laughing softly, "is Roma aware of this quite touching, and I have to say, inexplicable faith you have in his powers? What on earth do you base it on?"

When she didn't answer, he laughed again, and motioned for her to sit down on one of the huge blocks of stone that littered the floor. She ignored him.

"Not that I didn't find him useful," he went on, still smiling. "He can be rather formidable. In fact, at one time I considered enlisting his support. But then, there is that tiresome Persean code he lives by. Bleak. Inflexible. I'm sure you must have noticed it. They're supposed to be quite incorruptible."

"You don't believe it?"

"No one is incorruptible. It's a question of discovering the right incentive. In Roma's case, I found I didn't have the time."

She looked away, letting her eyes wander to the edges of the light. What would it take to get away from him? Howard had walked through the labyrinth with the sureness of familiarity. How would she find her way out of this lightless trap without him? Would it be better to fall down one of the pits outside than take whatever Howard offered? On the whole, she decided, it would.

"Now," he said, as if reading her thoughts and finding them amusing, "if you have quite finished assessing your chances of escape, perhaps we can talk about the dissolution sequence."

"I told you, I don't know where it is. We didn't find it." She didn't mention the obvious, that Roma might be finding it while Howard was wasting time here with her.

He sighed. "You woke up saying you had figured it out. Please don't make me remind you of that again."

"But that had nothing to do with the dissolution sequence! It was about Vincent."

"Vincent?" He sounded puzzled.

"Yes. I think I know where he went."

"You can't expect me to be very satisfied with that," he said ironically. "I already know where Vincent went."

*But not the significance of it, I'll bet*, she thought.

"That's all it was," she insisted.

He shook his head. "You expect me to believe that you woke up in a state of excited discovery over the whereabouts of someone you have never met, who means nothing to you?"

She realized then that it was pointless to tell him, to explain. Even if she succeeded in convincing him, it might, in some obscure way, be dangerous.

"You're boring me, Dr. Alexander. And wasting my time. Tell me where it is."

"I don't know!" she yelled in exasperation.

He looked at her for a long moment. "You know," he said, his gaze softening, "this is really all so unnecessary. You have been listening to the babblings of frightened and misinformed people whose own hysteria and lack of discipline brought this chaos upon us all. It is convenient to have a scapegoat when things beyond your ken go awry, so naturally they blamed me. I am not a violent man. I will use force, when necessary. But only then. I have no real intention of hurting you. But you must see, Roma is incapable of making the logical, correct choice about the gate. He is obsessed with the necessity for shutting it down, for destroying the matrix."

"It is destroying time."

"Yes!" he said, his voice echoing in the empty space around him. "But it can be stopped. Fixed. We know, now, what is wrong. It doesn't have to be destroyed; that's insane! Give up what we have learned here? Give up my work?"

"Give up the loot?" she asked mildly, watching the disrupter.

"I will make you see!" he cried, and she heard genuine anguish in his voice. For a moment she thought he would fire. When he didn't, she nodded slowly and sat down. He sat opposite her, propping the handlight next to him so they were islanded in a pool of light.

"Throughout time," he began, as if lecturing to an appreciative audience instead of a captive one, "there have been the many who live in history and the few who make history. Do you agree?"

"Perhaps."

"You do agree, Dr. Alexander," he said earnestly. "You are a scholar. You are a student of history. You are quite annoyingly bright," he added with a charming smile, "though your personal judgment is clouded at present. Still. I am very impressed with what you have accomplished. I don't know that I have ever encountered anyone with just your combination of intelligence and . . . well, let's call it intuition."

"Thank you," she said dryly.

"I don't suppose," he said thoughtfully, the dark eyes watchful, "that I could persuade you to abandon your quite misplaced investment in Gianni Roma and, shall we say, come over to my side? After all, I doubt if he could ever appreciate your potential."

She let her astonishment show. "What can you possibly imagine I would be able to do?" She could have bitten out her tongue the minute the words were out. His smile deepened.

"I am one of those who will not occupy history but make it. Literally. I have the power to do what no other man has ever been able to do. I have the ability, within my grasp, to understand history. Not just this little event, or that small consequence, but understand the great pattern that is history in all its infinite variety. The man who understands a thing controls it. I will control time, Dr. Alexander. May I call you Virginia?"

"Please do." She strove to keep the sarcasm out of her voice.

"Thank you. Now I invite you to consider the consequences of controlling history. Haven't you ever thought about what it would be like to live without war? Without famine? Without disease? To see all the creative energy the human race is capable of put to constructive rather than destructive use? That can happen, now, because one man exists who can control history. Who can determine the appropriate, the optimum choices, however many times it is necessary to achieve the desired ends. Divisiveness can be done away with in all its forms, and humanity can be welded into a unified force. All that is best, finest, most worthy of praise. Humanity will be exalted." His voice throbbed with passionate sincerity. She could almost hear the crowds roaring.

*All that is best*, she thought, *according to the fanatic standards of John Howard*. The rest would be weeded out. *Chosen* out of existence.

She swallowed, listening to the voice that was like black velvet, deep, silky and caressing.

"Virginia, even a man with a great vision requires help. The ranks here have thinned out, as you will have noticed."

"So you propose to make do with me?"

He shook his head. "You undervalue yourself. Not that I want you to run away with the idea that I need you, particularly. Or, whatever Roma's reactions may have been, that I will fall so far under your spell that I will . . . shall we say, lose sight of the essentials. I have achieved what I have because I am able to keep everything in perspective, and people, by and large, do not really interest me personally. I think you have the potential to be the exception."

The really terrifying thing, she thought, was how many people would be led by that silken voice into following. It had happened in history many times, but it would never happen again, after this one last time. John Howard would sway, solicit, seduce, and people would flock to his banner. There were plenty of people who wanted uniformity over diversity, purity over compassion and acceptance. Oh, yes, it would sell. Even as she loathed his words, she felt the pull of his personal magnetism and charisma.

"I don't want to be left here in the dark," she said, allowing a tremor in her voice. She watched him taking pleasure in her fear. If she had ever had the slightest idea of signing on with Howard the Mad, that would have killed it stone dead.

"As I see it," he said easily, "you have two options. You can tell me what I want to know, as a token of your good faith. We can then leave here together. I will even spare the life of the noble but wooden-headed Persean. That option would be my first choice, Virginia, because you really are very beautiful and very beguiling. I've been thinking of who it is you remind me of, and I think I've got it. Nefertiti, 'The Beautiful One Has Come,'" he quoted. "The same lovely long neck, the same delicacy, the tilt to the eyes, except of course, her hair and eyes were dark.

Or, you can continue to refuse, in which case I may have to leave you here to think it over. And, yes, in the dark. Actually, there is a third option. As beautiful as she was, as fascinating as Akhenaten may have found her, he almost certainly took this option when The Beautiful One displeased him for one reason or another. He broke her lovely neck and found a new queen. When the need is great enough, everyone is expendable."

"Everyone except you."

He inclined his head with a smile. "As you say. Now what is it to be?"

She dropped her eyes for a moment, as if considering. As she didn't know the location of the sequence, he was obviously going to be displeased. The question was, would she survive his displeasure?

"I'm waiting for your answer. But not for much longer." His voice was dark, annoyed that it was taking her so long to make what was obviously the only possible decision.

*What answer can I give him that won't get me killed?*

The answer presented itself with sinuous grace. If it had been false, if there had been nothing behind it but pretense, it would have failed. But when she looked into the bright, deadly gaze lifting up behind Howard and screamed, her sincerity was absolutely convincing. Its quavering echo reverberated off the stone walls. Howard jerked around and dove for the floor, firing the disrupter at the snake in the same motion. The explosion sent shattered rock and roasted cobra up in a foul cloud between them. It also shattered Howard's handlight. It flicked through her mind that if the cobra had finished positioning for its strike before she screamed, Howard would be dead. Bad timing. On that thought she was running into the darkness.

*Osiris, let me have counted correctly*, she pleaded, knowing Howard would be only a few steps behind her. He had been on his feet before she cleared the doorway. Her outflung hand brushed along the wall, telling her when she came to a crossing. She threw herself around corners with confidence born of desperation. There was a moment when she believed that she was going to make it back to the lighted corridors. She could see ahead, not actual light, but a slight lifting of the darkness. A shot from his disrupter, aimed up the corridor in the direction of her running footsteps, crashed off the wall ahead. He would have seen her in the flash. She dived into a side corridor just ahead of the next blast, and felt the stinging fragments of rock stab into her legs and back. Then she hit something hard, and with a soul-killing roar the world fell in around her.

# Chapter 36

## 1357 B.C.E.
## Abydos

*If I hadn't been running so fast*, she thought through the haze of pain, *I would be dead and this would be over. For me*. When she was reasonably certain that the rest of the corridor was not going to come down on top of her, she dragged herself out from under the debris. She knew what had happened; she was running hard when she struck the edge of a collapsing wall and her momentum had carried her past the main fall. If she had been moving cautiously, she would be under it. Her mind veered away from the image of what those huge stone slabs would have left of her body. Her lungs told her the air was full of dust and rock fragments, and she strove not to cough, not to make a sound. Howard might be dead beneath the fall, but somehow she doubted it. She reached out both hands and explored the darkness. Inches from her body lay several tons of rock mixed with bricks from the ceiling. She was on the wrong side of an appalling barrier. She could go down the corridor in which she now stood, and try to find her way around. But it was one she had never been in, and she knew that unless she was very lucky, she would not be able to find her way back through the darkness to the cross corridor the deadfall now blocked. The way out.

She stretched on tip-toe and could not feel the top. She moved sideways, trying to think. Then, miraculously, a tiny thread of light flowered through the chinks between the slabs of the fall. Not miraculous, she realized, but only the would-be ruler of history, coming to have another try at killing her. He was on the other side of the barrier, and he had another light.

Rocks and dust tumbled out into the hallway near one wall. The fall must be lower there, and thinner. He would be through in moments. The majority of the fall was made up of huge slabs of stone, wedged tightly from wall to wall. If she could climb it, she would be out of the range of his light. She might even be able to climb over the barrier. *Climb*? All the demons of her fear settled on her back and she shook. She threw a hunted glance down the black corridor behind her. Howard would be behind her with a light and a disrupter. She could not keep far enough ahead of him for long. He knew the labyrinth here, and she didn't. It was certain death to move down that corridor, and she knew it, imagining the disrupter's effect on her unprotected back.

A sound from the barrier, the sound of Howard's malevolent nearness, drove the phobic fear from her mind. Making her decision, she bent down and pulled off her boots, thrusting them out of sight among the loose debris at the bottom of the fall. As silently as bare feet allowed, she went up the fallen stones like a cat. *This is suicide*, she thought fleetingly; *the stones haven't had time to settle. The whole thing could collapse. With any luck, on top of Howard.*

She stifled a yelp as her foot came in contact with the sharp edge of stone. *No blood,* she prayed. *He'll see it.*

She went up the barrier with a speed driven by panic and a sure-footedness she could never have achieved under normal circumstances. She was almost in the dark now, moving above the range of the small flickers of light penetrating the barrier from below. Desperately she felt above her for a small opening, a ledge that jutted out, anything that would shield her from below. But it wasn't going to work, she realized. There was another crash nearby, and she heard a soft expletive. *Dear God, he's nearly through.*

She took a cautious step sideways, feeling with scraped fingers for any sign of an opening. Almost dead center of the corridor she found a slab that formed a small ledge. Laughably small, and almost out of reach. The rock she stood on shifted under her weight. Assuming she could get to it, was there any chance at all she could elude Howard's vengeful search?

Two things happened simultaneously. Howard stepped out into the corridor twenty feet below her, just as she hauled herself onto the ledge. The stone she had been standing on fell forward and down, setting off a small avalanche of the looser stuff. On hands and knees, she swayed perilously on the ledge, then felt it tilt underneath her. She slithered forward across the ledge, stopping herself just before her shoulders went over the edge.

It was a ridiculous position, and one that was going to be virtually impossible to sustain. She was clamped onto the tilted stone, canted outward and down. Howard's last push brought a rain of small stones out with him, merging with the ones she sent down as her treacherous perch settled into its appalling new angle.

He shone the small handlight across the barrier, and down the hallway. If it had been strong enough to reach the ceiling, he would have seen her. As it was, he looked up into darkness, speculating on the height of the fall even as she had done. She froze against the stone, the blood rushing to her head. *Don't black out*, she warned herself. *Don't make a sound. The consequences would be bad.*

"Virginia?" said Howard to the darkness. She held her breath, and willed her heartbeat to quiet. "This is childish. You can't possibly get away. This corridor leads to a dead end. I have only to outwait you."

He moved a little way down the corridor, the light lifted high. It did not reach to the end. She could feel him wondering. Was she down there, cowering against a wall? Or was she hidden in the rocks of the fall? His instincts were good. He turned and came back to the uneasily piled stone. She had to remind herself that though she could see his face quite clearly, he could not see her. Unless he climbed up.

"Virginia," he said again. "You are out of time. In another moment only the third option will remain."

*As if there had ever been any others*, she thought grimly. *Roma, where the hell are you? You have to have heard the sound of all that falling rock.*

Again, the uncanny reading of her thoughts.

"Hoping for rescue? I can hardly wait for him to try. In

spite of everything, I really don't want to kill you, Virginia. I'd much rather kill Roma."

The silence suddenly enraged him. He began to talk, then, and the beautiful voice told her exactly what he was going to do to her when he found her. His words crawled over her skin, and she longed to cover her ears, but dared not lose her hold on the treacherous stone slab. Her head pounded unbearably, and she knew she was going to pass out. Her fingers and toes were numb, and in another minute she would lose her grip and fall out and down. And then she would die.

A new terror gave strength to her failing hold. *Roma.* He would come, was already on his way, unaware of Howard's presence in the labyrinth. He would be hurrying, probably with a handlight to give away his position. He would turn the corner, and in that moment of exposure Howard would shoot him.

Disrupter fire exploded a foot from her body, and she barely retained her hold, swallowing a cry as flying rock shards hit her. Howard the hunter, trying to flush her out. Like a wild, hunted thing she tried to merge her body into the stone, waiting for the next shot to bring down the wall around her. She prayed, and if God and Osiris and even Roma were all jumbled together, she could only hope her plea would reach the correct ears in the end.

She drew in a breath, to shout a warning for Roma as soon as she heard him, knowing it would probably be the last sound she ever made.

Then she heard Howard's footsteps as he turned and

moved down the corridor. The light dimmed and was gone. He didn't come back. *It must not be a dead end*, she thought. *Liar.*

She must have passed out in the darkness after all, if only for a moment. When she opened her eyes, Roma's face was almost on a level with her own.

"Wake up," he was saying. "I need your help."

She tried to nod, but found she was paralyzed.

"Howard," she tried to say, but it came out a whimper.

"I know," he said softly, "I heard him talking. Fortunately he still loves the sound of his own voice, so he didn't hear me coming."

There was a small handlight clipped to his belt, and he was climbing with one hand, keeping one eye and his disrupter trained on the corridor behind him. There was a sizable gap between them, left by the falling and shifting of stone she had caused in her crazy ascent. The stone all around them was unsteady.

He pulled himself up another foot. Pushing his disrupter into the holster, he stretched out an arm.

"Okay, give me your hand."

"I can't."

"You can. Do it now," he said sternly.

She gritted her teeth and pried her fingers loose, extending her hand a few inches.

"Further!"

She stretched her arm, and felt herself sliding toward the drop. His fingers closed over hers.

"Let go with your other hand."

"No," she cried, trying to dig fingers and toes into solid rock.

"Let go!" he roared, and jerked her loose.

She slid off the rock into space. The slab crashed down from beneath her, mercifully missing any others or they would have gone down in a massive rockslide. For one hideous moment she thought she was going to do a swan dive all the way to the floor. Then she found herself swinging from his hand right side up. The relief to her head as the blood started to flow the right direction almost made her forget the painful strain on her arm. Roma gathered his strength and pulled her around in a gentle arc until she faced the barrier and could force her aching hands and feet to find a hold among the stones.

"Now. You'll have to help me. Use your hands and feet. We're going down fast."

Somehow Virginia climbed down. Roma went down beside her, his hand never more than an inch from her own. She was not expecting the step that took her onto the floor, and it jarred her so badly she bit her tongue and her knees buckled. Then he was pushing her ruthlessly though the narrow opening between the rock fall and the side of the tunnel. She looked up the slope at the darkness above her and closed her eyes.

ꝏ ꝏ ꝏ

She did not remember one step of the journey back to Roma's room. She knew when they got there because he stopped and dropped to a crouch, dragging her down with him. The door opened and he commanded the lights, ready to fire if anything breathed in the room. It was empty. Once they were inside, he dropped her onto the bed and went to the hidden compartment in the wall. She watched him pulling some kind of equipment out and arranging it along the shelf near the computer viewscreen. He began to work at the computer, using a lightening fast combination of spoken words and hand signals. She heard "security," and "sensor net," and other things that would have been unintelligible even had she been fully conscious.

Then he was crawling around the room, passing an instrument of some kind over the floor and the walls. In the mural above the bed, just over his head, he found what he was looking for. He yanked another tool out of his belt and jammed it into the wall. There was a small electronic pop and he dropped something onto the floor.

"He must have been watching us from the beginning. All of us," he said. "And my sensor sweeps never discovered it."

Savagely he ground the thing beneath his heel.

Then the burst of activity was over. Virginia had followed it all with her eyes, not moving from where he had dumped her. She was utterly unaware that tears were streaming down her face.

"Drink this," Roma was saying. He raised her up, holding a glass to her lips. Her teeth chattered against it and her throat felt so constricted she was afraid she would drown.

"No, I don't want it," she muttered, trying to turn her head.

"Do what I tell you," he demanded.

"I am really tired of people telling me that," she said angrily, and saw he was laughing as he jammed the glass against her mouth. She opened her mouth and swallowed. It kicked her back into consciousness in two seconds flat.

After a few more swallows, she sat up and surveyed the damage. Her hands and feet were covered with cuts and bruises. She hurt in a dozen places where she had hit or been hit by falling rocks. The jumpsuit she wore was shredded from the edges of disrupter fire and splintered stone. There was blood everywhere.

"I've ruined your clothes," she said inadequately.

"I have more."

He helped her peel the jumpsuit off, and picked the rock fragments out of her back. Fortunately, most of them had lodged in the tough, protective fabric of the suit. He swabbed something from the medical kit over the cuts and bruises, and she was relieved that whatever it was didn't sting. Then he wrapped his black robe around her, and laid her, gently this time, back on the bed. She was asleep before he had drawn the blanket up to cover her.

# Chapter 37

## 1357 B.C.E.
## Abydos

When she opened her eyes Roma was standing over her, shaking her by the shoulder. It took a long moment before she recognized him.

"I was dreaming," she gasped.

"I noticed."

"Howard," she started to shake. "Where is he?"

He frowned in frustration. "I don't know. He's using some kind of damping field. The security sensors can't locate him. He did a pretty thorough job of raiding our equipment after he got rid of me. All but what I had hidden."

She tried to sit up and moaned as the impact of her rock-climbing expedition made itself felt.

"I feel like the bloody wall fell on me."

"You look terrible," he said, straight-faced.

"Thank you. I'll work on it."

He handed her a folded pile of clothing.

Another liberal dose of the drink he gave her the night before and she began to feel she might live.

"If you feel up to it, I'd like to hear about Howard." His tone was carefully neutral.

She swallowed, wishing for an irrational moment that

she need not remember.

"He got in here. I don't know how. I don't suppose you believe that."

"I do, as a matter of fact. I came back and saw the security lock had been opened. From the outside. Where had the bastard been? I should have known it was too much to hope that he was blasted into oblivion like all the others."

"He said the gate effect caught him just after I found the way into Amenti and left him trapped between times. Like you were. Except he had a functioning transcomp with him, so when you recalibrated the gate and it stabilized, he was able to complete his transfer. He's been here ever since, watching us."

"I hope he found it entertaining."

"He said he did," she said bitterly, and shivered. "He seems to think we found the dissolution sequence, and he wanted me to give it to him."

"If he's been watching our every move, why did he think we found it?"

"Roma, he was in here while I was sleeping. I woke up and heard him breathing. In the dark, I thought he was you. I said something that made him think I knew where the sequence was. Good God, I forgot to tell you! At least, I didn't forget, exactly, because so much happened after that, but—"

"Forgot what? What are you talking about?"

"Roma."

The excited lift in her voice pulled him a little way out of his dark abstraction.

"I want to show you sometning. In Vincent's room."

"The sequence wouldn't—"

"It isn't about that. It's something else. It would be easier if I could show you. I think you'll be glad. . . . "

He looked disbelieving, but made no objection. As they made ready to leave, he turned to the computer screen. It displayed a grid overlaying the map of the labyrinth. Small red lights winked from the rooms of the travelers, several corridors, and the gate control room. Malevolent little spying eyes, she guessed. Howard's eyes. Roma noticed her shiver.

"We'll deal with them," he promised grimly, picking up the disrupter, "and anything else we come across." His voice was quiet, and his tall body looked relaxed, but Virginia, looking into his eyes, was not misled. He was an armed weapon, every bit as deadly as the weapon he wore near his heart.

They wove a complex pattern through the labyrinth. Having transferred the sensor map to his transcomp, Roma took them in a seemingly random pattern through the corridors, finding and smashing the surveillance bugs. They went to the travelers' quarters beginning with Daedalus, then Lantis and Cassandra, and then Vincent. Seeing her about to speak, Roma shook his head and mouthed the words: "Not yet."

Roma looked around disbelieving, but made no objection.

Confronted again with the silent room littered with images from Vincent's imagination, his expression grew stonier. Before he would allow her to speak, he scanned the room for the surveillance bug he knew would be there. He found it and smashed it, with a violence that told her he was imagining something else underfoot.

They went to Temogen's room, and then to Howard's.

"Just in case he's as suspicious as I am," said Roma, sweeping the room. And, indeed, he found a bug buried near the viewscreen. Virginia looked at it wonderingly.

"In his own room?" she asked finally.

"He'd want to know if he had any uninvited visitors. As he violated the privacy of others, he would naturally assume his own was at risk."

When all the little electronic snoopers were reduced to dust, they returned to Vincent's room.

"All right. Show me whatever it is." *And get it over with.* He didn't exactly say it, but the words hung there in the air.

She picked up a handful of pages, covered with the lyrical drawings of intricate machines and smiling angelic faces.

"He was so good," she began.

"I suppose. I know very little about art." His tone suggested he didn't want to know more. "He was forever at it. It used to make Daedalus crazy. He wanted him to be all for science."

"Roma, listen. Look at these. Really look. Don't they remind you of anything?"

"I'll tell you what they remind me of," he said, his voice shaking. "They remind me that he's gone, dead probably, along with Cassandra and Lantis and all the others. Except Howard, and before God, I'll see that he pays for it. All these remind me of is how much Howard destroyed."

"It's everywhere. The smile on the woman's face . . . it's Cassandra, isn't it? The intricate machines, the winged creatures. Young, crude by comparison with what he will later achieve—even the mirror-writing. Think, Roma, about an illegitimate boy, unloved, unappreciated by his family, sent away from home to another town. An accident, he dies, there was plague everywhere then . . . something happens. Another boy, looking for somewhere to belong, someone to be, takes his place. In Verrocchio's workshop. Where he draws an angel so beautiful that the master will no longer work on the commission, because he perceives in the young apprentice a genius that far eclipses his own. Howard didn't destroy Vincent. He isn't dead. He has love, and honor, and when he does die . . . " her voice trembled, "he will have had more influence than perhaps any other artist in history. The world will mourn, and the great will stand at his deathbed. Legend has it, he will draw his last breath in the arms of a king." She dashed tears out of her eyes, holding up the drawings in her hand.

"Vincent?" He said it wonderingly, looking at the drawings. He nodded slowly, repeating the name they both knew, but hardly dared believe.

"It's probably the same for the others," she went on. "You've got to stop thinking of them as dead. They went somewhere in time, and they will live their lives. Not the lives they had planned, certainly. But like Lantis said, they have the advantage of knowing more about history. . . . "

He drew in a sudden breath, and cut across her words. "Lantis. What was it he said in his last journal entry?"

"That Howard had promised to give them the crystals and help restore time . . . that he wanted them to check—"

He waved her to silence, impatient. "No, not that. The part about Vincent."

She closed her eyes. He said Vincent believed that real truth was to be found not in science but in. . . .

Her voice trailed off, and she looked around the room in dawning comprehension.

"Art!" he finished for her, snatching up a handful of drawings. "We've been so certain Lantis would have left a memory crystal with the sequence. Crystals! We use them to store data, record information, everything. But Howard would have looked for the same. And Lantis, canny little engineer, would have known that! So he didn't leave the information on a crystal. He left it hidden in plain sight, a trick so ancient no one considered it! He left it on a piece of paper in the only place it would be unremarkable. Here, among the drawings."

He was gathering them up as he spoke, looking at each carefully.

"Are we looking for numbers?" she asked, staring at the drawings in her hand.

"Nothing so crude. Oh, the numbers will be on the paper, but probably not visible. Here!" He held up one of the fabulous, anachronistic machines. Deep among flywheels and levers rendered with a poetic love of form and shade was a small section of criss-crossed lines drawn with pedantic precision. A small section of lattice. Once noticed, it leaped to the eye that it was by a different hand.

"The lattice. This is it." He laughed, shaking his head. Then he looked up.

"Virginia. Thank you for telling me. About Vincent."

"He was . . . very dear," she said with a smile.

"My life does not permit me a family," he said slowly. "But he somehow . . . came close. Kin."

"You should be proud. Your boy very definitely made good. And I think he was happy, Roma. He got to be what he was meant to be."

He closed the distance between them and, putting a hand under her chin, lifted her face.

"I find it extraordinary, Dr. Alexander, that inside you are even more beautiful than you are outside." He was looking at her with an expression she had never expected to see in his eyes, and she said the first thing that came into her head.

"And Howard bet you'd never notice my potential."

He laughed softly, for a moment, against her mouth. "I hope he continues to underestimate me."

When he drew away from her, she felt as if every nerve ending in her body had lighted up like a roman candle. She was glad to see that he was having a little trouble breathing on his own.

"Virginia, time is running out. We have to find the crystals before Howard can retrieve them."

*Take it lightly*, she thought.

"Yes. I know."

He smiled at her, and the smile lingered as he looked down at the drawing in his hand. "Too bad Howard didn't leave a piece of paper with the numbers on it. But we could hardly expect—"

Virginia started to laugh then, the combination of discovery, relief, and sheer sexual excitement going to her head like a powerful drug. He stared at her, stupefied.

"But he did. He did just that, or very nearly," she gasped. I know what the scroll means. The fake *Ban of Akhenaten* on Howard's viewscreen. I should have figured it out sooner, except it addled me, finding the actual *Ban.* It has been a rather special part of my life and—"

"You know where he hid the crystals?" His face mirrored the disbelief, the dawning hope in his voice.

She shook her head. "No. But you probably do. We need to look at it again, to be sure. But I know I'm right."

"Put the fake *Ban* from Howard's notes up on the screen," she asked. They were back in Roma's room, Howard's data crystals arranged by the viewer.

He did so, never taking his eyes off her face.

She leaned over his shoulder, pointing at the hieroglyphic columns that had so baffled her.

She pointed to the hieroglyphics that did not fit in the *Ban.* "You have to understand that each hieroglyph can mean many things. It may represent a letter of the alphabet—a sound, that is—or an idea. They take on different meanings in different contexts, in different positions relative to each other, any number of things. The Egyptians wrote from left to right, but also right to left and top to bottom depending on the surface inscribed."

Seeing him growing restive, she hurried on. "I'm boring

you with all this so you will understand that it is not just a case of reading a text. You have to understand the context. This is written as if it was a story text, like something out of *a Tale of Two Brothers*. But if you delete all the extra words, and forget about the arrangement, and just deal with the hieroglyphs themselves, it all comes down to something very simple and sensible. Numbers."

His hand closed around her wrist so suddenly she yelped.

"Numbers!" He was with her at last.

She nodded. "I would have seen it sooner, except I was so taken up in finding the *Ban*. One, two, nothing," she began reading, "nine, twenty, four, five, ten, nothing, nothing, one hundred. Plus these here have the double repeat sign, and these the triple. All together, about twenty-five number combinations. Now, why would Howard go to the trouble of cluttering up a translation of the *Ban* with a lot of numbers?"

Roma was looking at her with wry appreciation. "Howard would, as I said, have no need to write down the names of the places he hid the crystals. But he might well not wish to trust to memory the coordinates needed to set the gate!"

"Do you recognize these numbers?"

He shook his head. "Not in this order. He may have scrambled them. . . . "

She continued looking over his shoulder, then looked closely at the false text.

"Perhaps this will help . . . this sign here is reversed from the way it is usually written. So is this . . . it's one of the things that threw me off at first." She traced the two signs on the screen. "If you reverse those numbers. . . . "

He nodded. "It's probably a little more complicated than that, but the intelligence program should be able to finish the job." He became absorbed in his work, and it was some little time before the computer spread a series of coordinates across the viewscreen, neatly arranged in clusters.

"That's it," his fingers hovered over the first set of numbers, "the Yucatan station at Chichén Itzá, and Atlantis. That still covers quite a lot of territory. Still, now we know where to start looking. Have you ever been to either of those places?" He was pushing his disrupter into its holster, preparing to go to the gate.

Virginia shrugged. "I've been to Chichén Itzá. And just for the record, I don't even believe in Atlantis."

"Well, it doesn't matter," he was saying absently, gathering up a carrysack and pushing things into it. She saw a bundle of what looked like rope, and a knife, and some other small items she did not recognize.

# Chapter 38

## 1357 B.C.E. Abydos
## 1200 C.E. Chichén Itzá

As they walked into the control room, he accorded her a brief glance. "I've been thinking," he began.

"This is the part," she said slowly, "where the hero tells the heroine that he will be right back after he finishes saving the universe, and will she please wait right here until he does."

"You know how dangerous the gate is. I think I've stabilized it, but we did that every time we used it, and people still disappeared."

"And many of them were not using the gate at the time. It could happen to me right here, while you are gone. Or even before you leave. Isn't that right?"

"The risks go way up if you are using the gate. It is my responsibility to protect—"

*Women and camp followers to the rear.*

"Roma." Something in her tone got through to him, and he paused, his carryall swinging from his hand. "I am not one of your responsibilities. You have no authority over me or my actions. It's going to take both of us. You know I'm right."

He sat down on the step to the gate pad and drew her down beside him. Reaching out a tender finger, he traced the line of her cheek and jaw.

"Virginia. Listen carefully. There are two crystals. In order to go after them, I'll have to replace the coordinate relay module. Howard will be exerting all his abilities to stop us from getting the crystals. I've set security lockouts around the control room. It's probably safer here than using the gate."

"You've killed all his little bugs. How would he know we've discovered the sequence and gone after them?"

"He'll know when the gate initializes that we've gone somewhere. He knows I won't stop until I find them. I think he'll figure it out pretty fast. What I can't imagine is either leaving you here or letting you go through the gate. Howard may have taken your escape last night personally. When I heard the rockfall, the disrupter fire. . . ." His voice trailed off, and she had a fleeting vision of him, running in desperate haste through that confusing snare of tunnels, wondering what he would find at the end.

"Roma," she made his name a caress. "What makes you think I need your permission?"

She stared him down, a tender smile hovering on her lips, until he finally nodded, bowing to the inevitable.

"Has anyone ever told you that you are a stubborn, intractable woman?"

"Many times."

He pulled her against him for too brief a moment, then got up and began rummaging in a large cabinet. "We have access to something that will, I hope, help us."

He took out a black suit, made like a coverall.

"This is a transfer suit. It will boost the power of the transfer. We used them when we went somewhere with no gate on the other side. Daedalus mentions in his notes that he believed using the suits would also amplify the stability of the gate system. This mechanism here," he showed her a small flap on the chest that covered the series of buttons, "contains a transfer crystal tuned to a particular gate or time. In this case, to the main gate here, so it's strictly a one-way trip. Should anything go wrong with the gate on the other side, the transfer crystal will return you to this gate when you activate it."

He was helping her slip it over her clothes. The suit molded itself around her, fitting closely at wrists and ankles. There were numerous pockets in the arms and legs. He pulled out a second suit for himself. He pointed to another button in the chest control panel.

"This one is a communicator link. If you hit it, the suit will open a voice link and send a locator signal."

He handed her a transcomp.

"It's set to register the power crystals. When you get close to one, it will blink and activate the tingler."

"Where are we going first?"

"Chichén Itzá."

When she was ready, she moved to the gate pad. She looked back and tried to smile. Then it happened. All the will, all the resolution and confidence she suddenly knew to be false drained out of her. The feeling of wrongness came over her in a sickening wave, like a premonition of the dissolution of mind and body.

He was taking out equipment from a variety of cabinets and chests, and stuffing it in her pockets. His hurried explanation of their purposes went by in a blur of sound. She nodded, and repeated his instructions, but it was meaningless.

"Remember. If you have to, for any reason, the transfer crystal in the suit will bring you back. But the gate at Chichén Itzá is still active, according to the time grid, so it will be easier and safer if we can use the gate controls to return."

Safer. *Easier*, somewhere in a ruined city of immense proportions, to find one hidden power crystal. To let this horror take her through space and time, probably nowhere. Her phobia, that paralyzing fear that owes nothing to rational thought, that sucked resolution and will out of the body, that disconnected the mind, poured through her like dirty water.

"I can't."

He looked around, alarmed at the sound of her voice.

Hating herself, shaking with shame and defeat, she sat down on the step of the pad.

"Oh, God, I'm so sorry. I can't do it. I really can't. I can't drive. I can't fly, unless I dope myself into a stupor. And I can't do this."

"It's all right." He wasted no time arguing. His hands were busy at the console, entering the coordinates to the void. "I'll leave you the disrupter. I prefer that. It's all right." He said it one too many times.

There were too many things she could not do, she realized, and watching Gianni Roma take his last step into what was almost certainly oblivion, leaving her behind, was at the very top of the list. Going through the gate to Chichén Itzá would have to take second place. She stood up and stepped onto the pad. He did not argue with her. Perhaps, she reflected later, it was the finest thing anyone had ever done for her.

He continued looking at her for a moment, then smiled and hit the switch. A second later he was beside her on the pad. And then the gate took them.

ꝏ ꝏ ꝏ

*This is not air!* was Virginia's first anguished thought. The humid, steaming atmosphere of the Yucatan hit her and wrapped itself around her like a wet wool blanket. "Oh, God, I hate humidity," she said aloud. Roma wiped at the sweat that had broken out on his face. They were standing in the doorway of a small building at the southwest corner of a huge plaza. Embedded in the lintel she recognized the curiously pulsing threads of crystal. The building itself, probably a storeroom or outbuilding of some kind, was half buried in piled earth and a riot of decaying vegetation. A ruin carefully recreated by the travelers when they abandoned the gate.

Roma scrambled up the side of the mound of dirt in front of the door, and reached a hand down to help her. They lay looking across the plaza at the ruined city of the

Maya. Not so terribly ruined, either. The great structures were all still intact. When people visited these ruins in her own time and saw the bleached and scoured stone of the towering walls, they imagined the cities to have been the same in the time of their zenith. They thought these buildings of stone had been gray and austere.

Her eyes ached from the glare of color in the westering sun. Great murals of red, terra-cotta, and the vivid Maya blue stretched across temples. Towering polychrome figures of gods and heroes adorned countless stelae. They threw eerie black shadows across the grass-grown floor of the plaza.

"The place is huge," she said. "It will take hours, perhaps days to search all of it."

"The tinglers will help. We'll have to separate. Keep out of sight." He stood up and moved to the edge of the plaza.

"I'll go to the right, due east. We'll meet on the far side, at the northeast corner. If you see anything that worries you, anything that shouldn't be here, hit the communicator button."

She nodded, wondering what *should* be here, and edged to the right along the edge of the shadows. Not for a mound of power crystals would she have stepped out into that haunted plaza. The city could not have been abandoned for long. The thought that it might not *be* abandoned flitted through her mind like a cloud of bats, and she flinched. No, her reason asserted, Roma would not have allowed the travelers to establish a gate in an inhabited area. Roma. The thought of him was an anchor. She did not pause to consider that; merely took hold of her courage and started toward the first band of shadow. Making her way around the edges of the great open space took time. Before she was halfway down the west side of the plaza, her clothes were soaked and her lungs screaming in protest. *How did these people build a great civilization here? How did they build anything? How did they breathe?* Her respect for this ancient culture went up several notches. It was hot in Egypt, but the water and the air did not occupy the same space.

Virginia came to the edge of a rectangular space between towering terraces. She pulled herself up to the first terrace and looked down. There were huge stone rings at each side, high up on the walls. It was a playing field. She sat down for a moment to rest her laboring lungs, and watched the shadows creeping across the famous ball court. Here prisoners of war had been forced to play a complicated game with a heavy leather ball. No one was really certain how the game was played. Everyone was pretty certain, however, that the loser was beheaded as a sacrifice to the gods of the place. Sometimes, she remembered reading, the winners were sacrificed instead, as a special honor. Talk about a lose-lose situation.

She stood up and turned around, and found herself staring at a rack of skulls on the level above her. One of the heads still had a few dried scraps of flesh adhering to the bone. There were insects. She moaned and put her head down, trying not to be sick. She had no idea how long ago that unfortunate had lost his head in this place of blood, but it had definitely not been long enough. Had he died as a last plea to the inexplicable indifference of the gods of a dying culture? No one really knew why the Maya had abandoned these wonderful cities, the sites of such great beauty and terror. Quetzalcoatl, called Kukulcan here at Chichén Itzá, had come to the ancients, so the mythology ran, and had taught them the secrets of agriculture. He had been fair-skinned and he had taught them language and music. He had put an end to human sacrifice. But then the times of war had come upon them, and the peoples of Mesoamerica had returned to the practice of sacrifice in an effort to influence the brutality of nature and their fellows. It had not worked.

She stood up and moved on, looking now for an image of the feathered serpent, the God-King who must have watched the demise of his people and wept. Later, when conquerors had come, the remaining Maya and Aztec peoples had remembered the stories about Kukulcan promising one day to return. They looked at the fair-skinned Castilians, with their horses and their weapons of wonder, and had paused to consider. That hesitation had been their final destruction.

A great carving of the serpent loomed up on a gateway. She pulled the transcomp from her pocket and looked at it. No lights. No tingle. Nothing. She kept looking.

Over an hour passed, and she had almost completed one quarter of the perimeter of the plaza. At this rate, it would be dark before they completed just one circuit of the great open space before her. She had seen no sign of Roma across that great plaza, and expected to see none.

He had disappeared into the shadows as if one of them. She was definitely not prepared to stay here in this jungle at night. The city might have no human population, but other life most certainly thrived there. Birds called and chattered from the trees and empty buildings. Insects buzzed. She would be willing to swear she could hear the ground breathing.

Then she felt it, the first slight tingling sensation from the transcomp in her thigh pocket. She left it there and continued on. The tingling grew stronger when she turned to the north side, and she climbed the stairs leading to an open platform. Virginia was familiar with some of the recent work done on the great Mayan cities. She knew what the platform was. Scholars called it the Venus platform because it was decorated with symbols of both Kukulcan and the planet Venus, another important part of Maya cosmology. Winding through the trees behind the platform was a wide causeway, the paving stones still showing through the encroaching green. She also knew where it led. "Of course," she breathed, and a convulsive shiver ran through her body.

ஐ ஐ ஐ

It was a horrible place in the future, but it was indescribably worse here, in the past, so much closer to all the death. She stood on the edge of the deep natural sinkhole known as the Sacred Cenote. From the platform at the edge of the well, decorated with more images of Kukulcan, the Maya had flung men, women, and children into the dreadful pool as sacrifices and tools of divination. She thought about standing seventy-five feet above the surface of the dark water, knowing that you were going to be thrown down. Her sweat turned cold. The victim was usually a woman, she reflected. If the woman wasn't killed on impact, or failed to drown in the slimy water, and she could tell a good enough tale of messages from the gods, sometimes they fished her out. *Not often enough*, she thought, *looking at that hideous drop*.

Virginia looked down at the green water, and shuddered. The crystal had to be here. She examined the platform hopefully, but there was nothing to see but stone and moss. No amount of prodding or pulling at the carvings produced any hidden caches. She eyed the water. It was just like Howard to hide it down there.

She climbed down off the platform and began to search the edge of the well. The salt from her sweat stung her nose and eyes, and the insects were a torment. Finally, she acknowledged her first guess was the right one. Hating Howard with every breath, she pulled open one of her suit leg pockets. There was something like a pair of pitons, each with its own little crystal power supply winking up at her, and attached to them was a ridiculously small bundle of quarter-inch bars connected by fine, supple cord. This resolved itself into a ladder. She looked at it for a moment, unsure whether to laugh or cry. It couldn't possibly hold her weight.

Then she remembered Roma and hit the communicator button. Nothing happened. She looked up at the sun, setting behind the tree line. Another short while and it would be dark. Too late to retrieve the crystal. Last night, she reflected, trying to still the frightened jumping of her heart, she had done an almost equally impossible thing. She had climbed up that shaking barrier, to a height that would make her nose bleed if she thought about it for long. Impossible for the phobic person she had become, yet she had done it. So it was not impossible to consider climbing down. She would climb down and find the crystal.

Her stomach lurched, and she prayed Roma would come and make it unnecessary for her to go down into the well. Thinking of him, she remembered that shameful performance in the gate, after she had insisted on going and then had given into panic. It might go a small way toward making up for her sad performance if she could do this one other impossible thing.

She lay on her stomach at the edge of the Cenote platform, under the image of Kukulcan. With her head hanging over that dreadful drop, she held first one piton, then the other against the rocky side of the well. When she thumbed the switch, the pitons hummed and with a tiny jerk embedded themselves in the stone. The gossamer ladder she unrolled carefully, letting the bottom drop into the well. It was barely a foot and a half wide. Without letting her thoughts dwell on where she was finding the courage, she turned around and levered her legs over the side, feeling for the ladder. She got both feet on a rung, and taking a firm handhold, knowing if she paused for too long she would die in this very spot, let the ladder take her weight.

The ladder stretched minutely and she fell against the rock wall, bruising her hands. Somehow she held on, and feeling with shaking legs and feet, found the next rung. She climbed down, blinking the sweat out of her eyes, clinging to the seemingly frail lifeline, feeling the ever-increasing tingle from the transcomp in her pocket. *I will not think about the drop*, she thought. *I will think about finding the crystal, about putting it into Roma's hand. I will not think about the drop.* Word by word, she talked herself down that frail-seeming ladder.

Just above the waterline, she found herself looking into a crevice in the wall, little more than a vertical crack. The power crystal was there, in a tiny box made of jade. *Mayan*, she thought with part of her mind. Not bad. Had she come here as an archaeologist or tourist, she would have seen the splendid little box and very little else. The crystal would have been meaningless, a pretty geological oddity to the uninitiated. Howard thought of everything.

She laid her forehead against the clammy limestone for a moment, and offered the most devout prayer of thanksgiving she had ever made in her life. She slid the crystal into one of her sleeve pockets and dropped the jade box into the Cenote, her private offering to Kukulcan—hoping he still didn't appreciate human sacrifice. Then she started to climb back up. Her hands had passed from sore to agony by the time the top of her head drew level with the rim. *Gloves*, she thought, *why didn't he think of gloves. Maybe he did*, she admitted. She had not really been paying that close attention. She made one final effort and pulled herself up over the edge. And looked straight into Howard's dark, compelling, and utterly mad gaze.

She screamed. Her grip on the ladder loosened, and she would have fallen had he not grabbed her arms and hauled her up, holding her with her toes barely on the lip of the well.

"Dr. Alexander, we meet again," he said pleasantly.

He held her on tiptoe, and the muscles in her legs, already punished by the climb, began to knot.

"You have something that belongs to me, I think," he continued in the same tone.

He saw denial in her eyes and gave her a shake. One foot slipped off the edge, and she clutched at him.

"Don't bother to lie, Dr. Alexander. I know you have it. Please don't put me to the trouble of searching you for it."

His eyes hardened, and he shook her again. She gritted her teeth against the fear, denying him another scream.

"How did you get here?" she forced the words through stiff lips.

He smiled. "Now, the part where the heroine encourages the villain to talk about himself until the hero can arrive is over. The hero, whom I must suppose to be Roma, is impotent, and I am not, whatever you may think, the villain. Merely the visionary. It really is a pity, but small lives must sometimes be sacrificed in great causes. And now, if you do not give me that crystal I am going to take it from you, and then I will pitch you over the edge. You will not enjoy either process."

Never taking her eyes from his, she managed to pry the

fingers of one hand loose and reach for a leg pocket flap. Her leg cramped unbearably, and she had the sickening sensation of her toes slipping toward the edge. Her terror of heights swept over her and she felt her stomach wrap itself around her spine. *Dear God, I'll go over backward.*

"Hold me," she pleaded, feeling her feet lift from the slimy stone.

"Certainly," he promised, smiling. Then, with no change in tone, he added, "Roma, if you take one more step, so much as move a muscle, I will drop your red-headed bitch straight into hell."

She swiveled her gaze and could see Roma, at the edge of the platform, his disrupter held in front of him with both hands.

"Step back, Howard."

Howard laughed. "Not likely. But I do congratulate you. I really didn't think you would get this far. Fortunately I believe in being prepared, even for so unlikely an eventuality."

He shook her again, ever so slightly, and she could not restrain a little whimper of fear, or her convulsive grasp of his arms.

They stood there, breast to breast, in a travesty of a lover's embrace with her feet poised above that hideous drop. She managed to get one toe back on the edge.

"Now," he said, speaking to Roma but never taking his eyes from hers, "you will drop the disrupter. Slowly and very, very carefully."

She gave her head a minuscule shake.

"He's not going to do it, Howard."

"I think he will. Because I think that now he has tasted the goods."

She wished it was something exalted like concern for the future of the universe that strengthened her resolve. But it was pure, stinging rage that gave her the strength to give a violent wrench and launch herself into space. It felt as if she hung there an endless moment, a flightless bird buoyed up by fear. *Don't scream*, she reminded herself, *or you'll drown. If the fall doesn't kill you.* Then came the nightmare sensation of falling, falling. A moment later, her feet hit the surface and the warm, turgid water closed over her head.

The momentum of her fall took her down, down like a sack full of lead, to join the other broken bodies on the bottom. She clawed at the seal over the control panel on her suit with terror-splayed fingers. Her ears filled with water, and she was deafened by the sound of her own thrashing. Most of the well was in shadow by late afternoon, and the water was dark when she forced her eyes open and turned her head upward. She had no time to feel surprise that she had survived the fall. She had room for only one thought, to get to the surface. She kicked desperately, floundering, and knew that she was not going to make it back to the air. Her mouth was filling with water when she finally managed to rip open the chest flap and find the return button on her suit.

# Chapter 39

## 1357 B.C.E.
## Abydos

She hit something—hard—and drew in a lungful of air, coughing and retching. From somewhere there were arms around her, and she struggled against them. The bony arms of previous victims? Kukulcan welcoming her into the Mayan version of heaven? She hit out and connected with something that was neither bony nor cold, but warm.

"Stop it," said Roma's voice.

Her eyes snapped open, and she looked into his eyes. Then she closed her eyes again, and laid her face against his chest. That was all she wanted in the whole benighted universe, not to move from this spot ever again. Finally, he drew back a little.

"You smell like a swamp," he said.

"Thank you," she said in an exhausted voice.

She took his hand and opened it, palm up. And into it she dropped the crystal.

"One for us," she said.

Another fit of coughing shook her, and he held her head while she choked up another lungful of water.

"What happened," she finally managed to ask, "after I took the dive?"

"When you went down he lost his balance. He went over a second after you did. I can't believe his luck."

"Luck?" she shuddered, thinking of that hideous well and its clutching burden of death.

"He may not be dead."

"Did he scream?"

"No."

Virginia began to cry, then.

He held her again, rocking her gently until she stopped. When she raised her head, he was smiling.

"Come on. You're dripping on the console."

This time Virginia remembered every step back to his room. He held her tightly against him, sodden and stinking to heaven of what she hoped profoundly was rotting vegetation, through the labyrinth toward sanctuary.

When she stripped off the transfer suit and the jumpsuit she wore under it, and watched him kick them out into the hallway, she wondered if she had now managed to destroy the last of his clothes. She stumbled into the shower and let the hot water sluice the mud and weeds from her hair and body. When she finally felt she had scrubbed off everything but skin, she pulled on the robe and went back to curl up on his bed. She watched him busy over the deadly looking disrupter, checking settings and power cells and whatever made it disrupt. Her eyes lingered on the smooth planes of his face, remote in concentration, the strong neck and shoulders. He looked young, she realized, until you looked into his eyes.

"If he's not dead," he said without looking around, "he'll try for the other crystal. Howard had to have used his transcomp to go to the Yucatan gate, so he'll have exhausted the transfer crystal. He's lucky he got there at all. He'll have to replace it with one from the Mayan gate, and that will mean retuning it."

"Can he do that?"

"It will take time. The crystals in the gate will be tuned for that gate, that time. Each set is tuned to its own time and matrix. With the right tools, it should take him about seven hours before he can go after the other power crystal."

"You think he has the right tools?"

"I think," said Roma a trifle grimly, "we have to assume he does."

He turned around then, his expression softening. "Meanwhile, it will take the main gate console about six hours to recalibrate, before we can use it again. That will give us a one-hour lead." He came and sat beside her.

"I want you to promise me something," he said.

She waited.

"I want you to promise me that you will let nothing come between you and the goal we have set for ourselves. The mission, if you will. Nor will you expect me to. We have to initiate the dissolution sequence. Will you promise?"

She nodded, wondering.

"I want to hear you say it," he persisted.

She was flooded suddenly with a painful wash of understanding. She swallowed, and looked him straight in the eye

"I promise."

"You will not let anyone, anything you feel, stop you."

"I promise," she said again, her heart in her throat. "Why are you insisting on this now?"

He smiled. "Because I am going to touch you, hold you. And I was afraid that once I did, I wouldn't be able to ask you."

He pulled her into his arms and held her body to body, mouth to mouth.

"Roma—" she said against his lips, and knew she was crying.

"Shhh," he whispered. "With all this talk of time and infinity, past and future, I've always known that there is only one moment in all of time that is real. This one."

Later, when they could permit the commonplace of speech between them, he raised his head. "Virginia. What happened to you in the gate? Before we went to Chichén Itzá?"

She stirred, and he drew her closer against him.

"Tell me."

"I was a grad student, on a dig in Abydos. I was in love with my professor's senior assistant. His name was Hickson. One night, one of the diggers came running with a message from H.L.—the professor in charge of the dig—to come up to another site with the Jeep. This site. The labyrinth. He had found something here. It was a special night. And we drove through the desert, believing that it was going to last, that we had found perfection and it was never going to abandon us. When we got here, H.L. showed us the gold statue of Osiris. The one that's out there now, in the vestibule. We carried it out to the Jeep, and drove down the mountain." Her voice faltered.

"Tell me," he said again, very softly.

"Hickson hurt his hand, loading the statue, so I was driving. We blew a tire and the Jeep went over the cliff. H.L. got out, and I was thrown clear. But Hickson was pinned underneath the statue. He went to the bottom of the cliff. After a few months, I pulled myself together enough to finish my dissertation. H.L. gave me a job in the museum, a nice safe job. I walk to work. I don't go out on digs. I don't drive a car. And I can't bear the sensation of being in the air. I'm terrified of falling."

He said nothing for a while, letting her story fill the silence. Then, "Are you ready to let him go, now?"

"Let him go?" she echoed.

"Yes. If he loved you, he wouldn't have wanted you to be a prisoner of the past. He might even have hated you for using him like a chain, a fetter around your life."

She didn't answer, so he lifted himself on his elbow and looked into her face.

"For someone who is terrified of falling, you did quite a dive into that well."

"I read somewhere, when I was a child, about someone falling a long distance into water. The secret to surviving it was not to scream. If you screamed, then when you hit the water you were out of air."

"You didn't scream."

She smiled. "I know. And yes, Roma. I am ready to let

him go. I have." *And now, somehow, I'll have to find a way to let you go.*

He buried his face in her hair for a moment.

"So, tell me about the Persean Order," she said against his shoulder. "Why no family?"

He settled himself again. "It is an honor to be accepted at the School," he began, "but it requires a lifetime of training and discipline. A man with a family has a price, a point of vulnerability. He can be bought, coerced, used. When people hire a Persean to protect and defend them, they know that he is not subject to outside pressure."

"So no involvement? No personal relationships?"

"No commitments. And not with a client. It . . . clouds the judgment."

"What a good thing," she said, "that I am not a client."

"Isn't it?"

The computer, in its soulless way, had watched the clock. When it sounded its small, electronic beep, she felt the muscles in his body tense. "It's time."

She tightened her arms for a moment. "*No, 'tis the nightingale*," she quoted against the uprush of loss.

"What?"

"Just a line from . . . a very old story."

# Chapter 40

## 1357 B.C.E.
## 1995 C.E. Abydos

They stood in the gate control room. Roma checked the sensors and seemed satisfied.

"Did you bring everything you're taking with you? We won't have much time, once we replace the last crystal."

She nodded. Her bag lay beside the console. Roma, wearing a transfer suit, had filled the pockets with his equipment. She wore his very last jumpsuit. Her own clothes were stuffed in her bag, along with the other things she was taking back. Her fingers found the Medusa medallion over her heart. He had sketched a salute when he fastened it there.

Roma began pulling crystals out of their housings, inserting others, pressing an intricate pattern of touch-pads and keys on the console. The viewscreen displayed a lighted, complex series of equations and formulae that formed and reformed as he worked.

A panel was open on the side of the console, and Virginia could see into the time gate controls. It gave her the sensation of falling. She looked away, and saw Roma had taken out the power crystal. He knelt down and inserted it in a delicate web of transparent wires just inside the panel. There was another web beside it, empty. The crystal spars that arched up the walls and into the ceiling pulsed with unearthly radiance, and the air rang with crystal dissonance.

He stood up. "It's a two-part sequence. The first, this one, Daedalus believed would rebuild enough stability in the gate to begin the realignment of the crystal matrix. But we have to have the other crystal to complete the dissolution. When we put the last crystal into the net and initialize the sequence, time will be repaired as much as possible. Then the matrix will die."

He put his arms around her. "What is lost in this line, will remain lost. We can't undo that. But our timeline will separate from this one, and heal at the points of collision. There, time will reassert itself. Your statuette will return home, Virginia. And so will you. Now we have to go after that crystal, before Howard can beat us to it."

"Roma," she was crying again. "Where will you go?"

"I'll go home, too. Alone."

"Let me come with you." She knew as she said it that it was pointless.

"You know I can't. When time finally reasserts itself here, inside the matrix, we will be sent where the gods of time have ordained. And then the matrix will collapse, and the door will shut."

There was a slight sound behind them. "Poetic, but untrue."

Howard yanked her back against him with such violence the breath was driven out of her body and she could not breathe. Her ears rang, but she could hear him talking in his unruffled, elegant voice.

"Roma, don't be childish. You know you can't fire your disrupter in here," Howard was saying. "If you misjudged by a fraction of an inch, the backwash would hit the console. At the same time, you would certainly kill Dr. Alexander. Or, of course, I would. I might, anyway."

Something cold pressed against her temple, and she knew it was Howard's disrupter.

"The same reasoning applies to you, Howard. Shoot her, and you kill the console. You don't even want to think about what that would mean. Impasse."

"You think so?" asked Howard. He dragged her back, shoving the disrupter under her chin. Roma's, straight-armed in front of him, never wavered.

Howard lifted his other hand, and held up the remaining power crystal.

"You see," he said gently, "I'd already retrieved it when we met at the Cenote. You didn't manage to kill all my little bugs, after all."

Roma was silent.

"Oh, your equipment is good, Roma. It's just that mine is better. You slowed me down, inconvenienced me. But money really can buy anything, and for every lock you brought with you, I brought a key. Foresight is everything. Now let's talk."

Roma waited, never taking his eyes off Howard.

"Enter the first part of the sequence. Repair the broken event strings. Well and good. But you don't need to destroy the matrix. We know now what not to do. So long as we don't cross over timelines, the event strings will not break down. The gate will function as it was designed to." Howard's voice was persuasive.

"Still trying to complete the mission?" asked Roma mildly.

"In a way. The mission always was to reorder time, wasn't it? The *real* mission, to find a way to defeat the Cataclysm. We can do that. The data is all there, in the matrix. Recordings of trillions of event strings. And we can plant more recorders. We have an infinity of time at our disposal."

"We." Roma's voice was devoid of emotion.

"Yes! Join me, Roma. Try to overcome that Persean strait-jacket in which you've immured your mind. Think of what we can do for history, for humanity! I've already explained part of it to Dr. Alexander. And you can even keep her with you, if you like. Or not. Think about it."

They hadn't found all the bugs, and he had listened, watched. . . . God, she wanted him dead.

Slowly he began to move, still holding her in front of him, the disrupter digging painfully into her throat. "Now. Dr. Alexander and I are going to go up into the matrix. Once the power crystal is destroyed, you can't destroy the gate. It will be stable. You can decide then whether you're going to be immortal . . . or the obvious alternative." He was backing toward the elevator. *I've always despised women who let this happen to them,* she thought. *It's such a cliché.*

They were in the elevator and rising, and then the radiance of the matrix flooded through the opening doors. Howard flipped a switch on the elevator control panel. The lights on it died.

Finally he released her. "To the first ladder," he said, pushing her ahead of him. "Get off at the fourth level." She followed his instructions, climbing the ladder ahead of him, trying not to wonder how Roma was going to get up there without the elevator. They stepped off on the catwalk, and he motioned her into the matrix, driving her toward the center, toward the well of eternity.

When they reached it, he looked down briefly at the nonexistent colors, the sounds out of hearing range somehow visible, the event strings forming and unforming, and smiled. He held the crystal poised over the abyss.

"I considered keeping it, against the possibility that I might need it in the future. I couldn't trust Roma so long as it exists. And then, as I will have the future, I can always get another."

"You believe Roma will join you?" Her tone of disbelief angered him, and the dark eyes looked at her with an expression of absolute malice.

"Yes. In the end, he will. Because of you."

She shook her head. "No. He won't. And so you will finally be alone."

"You think that frightens me?"

"Yes."

The hand holding the crystal shook for a moment, then flew up, the fingers splayed as Roma's body slammed into his from behind. The crystal went up in a wide arc, disappearing somewhere in the matrix. Roma and Howard were down, struggling on the edge of annihilation. She flinched at the sickening sound of bone crunching on flesh. There was no question that Roma would win, she thought. Howard, for all his brilliance, was no match physically for the Persean's skill and strength. Then Roma gave a grunt of pain, and his grip faltered. Howard, knowing his disrupter would be too dangerous to use inside the matrix, had come prepared with a different kind of weapon. The hilt of a knife stood out from Roma's side. Roma's fingers closed on it and pulled it out of his body. She would hear that sound until she died. Somehow he retained his hold on Howard, and turning his head, he jerked his head at the matrix.

"Find the crystal," he said between painful breaths.

Gritting her teeth against the crystal vibration, she crawled into the matrix. It was hypnotic, watching the fire dancing and streaming through the crystal all around her. *Find one little piece of crystal. In all this. Dead easy.*

It could be anywhere. The field in which the matrix was suspended would keep it from falling through to the floor. Her eyes were strained by the effort to look everywhere at once. It had hit here, surely, she thought, gauging the place she had seen the crystal strike fire. Her existence narrowed to a few feet of lattice, as she crawled over the catwalks, trying to see one little leaf fragment in this forest of crystal. It was impossible. There was no possibility of succeeding. Just then she put her seeking hand down on a small, faceted shard and knew she had found it. She ran back through the shimmering wastes of time, the crystal clutched in her hand. The crystal that would dissolve this gateway that should never have been built.

Roma was lying against the railing, his arm around Howard's neck in a choke hold. He held the knife under Howard's chin with his other hand. His face was white from blood loss.

"Take it down and put it in the console. Where I showed you," he said through clenched teeth.

"No!" It was a long cry of desperation and frustrated fury. Howard twisted unavailingly in Roma's grasp, his legs flailing out. Virginia took a hasty step sideways to avoid becoming entangled, and trod in the pool of blood that had gathered near Roma's body. She slipped and staggered, coming perilously close to the edge. Her desperate struggle to regain her footing distracted Roma. His concentration weakened for a critical instant, and Howard elbowed him viciously in the stomach. Howard wrenched himself free, though the knife left a long, ugly cut where his neck and shoulder joined.

He seized Virginia by the arm, forcing her hand down to take the crystal from her. Somehow she held on to it, her fist clenched so tightly the crystal dug into her palm. They struggled across the slippery floor. She felt her feet slide as Howard levered her body toward the railing. His intention was clear. She twisted in his hold. Hitting hard against the railing, they went over. And she felt Roma's fingers close around her ankle, and hold.

Howard held onto her wrist, and they slammed together

against the rim of the edge, only Roma's grip on her foot holding them above the boiling sea of time. Stretched between them, the pain was blinding, intolerable. Somehow she still had the crystal.

"Push your other foot back to the railing," said Roma's voice. Then he had her other ankle, and was pulling them up. She could hear the air whistling in his tortured lungs, feel his hands bruising her flesh.

Then she was dragged up until her body folded over the railing and her feet found the floor of the catwalk. Roma reached over her for Howard, still holding her wrist, swinging below her. His grasp eased the intolerable strain on her arms, as he began to pull Howard up. Bent double as he was over the railing, blood from the knife wound in his side ran down his arm and onto Howard's hands. They both felt the moment when his grasp weakened and slipped.

Howard's look was one of incredulity as he felt the space between their fingers lengthen, and found nothing at all between him and eternity. He went down, and this time he did scream.

They made their way back to the elevator. There was a small plug of some kind attached to the control panel on the wall. She looked a question.

"Override module," he said with a ghost of a smile. "Extra security never hurts."

His voice was weakening, and by the time they reached the console his knees buckled. She lowered him to the floor. "You'll have to do it," he said weakly, indicating the open panel. He handed her the crystal. "Push it gently into the empty membrane next to the other one."

With shaking fingers she obeyed, dropping the crystal into its web of connecting fibers. Instantly it glowed to life.

"Now, hit the switch."

Her fingers poised over the touch pad she knew would initiate the sequence. She looked at him.

It flashed before her eyes then, the gate repaired but intact. A future in which both of them could live and not be separated. She closed her eyes against the rush of longing.

"Roma?"

"You promised. Remember?"

She threw the switch, and went to help him up onto the gate pad. She took his weight against her, and they stood there for a moment, locked together, until he drew gently away from her. She could still feel the imprint of his body on her own when the gate effect took them.

ꝏ ꝏ ꝏ

A cool breeze stirred her hair, teasing her face. She opened her eyes. Osiris stared over her head with the same serene indifference he had always shown. She was standing in front of the statue, and the dawn was breaking behind her. She drew in a deep breath, aware of a sense of belonging. This was her time. She was meant to be here.

She opened her bag and pulled out the souvenirs she had brought back with her from her sojourn in time. An azure crystal, almost as blue as Lantis's eyes. A priceless jade comb, set with pearls. A drawing of an angel with a softly rounded face and a mysterious smile. And a round medallion showing the intricately carved face of Medusa, pinned over her heart. *My medals.*

Her eyes blurred. Was she right about where they had gone? Images crowded behind her eyes. A great city rose against the sea, built of red and black and white marble. It would be a secret wonder in the ancient world, designed by a boy who loved to build, powered by the mystery of crystal. An old man seeking sanctuary built a dancing floor for 'Ariadne of the beautiful tresses,' and for her father the king a labyrinth to house a monster. The towers of Ilium fell and burned, fired by lust and betrayal, failing to listen to the confused voice and dark dreams of the lost prophetess who truly knew the future. A savage with a sophisticated mind forged an empire on the edges of the steppes and shook the world. And a boy with beautiful hands and a sensitive face would grow into an old man, concluding that everything in his life had served only one end, his art. She looked down at the blood on her clothes. Roma's blood. Where in all the mists of eternity had he truly gone? She pushed her relics into her bag and walked to the Jeep. The keys were still in the ignition. She got in and started the engine. Slowly, she drove through the sand and out of the ruined temple at Abydos into the morning. There was no need for hurry. She had plenty of time.